CRIME CLASSICS

My Friend Mr Campion
and other mysteries

CRIME CLASSICS

My Friend Mr Campion
and other mysteries

ALBERT CAMPION INVESTIGATES

MARGERY ALLINGHAM

ABOUT THE AUTHOR

Born in Ealing in 1904, Margery Allingham was an eminent crime writer who is today best remembered for her Albert Campion detective stories. Hers was a family with a strong literary tradition and, encouraged by both her parents, Allingham started writing at a young age, publishing her first novel, *Blackkerchief Dick*, in 1923 when she was just nineteen.

Albert Campion was first introduced as a minor character in *The Crime at Black Dudley* in 1929. Following pressure from her American publishers, who were very taken with the character, Allingham built an entire series around the unassuming and resourceful amateur sleuth. She wrote prolifically throughout her life, producing more than 40 novels as well as many stories and novellas.

Ranking amongst the very best of English crime writers of her age, Allingham was once extolled by *The Sunday Times* as having 'precious few peers and no superiors' in the genre.

She died of cancer in 1966.

This edition published in the UK by Arcturus Publishing Limited
26/27 Bickels Yard, 151–153 Bermondsey Street, London SE1 3HA

This edition published in Australia and New Zealand by Hinkler Books Pty Ltd
45-55 Fairchild Street, Heatherton Victoria 3202 Australia

Cover artwork by Duncan Smith
Typesetting by Couper Street Type Co.

AD001969EN

the UK

CONTENTS

MY FRIEND MR CAMPION

From my point of view one of the oddest things about my friend Mr Campion is that here we are in 1935, I've known him for eight years and I haven't the faintest idea who he is or what sort of yarn I shall be called upon to retail about him next. I know his name is assumed and, of course, from time to time I have been able to pick up odd pieces of information he has let fall in the course of the various of his adventures I have chronicled, but who he is and what his real name is I am not merely not at liberty to divulge: I simply do not know.

We met first, as later I found out, in what was a highly characteristic fashion. Early in 1927 I was writing *The Crime at Black Dudley*, a book about an exciting and mysterious affair taking place in a strange, gaunt old house. I was a quarter of the way through the book and the perfectly good hero was behaving very well indeed in the most trying circumstances. There was a dinner-party and I was peacefully describing it when I noticed that there was one character too many – or rather that there was a stranger in the little party I had so carefully assembled.

I don't want it to be thought that I am one of those dear old ladies who just write down the first thing that comes into their heads and hope the finished page will be entertaining. Rather am I one of those pernickety souls who plan and re-plan, who build up and weed out and scrape and niggle away in their minds until they know just exactly what sort of story they are going to write, who the characters are and all about them.

Moreover, I have very strong views on the subject. I believe that an author who cannot control his characters is, like a mother who cannot control her children, not really fit to look after them. So this stranger at the Black Dudley dinner-table startled me and made me feel terribly uncomfortable.

Campion butted into the conversation, I remember, with a most unsuitable remark, in tone much too flippant for the grim proceedings, and I became aware of him as vividly as if I had turned my head and suddenly seen him.

At first sight he was not exactly prepossessing but lately he has looked much better but then he's getting on, all of thirty-five, and age is hardening him a bit.

In 1927 he was just as I then described him: a tall, pale young man with sleek yellow hair, enormous horn-rimmed spectacles and an abysmally foolish expression. As is everyone else who does not know him I was fooled by that expression and I had no idea of the hidden shrewdness, the quick, practised brain or the lovable disposition concealed beneath that negligible exterior.

I tried to turn him out of my story; I did not think his line in imbecile chatter an adornment to my sober tale, but all my efforts to shake him off were of no avail. As soon as I got going on a conversation between two characters out leapt an absurd remark and the pale young man was there again.

Dismayed, I gave up work for a week and thought I had lost him but as soon as I returned to the Black Dudley dinner-party there he was, smiling inanely and chattering away like a cross-talk comedian.

In the end I gave up the struggle and after that he took over possession. The hero, a plumpish young barrister, muffed his high spots and Campion popped up at the last moment and saved the situation very neatly.

In spite of myself I began to like him, he was so resourceful, so courageous and always a perfect little gentleman, but I could not get used to his wisecracks or his habit of saying the silliest thing at the most awkward moment.

That Black Dudley business was certainly his affair but I was not happy about him. He seemed to be on some very shady business, for two or three embarrassing moments I thought he was a crook and, because in the penultimate chapter of my book he faded out of the story as suddenly as he had come into it, I never found out quite what his status was.

I met him next when I was writing *Mystery Mile* and when (in the first chapter) I found him on board the SS *Elephantine* I was pleased to see that he looked a little less effete.

Of course, I had planned a story with him in mind but in *Mystery Mile*, as afterwards in every Campion story, I did not actually plan his part. From the very beginning he always saw to that himself and now I have come to rely on him in the same way that one relies upon an old and trusted collaborator.

It was in *Mystery Mile* that we really got to know each other. Early on he handed out his visiting card:

MR ALBERT CAMPION
Coups neatly executed
Nothing sordid, vulgar or plebeian
Deserving cases preferred
Police no object

PUFFIN'S CLUB
THE JUNIOR GREYS

and in the course of the story I saw for the first time the inside of his flat over the Police Station in Bottle Street and met for the first time Magersfontein Lugg, his "gentleman's man", as he called him.

I have always liked Lugg. Though by that time I had reached the stage when I took everything Campion told me with a grain of salt, I believed him when he said that Lugg had been a burglar and that he was "a very useful chap". He certainly was extremely useful in the later stages of *Mystery Mile* and it was then that his huge, white, miserable face became as familiar to me as Campion's own.

It was down at *Mystery Mile* that I met Biddy Paget. Campion met her there too and it was all rather uncomfortable for a while because I was rather fond of Campion and, though I could understand Biddy preferring the American, young Marlowe Lobbett, I did not like to see my hero slighted.

However, although I never thought him quite so light-hearted again, when next we met – and he handling a very delicate little job for the Treasury – he seemed perfectly happy.

That story was called by us *Look to the Lady* and by the Americans *The Gyrth Chalice Mystery*, and when it was done I thought I knew all there was to know about Campion except his name, but he had a surprise for me. Until I wrote *Police at the Funeral* I had never seen him handling a murder mystery and I had meant to leave it all to Inspector Stanislaus Oates of Scotland Yard but Campion turned up again in the first chapter, and I must say he astonished me. He subdued his natural exuberance to the gravity of the circumstances and fitted into that grief-stricken, terror-ridden Cambridge household without giving offence to anybody. Moreover, he was decidedly helpful, quite as much so, in fact, as he had been in the hand-to-hand fights in *Mystery Mile* and *Look to the Lady*. Frankly, I was delighted to discover that he had a brain capable of genuine observation and deduction as well as his natural ability to wriggle out of a tight corner or worst a dangerous enemy.

As usual, he got on well with all the other characters – from my point of view not the least of his charms – he even endeared himself to Great Aunt Caroline and he certainly saved Uncle William from arrest.

After that, when we were truly old friends, I chronicled his adventures in the Pontisbright heirloom case (which we called *Sweet Danger* and the Americans, for some reason, *Kingdom of Death*). Amanda Fitton turned up during that business and I thought he was going to fall for her and get tied for life to the little baggage, but perhaps the memory of Biddy still rankled; anyway, he escaped to go to the assistance of sweet old Mrs Lafcadio in *Death of a Ghost* (a title which, if you only think of

it, gives away the whole mystery). In that, to date the most
ambitious of his efforts, he distinguished himself.

His latest experience – he certainly leads an adventurous life
– is in another murder case. Campion thinks my account should
be called *Flowers for the Judge* and from that title anyone familiar
with English legal custom will guess what he has let me in for.

This is about all I can tell you about Albert Campion. I like
him and I like to consider myself his best friend but, even so, to
me he is still a mystery. I know he was born on May 20th, 1900.
I suspect he was at Rugby – he has just a touch of the Rugby
manner. He says he went to St Ignatius College, Cambridge,
and I know that he embarked on his exciting career in 1924. I
know that he belongs to Puffin's Club and to the Junior Greys
and that his address is 17a Bottle Street, Piccadilly, London
W.I., but who his people are, what his name is and what he does
on his holidays, so to speak, alas, I cannot tell you.

However, he is sometimes indiscreet. Sometimes he lets his
tongue run away with him. So – you never know. I live in hope.

Editor's Note

Taken from the transcript of a broadcast given in 1935.

Margery Allingham's hope that Campion's occasional indis-
cretions would reveal to her more about the details of his life
was fulfilled, but only minimally. Her conviction that he had
survived his early encounters with Amanda Fitton was misplaced.
In fact, he did get himself "tied for life to the little baggage".

The following has never appeared in any edition of *Who's Who*:

CAMPION, Albert (*pseud*; real name known to be Rudolph), "man come about the trouble"; *b* 20 May 1900; *s* of . . . and Lady K; *m* Lady Amanda Fitton; one *s*; *Educ*: Tottham, Rugby, St Ignatius Coll., Cambridge (2nd Cl. Hons, History Tripos); served War 1939–45 Intelligence Corps (SOE). *Relevant publications*: series of biographical studies by Margery Allingham (q.v.) 1929–68 and two by Youngman Carter (1969, 1971). *Recreations*; wine, collecting fine art, otherwise odd. *Address*: 17a Bottle Street, Piccadilly, London W.1. *T*: Regent 01300. *Clubs*: Puffin's, Junior Greys.

THE CASE OF THE MAN WITH THE SACK

There was a personal letter under the pile of greeting cards sent off a week too soon by earnest citizens who had taken the Postmaster-General's annual warning a shade too seriously.

Mr Campion tore it open and a cry from Sheila Turrett's heart fell out.

'My darling Albert, Please come for Christmas. It's going to be poisonous. Mother has some queer ideas in her head and the Welkins are frightful. Mike is a dear. At least I like him and you will too. He is Mike Peters, the son of Ripley Peters who had to go to jail when the firm crashed. But it's not Mike's fault, is it? After all, a good many fathers ought to go to jail only they don't get caught. I don't mean George, of course, bless him (you ought to come if only for his sake. He's like a depression leaving the Azores. It's the thought of the Welkins, poor pet). I don't like to ask you to waste your time on our troubles, but Ada Welkin is lousy with diamonds and Mother seems to think that Mike might pinch them, his father having been to jail. Darling, if you are faintly decent do come and back us up. After all, it is Christmas. Yours always (if you come) Sheila. P.S. I'm in love with Mike.'

On Christmas Eve the weather decided to be seasonable; a freezing overhead fog turned the city into night and the illuminated shop fronts had the traditional festive appearance even in the morning. It was more than just cold. The damp atmosphere soaked into the bones relentlessly and Mr Campion's recollection of Pharaoh's Court, rising gaunt and bleak amid three hundred acres of ploughed clay and barren salting, all as flat as the estuary beyond, was not enhanced by the chill.

The thought of Sheila and her father cheered him a little, almost but not quite offsetting the prospect of Lady Mae in anxious mood. Buttoning himself into his thickest overcoat, he hoped for the best.

The railway station was a happy pandemonium. Everybody who could not visit the East coast for the holiday was, it seemed, sending presents there, and Mr Campion, reminded of the custom, glanced anxiously at his suitcase, wondering if the box of cigars for George was too large or the casket of perfume for Mae too modest and if Sheila was still young enough to eat chocolates.

He caught the train with ease, no great feat since it was three-quarters of an hour late, and was sitting in his corner idly watching the hurrying throng on the platform when he caught sight of Charlie Spring. He recognized the face instantly, but the name came to him slowly from the sifting of his memory.

Jail had done Mr Spring a certain amount of good, Mr Campion reflected as his glance took in the other man's square shoulders and developed chest. He had been a weedy wreck six months ago standing in the dock with the light from the roof shining down upon his low forehead, beneath which there peered out the stupidest eyes in the world.

At the moment he seemed very pleased with himself, a bad omen for the rest of the community, but Mr Campion was not interested. It was Christmas and he had troubles of his own.

However, from force of habit he made a mental note of the man and observed that he boarded the train a little lower down. Mr Campion frowned. There was something about Charlie Spring which he had known and which now eluded him. He tried to remember the last and only time he had seen him. He himself had been in court as an observer and had heard Mr Spring sentenced for breaking and entering just before his own case had been called. He remembered the flat official voice of the police detective who gave evidence. But there was something else, something definite and personal about the man which kept bobbing about in the back of his mind, escaping him completely whenever he tried to pin it down. It worried him vaguely, as such things do, all the way to Chelmsworth.

Charlie had left the train at Ipswich in the company of some one hundred and fifty fellow travellers. Mr Campion spotted him as he passed the window, walking swiftly, his head bent and a large new suitcase in his hand.

It occurred to Campion that the man was not dressed in character.

He seemed to remember him as a dilapidated but somewhat gaudy figure in a dirty check suit and a pink shirt, whereas at the moment his newish greatcoat was a model of sobriety and unobtrusiveness. Yet, it was no sartorial peculiarity that haunted his memory. It was something odd about the man, some idiosyncrasy, something slightly funny.

Still faintly irritated, Mr Campion travelled a further ten miles to Chelmsworth. Few country railway stations present a rustic picturesqueness, even in summer, but at any time in the year Chelmsworth was remarkable for its windswept desolation.

Mr Campion alighted on a narrow slab of concrete, artificially raised above the level of the small town in the valley, and drew a draught of heady rain and brine-soaked air into his lungs. He was experiencing the first shock of finding it not unattractive when there was a clatter on the concrete and a small russet-clad figure appeared before him. He was aware of honey-brown eyes, red cheeks, white teeth, and a stray curl of red hair escaping from a rakish tweed cap in which a sprig of holly had been pinned.

'Bless you,' said Sheila Turrett fervently. 'Come on. We're hours late for lunch, they'll all be champing like boarding house pests.'

She linked her arm through his and dragged him along.

'You're more than a hero to come. I am so grateful and so is George. Perhaps it'll start being Christmas now you're here, which it hasn't been so far in spite of the weather. Isn't it glorious?'

Mr Campion was forced to admit that there was a certain exhilaration in the air, a certain indefinable charm in the grey brown shadows chasing in endless succession over the flat landscape.

'There'll be snow tonight.' The girl glanced up at the feather-bed sky. 'Isn't it grand? Christmas always makes me feel so excited. I've got you a present. Remember to bring one for me?'

'I'm your guest,' said Mr Campion with dignity. 'I have a small packet of plain chocolate for you on Christmas morning, but I wish it to be a surprise.'

Sheila climbed into the car. 'Anything will be welcome except diamonds,' she said cheerfully. 'Ada Welkin's getting diamonds, twelve thousand pounds' worth, all to hang round a neck that would disgrace a crocodile. I'm sorry to sound so catty, but we've had these diamonds all through every meal since she came down.'

Mr Campion clambered into the car beside her.

'Dear me,' he said. 'I had hoped for a merry Christmas, peace and good will and all that. Village children bursting their lungs and everybody else's eardrums in their attempts at religious song, while I listened replete with vast quantities of indigestible food.'

Sheila laughed. 'You're going to get your dear little village kids all right,' she said. 'Not even Ada Welkin could dissuade Mother from the Pharaoh's Court annual Christmas party. You'll have just time to sleep off your lunch, swallow a cup of tea, and then it's all hands in the music room. There's the mothers to entertain too, of course.'

Mr Campion stirred and sighed gently as he adjusted his spectacles.

'I remember now,' he murmured. 'George said something about it once. It's a traditional function, isn't it?'

'More or less.' Sheila spoke absently. 'Mother revived it with modern improvements some years ago. They have a tea and a Christmas tree and a Santa Claus to hand round the presents.'

The prospect seemed to depress her and she relapsed into gloomy silence as the car shot over the dry, windswept roads.

Mr Campion regarded her covertly. She had grown into a very pretty girl indeed, he decided, but he hoped the 'son in the Peters' crash' was worth the worry he saw in her forehead.

'What about the young gentleman with the erring father?' he ventured diffidently. 'Is he at Pharaoh's Court now?'

'Mike?' She brightened visibly. 'Oh yes, rather. He's been there for the best part of a week. George honestly likes him and I thought for one heavenly moment that he was going to cut the ice with Mother, but that was before the Welkins came. Since then, of course, it hasn't been easy. They came a day early, too, which is typical of them. They've been here two days already. The son is the nastiest, the old man runs him close and Ada is ghastly.'

'Horrid for them,' said Mr Campion mildly.

Sheila did not smile.

'You'll spot it at once when you see Ada,' she said, 'so I may as well tell you. They're fantastically rich and Mother has been goat-touting. It's got to be faced.'

'Goat-touting?'

Sheila nodded earnestly.

'Yes. Lots of society women do it. You must have seen the little ads in the personal columns: "Lady of title will chaperone young girl or arrange parties for an older woman". Or "Lady X would entertain suitable guest for the London season". In other words, Lady X will tout around any socially ambitious goat in exchange for a nice large, fat fee. It's horrid, but I'm afraid that is how Mother got hold of Ada in the first place. She had some pretty heavy bridge losses at one time. George doesn't know a thing about it, of course, poor darling-and mustn't. He'd be so shocked. I don't know how he accounts for the Welkins.'

Mr Campion said nothing. It was like Mae Turrett, he reflected, to visit her sins upon her family. Sheila was hurrying on.

'We've never seen the others before,' she said breathlessly.

'Mother gave two parties for Ada in the season and they had

a box at the Opera to show some of the diamonds. I couldn't understand why they wanted to drag the menfolk into it until they got here. Then it was disgustingly plain.'

Mr Campion pricked up his ears.

'So nice for the dear children to get to know each other?' he suggested.

'Something like that.'

Mr Campion sighed deeply.

Sheila negotiated a right-angled turn. Her forehead was wrinkled and her eyes thoughtful.

'This'll show you the sort of man Kenneth Welkin is,' she said. 'It's so petty and stupid that I'm almost ashamed to mention it, but it does show you. We've had a rather difficult time amusing the Welkins. This morning, when Mike and I were putting the final touches to the decorations, we asked Kenneth to help us. There was some stupid business over the mistletoe. Kenneth had been laying down the law about where it was to hang and we were a bit tired of him already when he started a lot of silly horseplay. I don't mind being kissed under the mistletoe, of course, but–well, it's the way you do these things, isn't it?'

She stamped on the accelerator to emphasize her point, and Mr Campion, not a nervous man, clutched the side of the car.

'Sorry,' said Sheila and went on with her story. 'I tried to wiggle away after a bit, but when he wouldn't let me go Mike suddenly lost his temper and told him to behave himself or he'd damn well knock his head off. It was awfully melodramatic and stupid, but it might have passed off and been forgotten if Kenneth hadn't made a scene. First he said he wouldn't be talked to like that, and then he made a reference to Mike's father, which was unforgivable. I thought they were going to have a fight. Then, right in the middle of it, Mother fluttered in with a Santa Claus costume. She looked at Mike and said, 'You'd better try it on, dear, I want you to be most realistic this afternoon." Before he could reply, Kenneth butted in. He looked like a spoilt kid, all pink and furious. "I didn't know you were going to be Father Christmas," he said.'

Sheila Turrett paused for breath, her eyes wide.

'Well, can you imagine anything so idiotic?' she went on. 'Mike had offered to do the job when he first came down because he wanted to make himself useful. Like everyone else, he regarded it as a chore. It never dawned on him that anyone would want to do it. Mother was surprised, too, I think. However, she just laughed and said, "You must fight it out between you" and fluttered away again, leaving us all three standing there. Kenneth picked up the costume. "It's from Harridge's," he said. "My mother was with Lady Mae when she ordered it. I thought it was fixed up then that I was to wear it."'

Mr Campion laughed. He felt very old.

'I suppose Master Michael stepped aside and Master Kenneth appears as St Nicholas?' he murmured.

'Well no, not exactly.' Sheila sounded a little embarrassed. 'Mike was still angry, you see, so he suddenly decided to be obstinate. Mother had asked him to do the job, he said, and he was going to do it. I thought they were going to have an open row about it, which would have been quite too absurd, but at that moment the most idiotic thing of all happened. Old Mr Welkin, who had been prowling about listening as usual, came in and told Kenneth he was to "give way" to Mike – literally, in so many words! It all sounds perfectly mad now I've told it to you, yet Mike is rather a darling.'

Mr Campion detected a certain wistfulness in her final phrase and frowned.

Pharaoh's Court looked mellow and inviting as they came up the drive some minutes later. The old house had captured the spirit of the season and Mr Campion stepped out of a cold grey world into an entrance hall where the blaze from the hearth flickered on the glossy leaves of the holly festooned along the carved beams of the ceiling.

George Turrett, grey-haired and cherubic, was waiting for them. He grasped the visitor's hand with fervour. 'So glad you've come,' he murmured. 'Devilish glad to see you, Campion.'

His extreme earnestness was apparent and Sheila put an arm round his neck.

'It's a human face in the wilderness, isn't it, darling?' she said.

Sir George's guilty protest was cut short as Mr Campion was shown upstairs to his room.

He saw the clock as he came down again a moment or so later. It burst upon him as he turned a corner in the corridor and came upon it standing on a console table. Even in his haste it arrested him. Mae Turrett had something of a reputation for interior decoration, but large country houses have a way of collecting furnishing oddities, however rigorous their owner's taste may be.

Although he was not as a rule over-sensitive to artistic monstrosities, Mr Campion paused in respectful astonishment before this example of the mid-Victorian baroque. A bewildered looking bronze lady, clad in a pink marble nightgown, was seated upon a gilt ormolu log, one end of which had been replaced by a blue and white enamel clock face. As he stared the contraption chimed loudly and aggressively.

He passed on and forgot all about the clock as soon as he entered the dining-room. Mae Turrett sprang at him with little affected cries which he took to indicate a hostess's delight.

'Albert *dear*!' she said breathlessly. 'How marvellous to see you! Aren't we wonderfully festive? The gardener assures me it's going to snow tonight, in fact he's virtually promised it. I do love a real old family party at Christmas, don't you? Just our very own selves . . . too lovely! Let me introduce you to a very dear friend of mine: Mrs Welkin-Mr Campion.'

Campion was aware of a large middle-aged woman with drooping cheeks and stupid eyes who sniggered at him and looked away again.

Lunch was not a jolly meal by any means. Even Lady Turrett's cultivated chatter died down every now and again. However, Mr Campion had ample opportunity to observe the strangers of whom he had heard so much.

Mike Peters was a sturdy silent youngster with a brief smile and a determined chin. It was obvious that he knew what he wanted and was going for it steadily. Mr Campion found himself wishing him luck.

Since much criticism before a meeting may easily defeat its own ends, Mr Campion had been prepared to find the Welkin family pleasant but misunderstood people, round pegs in a very square hole. He was mistaken. Kenneth Welkin, a fresh faced, angry eyed young man, sat next to Sheila and sulked throughout the meal. The only remark he addressed to Mr Campion was to ask what make of car he drove and to disapprove loudly of the answer to his question.

A closer inspection of Mrs Welkin did not dispel Mr Campion's first impression, but her husband interested him. Edward Welkin was a large man with a face that would have been distinguished had it not been for the eyes, which were too shrewd, and the mouth, which was too coarse. His attitude towards his hostess was conspicuously different from his wife's, which was ingratiating, and his son's, which was uneasy and defensive. The most obvious thing about him was that he was completely alien. George he regarded quite clearly as a nincompoop and Lady Turrett as a woman who so far had given his wife value for money. To everyone else he was sublimely indifferent.

His tweeds, of the best old-gentleman variety, had their effect ruined by the astonishing quantity of jewellery he chose to display at the same time. He wore two signet rings, one with an agate and one with a sapphire, and an immense jewelled tiepin, while out of his waistcoat pocket peeped a gold and onyx pen with a pencil to match, strapped together in a bright green leather case. They were both of them as thick round as his forefinger and looked at first glance like the insignia of some obscure order.

Just before they rose from the table Mrs Welkin cleared her throat.

'As you are going to have a crowd of tenants this evening, Mae, I don't think I'll wear it, do you?' she said with a giggle and a glance at Mr Campion.

'Wear what, dear?' Lady Turrett spoke absently and Mrs Welkin looked hurt.

'The necklace,' she said reverently.

'Your diamonds? Good heavens, no! Most unsuitable.' The words escaped involuntarily, but in a moment her ladyship was mistress of herself and the situation. 'Wear something very simple,' she said with a mechanical smile. 'I'm afraid it's going to be very hard work for us all. Mike, you do know exactly what to do, don't you? At the end of the evening, just before they go home, you put on the costume and come into the little ante-room which leads off the platform. You go straight up to the tree and cut the presents off, while all the rest of us stand round to receive them and pass them on to the children.'

Mrs Welkin bridled. 'I should have liked to have worn them,' she said petulantly. 'Still, if you say it's not safe . . .'

'Mother didn't say it wasn't safe, Mrs Welkin,' said Sheila sharply. 'She said it wasn't suitable.'

Mrs Welkin blushed angrily.

'You're not very polite, young lady,' she said, 'and if it's a question of suitability, where's the suitability in Mr Peters playing Santa Claus when it was promised to Kenny?'

The mixture of muddled logic and resentment startled everyone. Sir George looked helplessly at his wife, Kenneth Welkin turned savagely on his mother, and Edward Welkin settled rather than saved the situation.

'That'll do,' he said in a voice of thunder. 'That's all been fixed, Ada. I don't want to hear any more from either of you on the subject.'

The table broke up with relief. Sir George tugged Campion's arm.

'Cigar-library,' he murmured and faded quietly away.

Campion followed him.

There were Christmas decorations in the book-filled study and, as he settled himself in a wing chair before a fire of logs and attended to the tip of a Romeo y Julieta, Mr Campion felt once more the return of the Christmas spirit.

Sir George was anxious about his daughter's happiness.

'I like young Peters,' he said earnestly. 'Fellow can't help his father's troubles.'

Mr Campion agreed with him and the older man went on.

'The boy Mike's an engineer,' he said, 'and makin' good at his job slowly, and Sheila seems fond of him, but Mae talks about hereditary dishonesty. Taint may be there. What do you think?'

Mr Campion had no time to reply to this somewhat unlikely theory. There was a flutter and a rustle outside the door and a moment later Mr Welkin senior came in with a flustered lady. George got up and held out his hand.

'Ah, Miss Hare,' he said. 'Glad to see you. Come on your annual visit of mercy?'

Miss Hare, who was large and inclined to be hearty, laughed.

'I've come cadging again, if that's what you mean, Sir George,' she said cheerfully, and went on, nodding to Mr Campion as if they had just been introduced. 'Every Christmas I come round collecting for my old women. There are four of 'em in the almshouse by the church. I only ask for a shilling or two to buy them some little extra for the Christmas treat. I don't want much. Just a shilling or two.'

She glanced at a small notebook in her hand.

'You gave me ten shillings last year, Sir George.'

He produced the required sum and Campion felt in his pocket.

'Half-a-crown would be ample,' said Miss Hare encouragingly. 'Oh, that's very nice of you. I assure you it won't be wasted.'

She took the coin and was turning to Welkin when he stepped forward.

'I'd like to do the thing properly,' he said. 'Anybody got a pen?'

He took out a cheque book and sat down at George's desk uninvited.

Miss Hare protested. 'Oh no, really,' she said, 'you don't understand. This is just for an extra treat. I collect it nearly all in sixpences.'

'Anybody got a pen?' repeated Mr Welkin.

Campion glanced at the elaborate display in the man's own waistcoat pocket, but before he could mention it George had meekly handed over his own fountain pen.

Mr Welkin wrote a cheque and handed it to Miss Hare without troubling to blot it.

'Ten pounds?' said the startled lady. 'Oh, but really ..!'

'Nonsense. Run along.' Mr Welkin clapped her familiarly on the shoulder. 'It's Christmas time,' he said, glancing at George and Campion. 'I believe in doing a bit of good at Christmas time – if you can afford it.'

Miss Hare glanced round her helplessly.

'It's very-very kind of you,' she said, 'but half-a-crown would have been ample.'

She fled. Welkin threw George's pen on to the desk.

'That's the way I like to do it,' he said.

George coughed and there was a faraway expression in his eyes.

'Yes, I-er-I see you do,' he said and sat down. Welkin went out.

Neither Mr Campion nor his host mentioned the incident. Campion frowned. Now he had two minor problems on his conscience. One was the old matter of the piece of information concerning Charlie Spring which he had forgotten, the other was a peculiarity of Mr Welkin's which puzzled him mightily.

The Pharaoh's Court children's party had been in full swing for what seemed to Mr Campion to be the best part of a fortnight. It was half-past seven in the evening and the relics of an enormous tea had been cleared away, leaving the music room full of replete but still energetic children and their mothers, dancing and playing games with enthusiasm.

Mr Campion, who had danced, buttled, and even performed a few conjuring tricks, bethought him of a box of his favourite cigarettes in his suitcase upstairs and, feeling only a little guilty at leaving George still working like a hero, he stole away and hurried to his room.

The main body of the house was deserted. Even the Welkins were at work in the music room, while the staff were concentrated in the kitchen washing up.

Mr Campion found his cigarettes, lit one, and pottered for a moment or two, reflecting that the Christmases of his youth were much the same as those of today, but not so long from hour to hour. He felt virtuous, happy and positively oozing with goodwill. The promised snow was falling, great soft flakes plopping softly against his window.

At last, when his conscience decreed that he could absent himself no longer, he switched off the light and stepped into the corridor, to come face to face with Father Christmas. The saint looked as weary as he himself had been and was stooping under the great sack on his shoulders. Mr Campion admired Harridge's costume. The boots were glossy, the tunic with its wool border satisfyingly red, while the benevolent mask with its cottonwool beard was almost lifelike.

He stepped aside to let the venerable figure pass and, because it seemed the moment for jocularity, said lightly:

'What have you got in the bag, Guv'nor?'

Had he uttered a spell of high enchantment, the simple words could not have had a more astonishing effect. The figure uttered an inarticulate cry, dropped the sack, which fell with a crash at Mr Campion's feet, and fled like a shadow.

For a moment Mr Campion stood paralysed with astonishment. By the time he had pulled himself together the crimson figure had disappeared down the staircase. He bent over the sack and thrust in his hand. Something hard and heavy met his fingers and he brought it out. It was the pink marble, bronze and ormolu clock.

He stood looking at his find and a sigh of satisfaction escaped him. One of the problems that had been worrying him all day had been solved.

It was twenty minutes later before he reappeared in the music room. No one saw him come in, for the attention of the entire room was focused upon the platform. There, surrounded by enthusiastic assistants, was Father Christmas again, peacefully snipping presents off the tree.

Campion took careful stock of him. The costume, he decided, was identical, the same high boots, the same tunic, the same mask. He tried to remember the fleeting figure in the corridor upstairs, but the costume was a deceptive one and he found it difficult.

After a time he found a secluded chair and sat down to await developments. They came.

As the last of the visitors departed and Lady Turrett threw herself into an armchair with a sigh of happy exhaustion, Pouter, the Pharaoh's Court butler, came quietly into the room and muttered a few words into his master's ear. From where he sat Mr Campion heard George's astonished 'God bless my soul!' and rose immediately to join him. But although he moved swiftly Mr Welkin was before him and, as Campion reached the group, his voice resounded round the room.

'A burglary? While we've been playing the fool in here? What's gone, man? What's gone?'

Pouter, who objected to the form of address, regarded his master's guest coldly.

'A clock from the first floor west corridor, a silver-plated salver, a copper loving cup from the hall, and a brass Buddha and a gilt pomander box from the first floor landing, as far as we can ascertain, sir,' he said.

'Bless my soul!' said George again. 'How extraordinary!'

'Extraordinary be damned!' ejaculated Welkin. 'We've got valuables here. Ada!'

'The necklace!' shrieked Mrs Welkin, consternation suddenly welling up in her eyes. 'My necklace!'

She scuttled out of the room and Sheila came forward with

Santa Claus, who had taken off his mask and pushed back his hood to reveal the features of Mike Peters.

Lady Turrett did not stir from her chair, and Kenneth Welkin, white faced and bewildered, stared down at her.

'There's been a burglary,' he said. 'Here, in this house.'

Mae Turrett smiled at him vaguely. 'George and Pouter will see to it,' she said. 'I'm tired.'

'Tired!' shouted Edward Welkin. 'If my wife's diamonds–'

He got no further. Ada Welkin tottered into the room, an empty steel dispatch case in her trembling hands.

'They've gone,' she said, her voice rising in hysteria. 'They've gone. My diamonds . . . my room's been turned upside down. They've been taken. The necklace has gone.'

It was Mike who had sufficient presence of mind to support her to a chair before she collapsed. Her husband shot a shrewd, preoccupied glance at her, shouted to his son to 'Look after your mother, boy!' and took command of the situation.

'You, Pigeon, get all the servants, everyone who's in this house, to come here in double quick time, see? I've been robbed.'

Pouter looked at his master in mute appeal and George coughed.

'In a moment, Mr Welkin,' he said. 'In a moment. Let us find out what we can first. Pouter, go and see if any stranger is known to have been about the house or grounds this evening, will you, please?'

The manservant went out instantly and Welkin raged.

'You may think you know what you are doing,' he said, 'but my way was the best. You're giving the thief time to get away, and time's precious, let me tell you. I've got to get the police up here?'

'The police?' Sheila was aghast.

He gaped at her. 'Of course, young woman. Do you think I'm going to lose twelve thousand pounds? The stones were insured, of course, but what company would pay up if I hadn't called in the police? I'll go and phone up now.'

'Wait a moment, please,' said George, his quiet voice only a little ruffled. 'Here's Pouter again. Well?'

The butler looked profoundly uncomfortable.

'Two maids say, sir,' he said, 'they saw a man running down the drive just before the Christmas tree was begun.' He hesitated. 'They-they say, sir, he was dressed as Father Christmas. They both say it, sir.'

Everyone looked at Mike and Sheila's cheeks flamed.

'Well?' she demanded.

Mr Welkin laughed. 'So that's how it was done,' he said. 'The young man was clever, but he was seen.'

Mike moved forward. His face was pale and his eyes were dangerous. George laid a hand upon his arm.

'Wait,' he commanded. 'Mr Welkin, you'll have to explain, you know.'

Mr Welkin kept his temper. He seemed almost amused.

'Well, it's perfectly simple, isn't it?' he said. 'This fellow has been wandering about in this disguise all the evening. He couldn't come in here because her ladyship wanted him to be a surprise to the children, but he had the rest of the house to himself. He went round lifting up anything he fancied, including my diamonds. Suppose he had been met? No one would think anything of it. Father Christmas always carried a sack. Then he went off down the drive where he met a confederate, handed over the stuff, and came back to the party.'

Mike began to speak but Mr Campion decided it was time to intervene.

'I say, George,' he said, 'if you and Mr Welkin would come along to the library I've got a suggestion I'd like to make.'

Welkin wavered. 'I'll listen to you, Campion, but I want my diamonds back and I want the police. I'll give you five minutes, no longer.'

The library was in darkness when the three men entered, and Campion waited until they were all in the room before he switched on the main light. There was a moment of bewildered silence. One corner of the room looked like a stall in a market. There the entire contents of the sack, which had come so un-expectedly into Mr Campion's possession, was neatly spread out. George's cherubic face darkened.

'What's this?' he demanded. 'A damned silly joke?'

Mr Campion shook his head. 'I'm afraid not. I've just collected this from a gentleman in fancy dress whom I met in the corridor upstairs,' he said. 'What would you say, Mr Welkin?'

The man stared at him doggedly. 'Where are my diamonds? That's my only interest. I don't care about this junk.'

Campion smiled faintly. 'He's right, you know, George,' he said. 'Junk's the word. It came back to me as soon as I saw it. Poor Charlie Spring – I recognized him, Mr Welkin – never had a successful coup in his life because he can't help stealing gaudy junk.'

Edward Welkin stood stiffly by the desk.

'I don't understand you,' he said. 'My diamonds have been stolen and I want to call the police.'

Mr Campion took off his spectacles. 'I shouldn't if I were you,' he said. 'No you don't–!'

On the last words Mr Campion lept forward and there was a brief struggle. When it was over Mr Welkin was lying on the floor beside the marble and ormolu clock and Mr Campion was grasping the gold pen and pencil in the leather holder which until a moment before had rested in the man's waistcoat pocket.

Welkin scrambled to his feet. His face was purple and his eyes a little frightened. He attempted to bluster.

'You'll find yourself in court for assault,' he said. 'Give me my property.'

'Certainly. All of it,' agreed Mr Campion obligingly. 'Your dummy pen, your dummy pencil, and in the receptacle which they conceal, your wife's diamonds.'

On the last word he drew the case apart and a glittering string fell out in his hand.

There was a long, long pause.

Welkin stood sullenly in the middle of the room.

'Well?' he said at last. 'What are you two going to do about it?'

Mr Campion glanced at George, who was standing by the desk, an expression of incredulity amounting almost to stupefaction upon his mild face.

'If I might suggest,' he murmured, 'I think he might take his family and spend a jolly Christmas somewhere else, don't you? It would save a lot of trouble.'

Welkin held out his hand.

'Very well. I'll take my diamonds.'

Mr Campion shook his head. 'As you go out of the house,' he said with a faint smile. 'I shouldn't like them to be – lost again.'

Welkin shrugged his shoulders. 'You win,' he said briefly. 'I'll go and tell Ada to pack.'

He went out of the room and as the door closed behind him George sat down.

'Hanged if I understand it . . .' he began, 'his own son Kenneth was going to play Santa Claus, or at least seemed to expect to.'

Campion nodded. 'I know,' he said. 'If Kenneth had been playing Father Christmas and the same thing happened I think you would have found that the young man had a pretty convincing alibi established for him. You must remember the thief was not meant to be seen. He was only furnished with the costume in case he was.'

His host took the diamonds and turned them over. He was slow of comprehension.

'Why steal his own property?' he demanded.

Mr Campion sighed. 'You have such a blameless mind, George, that the wickedness of some of your fellow men must be a constant source of astonishment to you.' He paused. 'Did you hear our friend Welkin say that he had insured this necklace?'

George's eyebrows rose. 'God bless my soul!' he said. 'What a feller! In our house, too,' he added as an afterthought. 'How did you spot it, Campion?'

Mr Campion explained. 'I knew Charlie Spring had a

peculiarity but I couldn't think what it was until I pulled that clock out of the bag. Then I remembered his penchant for the baroque and his sad habit of mistaking it for the valuable. That ruled out the diamonds. They wouldn't be large enough for Charlie. When that came back to me, I recollected his other failing. He never works alone. When Mr Spring appears on a job it always means he has a confederate in the house. With these two facts in my hand the rest was fairly obvious.'

'You spotted the pen was a dummy when Miss Hare came this afternoon?'

Mr Campion grinned. 'Well, it was odd the man didn't use his own pen, wasn't it?' he said. 'When he ignored it, I guessed. That kind of cache is fairly common, especially in the States. They're made for carrying valuables and are usually shabby plastic things which no one would steal in the ordinary way. However, there was nothing shabby about Mr Welkin-except his behaviour.'

George poured out a couple of drinks. 'Difficult feller,' he observed. 'Didn't like him from the start. No conversation. I started him on shootin', but he wasn't interested, mentioned huntin' and he gaped at me, went on to fishin' and he yawned. Couldn't think of anything to talk to him about. Feller hadn't any conversation at all.'

THE CASE OF THE WHITE ELEPHANT

Mr Campion, piloting his companion through the crowded courtyard at Burlington House, became aware of the old lady in the Daimler, partly because her chauffeur almost ran over him and partly because she gave him a stare of such vigorous and personal disapproval that he felt she must either know him very well indeed or have mistaken him for someone else entirely.

Juliet Fysher-Sprigge, who was leaning on his arm with all the weariness of a two-hour trek round the Academy's Summer Exhibition, enlightened him.

'We were *not* amused, were we?' she said. 'Old-fashioned people have minds that are just too prurient, my dear. After all, I have known you for years, haven't I, and I'm not even married to Philip. Besides, the Academy is so respectable. It isn't as though she'd seen me sneaking out of the National Gallery.'

Mr Campion handed her into a taxicab.

'Who was she?' he enquired, hoisting his lank form in after her.

Juliet laughed. Her laughter was one of her most charming attributes, for it wiped the sophistication from her debutante's face and left her the schoolgirl he had known three years before.

'My dear, didn't you recognize her? That would have been the last straw for the poor darling! That's Florence, Dowager Countess of Marie. Philip's Auntie Flo.'

Mr Campion's pale blue eyes grew momentarily more intelligent behind his horn-rimmed spectacles.

'Ah, hence the disgust,' he said. 'You'll have to explain me away. The police are always doing it.'

Juliet turned to him with the wide-eyed ingenuousness of one who perceives a long-awaited opening.

'You still dabble in police and detection and things, then?' she said breathlessly and not very tactfully, since his reputation as a criminologist was considerable. 'Do tell me, what is the low-down on these terribly exciting burglaries? Are the police really beaten or are they being bribed? No one talks of anything else these days. I just had to see you and find out.'

Her companion leant back in the leathery depths of the cab and sighed regretfully.

'When you phoned me and demanded to be taken to this execrable exhibition I was vain enough to think it was my companionship you were after,' he said. 'Now it turns out to be merely a vulgar pursuit of the material for gossip. Well, my girl, you're going to be disappointed. The clever gentleman doesn't know a thing and, what's more, he doesn't care. Have you lost anything yourself?'

'Me?' Juliet's gratification at the implied compliment all but outweighed her disappointment. 'Of course I haven't. It's only the really worth-while collections that have gone. That's why it's so interesting. The De Breuil diamonds went first. Then the Denver woman lost her emeralds and the glorious Napoleon necklace. Josephine Pharaoh had her house burgled and just lost her tiara, which was the one really good thing she had, and now poor old Mrs Dacre has had her diamonds and rubies pinched, including the famous dog collar. Forty-two diamonds, my dear! – each one quite as big as a pea. They say it's a cat burglar and the police know him quite well, but they can't find him – at least, that's one story. The other one is that it's all being done for the insurance and the police are in it. What do you think?'

Mr Campion glanced at her affectionately and noted that the gold hair under her small black hat curled as naturally as ever.

'Both stories are equally good,' he announced placidly. 'Come and have some tea, or has Philip's Auntie Flo got spies everywhere?'

Miss Fysher-Sprigge blushed. 'I don't care if she has,' she said. 'I've quarrelled with Philip, anyway.'

It took Mr Campion several minutes – until they were seated at a table on the edge of the Hotel Monde's smaller dance-floor, in fact – before he fully digested this piece of information. Juliet was leaning back in her chair, her eyes roving over the gathering in a frank search for old acquaintances, when he spoke again.

'Seriously?' he enquired.

Juliet met his eyes and again he saw her sophistication vanish.

'I hope not,' she said soberly. 'I've been rather an ass. Can I tell you about it?'

Mr Campion smiled ruefully. It was a sign of the end of the thirties, he supposed, when one submitted cheerfully to the indignity of taking a young woman out only to hear about her hopes and fears concerning a younger man. Juliet went on blissfully, lowering her voice so that the heart-searchings of the balalaika orchestra across the floor concealed it from adjoining tables.

'Philip is a dear, but he has to be so filthily careful about the stupidest things,' she said, accepting a rhumbaba. 'The F.O. casts a sort of white light over people, have you noticed? His relations are like it, too, only worse. You can't talk of anything without getting warned off. The aunt we saw to-day bit my head off the other evening for merely mentioning these cat burglaries, which, after all, are terribly exciting. "My child," she said, "we can't afford to know about such things," and went on talking about her old White Elephant until I nearly wept.'

'White Elephant?' Mr Campion looked blank. 'The charity?'

Juliet nodded. '"Send your white elephant to Florence, Countess of Marie, and she will find it a home where it will be the pet of the family,"' she quoted. 'It's quite an important affair, patronized by royalty and blessed by every archbishop in the world. I pointed out it was only a glorified jumble sale and she nearly had a fit. She works herself to death for it. I go and help pack up parcels sometimes – or I did before this row with Philip. I've been rather silly. I've done something infuriating. Philip's livid with me now and I don't know what's going to happen when he finds out everything. I must tell somebody. Can I tell you?'

A faint smile passed over Mr Campion's thin face.

'You're quite a nice girl,' he said, 'but you won't stay twenty-one for ever. Stop treating me as though I was a maiden uncle.'

'You must be thirty-six at least,' said Miss Fysher-Sprigge brutally, 'and I'm rather glad, because presumably you're sensible. Look here, if a man has a criminal record it doesn't mean he's always going to be stealing things, does it? Not if he promises to go straight?'

Her companion frowned. 'I don't quite follow,' he said. 'Age is stopping the brain from functioning. I thought we were talking about Philip Graysby, Auntie Flo's nephew?'

'So we are,' said Juliet. 'He hasn't got the record, of course, but Henry Swan has. Henry Swan is – or, rather, was – Philip's man. He'd been with Philip for eighteen months and been perfectly good, and then this came out about him. Philip said he was awfully sorry, but he'd have to go. Philip couldn't help it, I suppose – I do see that now – but at the time I was furious. It seemed so unfair, and we had a quarrel. I said some beastly things and so did he, but he wouldn't give in and Swan went.'

She paused and eyed her companion dubiously. Mr Campion shrugged his shoulders.

'It doesn't seem very serious,' he said.

Juliet accepted the cigarette he offered her and seemed engrossed in the tip of it.

'No,' she agreed. 'That part isn't. But you see, I'm a very impulsive person and I was stupidly cross at the time and so when I had a wonderful idea for getting my own back I acted on it. I got Swan a job with the most respectable person I knew and, in order to do it, I gave him a reference. To make it a good reference I didn't say anything about the record. How's that?'

'Not so good,' he admitted. 'Who's the most respectable person harbouring this human bomb?'

Juliet avoided his eyes. 'Philip's Auntie Flo,' she said. 'She's the stiffest, thorniest, most conventional of them all. Philip doesn't go there often, so he hasn't seen Swan yet, but when he does and makes enquiries and hears about me – well, it's going to be awkward. D'you think he'll ever forgive me? He stands to get a fortune from Auntie Flo if he doesn't annoy her. It was a silly thing of me to do, wasn't it?'

'Not bright,' agreed Mr Campion. 'Are you in love with Philip?'

'Horribly,' said Juliet Fysher-Sprigge and looked away across the dance-floor.

Mr Campion had spent some time expounding a wise course of action, in which a clean breast to all concerned figured largely, when he became aware that he was not being heard. Juliet was still staring across the room, her eyes puzzled.

'I say,' she said unexpectedly, 'this place is wildly expensive, isn't it?'

'I hope not,' said Mr Campion mildly.

Juliet did not smile. Her cheeks were faintly flushed and her eyes questioning.

'Don't be a fool. You know what I mean. This is probably the most expensive place in London, isn't it? How queer! It looks as though Auntie Flo really has got her spies everywhere. That's her manicurist over there, having tea alone.'

He glanced casually across the room.

'The woman sitting directly under the orchestra?' he enquired. 'The one who looks like a little bull in a navy hat? She's an interesting type, isn't she? Not very nice.'

Juliet's eyes were still thoughtful.

'That's her. Miss Matisse. A visiting manicurist,' she said. 'She goes to dozens of people I know. I believe she's very good. How funny for her to come to tea alone, here of all places . . .'

Mr Campion's casual interest in the small square figure who

managed somehow to look flamboyant in spite of her sober clothes showed signs of waning.

'She may be waiting for someone,' he suggested.

'But she's ordered her tea and started it.'

'Oh well, perhaps she just felt like eating.'

'Rubbish!' said Juliet. 'You pay ten and sixpence just to sit in this room because you can dance if you want to.'

Her host laughed. 'Auntie Flo has a pretty turn of speed if she tracked us down here and then whipped round and set her manicuring bloodhound on us, all in half an hour,' he said.

Juliet ignored him. Her attention had wandered once again.

'I say,' she murmured, 'can you see through that mirror over there? See that man eating alone? I thought at first he was watching Miss Matisse, but I believe it's you he's most interested in.'

Her companion turned his head and his eyes widened.

'Apologies,' he said. 'I under-estimated you. That's Detective-Sergeant Blower, one of the best men in the public-school and night-club tradition. I wonder whom he's tailing. Don't watch him – it's unkind.'

Juliet laughed. 'You're a most exciting person to have tea with,' she said.' I do believe . . .'

The remainder of her remark was lost as, in common with all but one visitor in the room she was silenced by what was, for the Hotel Monde, a rather extraordinary incident.

The balalaika orchestra had ceased to play for a moment or so and the dance floor was practically deserted when, as though taking advantage of the lull, the woman in the navy hat rose from her chair and shouted down the whole length of the long room, in an effort, apparently, to attract the attention of a second woman who had just entered.

'Mrs Gregory!' Her voice was powerful and well articulated.' Mrs Gregory! Mrs Gregory!'

The newcomer halted as all eyes were turned upon her, and her escort expostulated angrily to the excited *maître d'hôtel* who hurried forward.

Miss Matisse sat down, and in the silence Mr Campion heard her explaining in a curiously flat voice to the waiter who came up to her:

'I am sorry. I thought I recognized a friend. I was mistaken. Bring me my bill, please.'

Juliet stared across the table, her young face shocked.

'What a very extraordinary thing to do,' she said.

Mr Campion did not reply. From this place of vantage he could see in the mirror that Detective-Sergeant Blower had also called for his bill and was preparing to leave.

Some little time later, when Mr Campion deposited Juliet on her Mount Street doorstep, she was in a more cheerful mood.

'Then you think if I go to Philip and tell him the worst and say that I'm sorry he'll forgive me?' she said as they parted.

'If he's human he'll forgive you anything,' Mr Campion assured her gallantly.

Juliet sighed. 'Age does improve the manners,' she said unnecessarily. 'I'll forgive you for disappointing me about the burglaries. I really had hoped to get all the dirt. Good-bye.'

'Damn the burglaries!' said Mr Campion and took a taxi home.

Three days later he said the same thing again, but for a

different reason. This reason arrived by post. It came in a fragrant green box designed to contain a large flask of familiar perfume and it lay upon his breakfast table winking at him with evil amusement. It was Mrs Dacre's ruby-and-diamond dog collar and it was not alone. In a nest of cotton wool beneath it were five diamond rings of considerable value, a pair of exquisite ruby ear-clips, and a small hooped bracelet set with large alternate stones.

Mr Campion, who was familiar with the 'stolen' list which the police send round to their local stations and circularize to the jewellers and pawnbrokers of the kingdom, had no difficulty in recognizing the collection as the haul of the last cat burglary.

The sender of so dubious a gift might have been harder to identify had it not been for the familiarity of the perfume and the presence of a small card on which was printed, in shaky, ill-disguised characters, a simple request and a specious promise:

Get these back where they belong and I'll love you for ever, darling.

Mr Campion had a considerable respect for the Law, but he spent some time that morning in acquiring a box of similar design but different and more powerful perfume, and it was not until the jewellery was freshly housed and the card burned that he carried his responsibility to Scotland Yard and laid it with a sigh of relief on the desk of Chief Detective-Inspector Stanislaus Oates, his friend and partner in many adventures.

The original wrappings he decided to retain. Its ill-written address might have been scrawled by anyone, and the fact that it was grossly overfranked showed that it had been dropped into a public box and not passed over a post-office counter.

He let the chief, who was a tall, disconsolate personage with a grey face and dyspepsia, recover from his first transports of mingled relief and suspicion before regretting his inability to help him further. Oates regarded him.

'It's my duty to warn you that you're under suspicion,' he said with the portentous solemnity which passed with him for wit.

Campion laughed. 'My cat-burglary days are over,' he said. 'Or am I the fence?'

'That's more like it.' The chief passed his cigarette case. 'I can't tell you how glad I am to see this lot. But it doesn't help us very much unless we know where it came from. These "cat" jobs are done by The Sparrow. We knew that as soon as we saw the first one. You remember him, Campion? – a sleek, handsome chap with an insufferable manner. These jobs have his trade-marks all over them. Pane cut out with a diamond and the glass removed with a sucker – no finger-prints, no noise, no mistakes.' He paused and caressed his ear sadly. 'It's getting on my nerves,' he said. 'The Commissioner is sarcastic and the papers are just libellous. It's hard on us. We know who and where the fellow is, but we can't get him. We've held him as long as we dared, three separate times this summer, but we haven't got a thing we can fix on him. I've been trusting the stuff would turn up somewhere so that we could work back on him from that angle, but, frankly, this is the first scrap of it I've seen. Where's all the early swag? This was only pinched five days ago.'

Mr Campion remained unhelpful. 'I got it this morning,' he said. 'It just came out of the air. Ask the postman.'

'Oh, I know . . .' The chief waved the suggestion aside. 'You'll help us just as much as you can, which means as much as you care to. Some society bit is mixed up in this somewhere, I'm sure of it. Look here, I'll tell you what I'll do. I'll put my cards on the table. This isn't official; this is the truth. Edward Borringer, alias The Sparrow, is living with his wife in digs in Kilburn. They're very respectable at the moment, just a quiet hard-working couple. He takes classes in the local gym and she does visiting manicure work.'

'Under the name of Matisse?'

'Exactly!' The Inspector was jubilant. 'Now you've given yourself away, my lad. What do you know about Margot Matisse?'

'Not much,' his visitor confessed affably. 'She was pointed out to me as a manicurist at a *thé dansant* at the Hotel Monde on Tuesday. Looking round, I saw Blower on her trail, so naturally when you mentioned manicurists I put two and two together.'

'Who pointed her out to you?'

'A lady who had seen her at work in a relation's house.'

'All right.' The policeman became depressed again. 'Well, there you are. It's quite obvious how they're working it. She goes round to the big houses and spots the stuff and the lie of the land, and then he calls one night and does the job. It's the old game worked very neatly. Too neatly, if you ask me. What we can't fathom is how they're disposing of the stuff. They certainly haven't got it about them, and their acquaintance just now is so respectable, not to say aristocratic, that we can barely approach it. Besides, to make this big stuff worth the risk they must be using an expert. Most of these stones are so well known that they must go to a first-class fellow to be recut.'

Mr Campion hesitated. 'I seem to remember that Edward

Borringer was once associated with our old friend Bertrand Meyer and his *ménage*,' he ventured. 'Are they still functioning?'

'Not in England.' The chief was emphatic. 'And if these two are getting their stuff out of the country I'll eat my hat. The customs are co-operating with us. We thought a maid in one of the houses which the Matisse woman visits might be in it and so, if you've heard a squawk from your society pals about severity at the ports, that's our work. I don't mind telling you it's all very difficult. You can see for yourself. These are the Matisse clients.'

Mr Campion scanned the typewritten page and his sympathy for his friend deepened.

'Oh yes, Caesar's wives,' he agreed. 'Every one of 'em. Servants been in the families for years, I suppose?'

'Unto the third and fourth generations,' said the chief bitterly.

His visitor considered the situation.

'I suppose they've got alibis fixed up for the nights of the crimes?' he enquired.

'Fixed up?' The chief's tone was eloquent. 'The alibis are so good that we ought to be able to arrest 'em on suspicion alone. An alibi these days doesn't mean anything except that the fellow knows his job. Borringer does, too, and so does his wife. We've had them both on the carpet for hours without getting a glimmer from them. No, it's no use, Campion; we've got to spot the middleman and then the fence, and pin it on them that way. Personally, I think the woman actually passes the stuff, but we've had Blower on her for weeks and he swears she doesn't speak to a soul except these superior clients of hers. Also, of course, neither of them post anything. We thought we'd got something once and got the Postal authorities to help us, but all we got for our trouble was a p.c. to a viscountess about an appointment for chiropody.'

Mr Campion was silent for some time.

'It was funny, her shouting out like that in the Hotel Monde,' he said at last.

The chief grunted. 'Mrs Gregory,' he said. 'Yes, I heard about that. A little show for Blower's benefit, if you ask me. Thought she'd give him something to think about. The Borringers are like that, cocky as hell.'

Once again there was thoughtful silence in the light airy office and this time it was Stanislaus Oates who spoke first.

'Look here, Campion,' he said, 'you and I know one another. Let this be a word of friendly warning. If you suspect anyone you know of getting mixed up in this – for a bit of fun, perhaps – see that she's careful. If The Sparrow and his wife are still tied up with the Meyer lot – and they very well may be – the Meyer crowd aren't a pretty bunch. In fact, you know as well as I do, they're dirty and they're dangerous.'

His visitor picked up the list again. Philip Graysby's aunt's name headed the second column. He made up his mind.

'I don't know anything,' he said. 'I'm speaking entirely from guesswork and I rely on you to go into this in stockinged feet with your discretion wrapping you like a blanket. But if I were you I should have a little chat with one Henry Swan, employed by Florence, Dowager Countess of Marie.'

'Ah,' said the chief with relief, 'that's where the wind blows, does it? I thought you'd come across.'

'I don't promise anything,' Campion protested.

'Who does?' said Stanislaus Oates and pulled a pad towards him . . .

Mr Campion kept late hours. He was sitting up by the open window of his flat in Bottle Street, the cul-de-sac off Piccadilly, when the Chief Detective-Inspector called upon him just after midnight on the evening of his visit to Scotland Yard. The policeman was unusually fidgety. He accepted a drink and sat down before mentioning the purpose of his visit, which was, in fact, to gossip.

Campion, who knew him, let him take his time.

'We pulled that chap Swan in this afternoon,' he volunteered at last. 'He's a poor weedy little beggar who did a stretch for larceny in twenty-three and seems to have gone straight since. We had quite a time with him. He wouldn't open his mouth at first. Fainted when he thought we were going to jug him. Finally, of course, out it came, and a very funny story it was. Know anything about the White Elephant Society, Campion?'

His host blinked. 'Nothing against it,' he admitted. 'Ordinary charity stunt. Very decently run, I believe. The dowager does it herself.'

'I know.' There was a note of mystification in the chief's voice. 'See this?'

From his wallet he took a small green stick-on label. It was an ornate product embellished with a design of angels in the worst artistic taste. Across the top was a printed heading:

This is a gift from the White Elephant Society (*Secy, Florence, Countess of Marle*) *and contains* – A blank space had been filled up with the legend: *Two Pairs of Fancy Woollen Gloves* in ink.

The address, which was also in ink, was that of a well-known orphanage and the addressee was the matron.

'That's how they send the white elephants out,' Oates explained. 'There's a word or two inside in the countess's own handwriting. This is a specimen label. See what it means? It's as good as a diplomatic pass with that old woman's name on it.'

'Whom to?' demanded Mr Campion dubiously.

'Anyone,' declared the chief triumphantly. 'Especially the poor chap in the customs office who's tired of opening parcels. Even if he does open 'em he's not going to examine 'em. Now here's Swan's story. He admits he found the jewellery, which he passed on to a friend whose name he will not divulge. That friend must have sent it to you. It sounds like a woman to me, but I'm not interested in her at the moment.'

'Thank God for that,' murmured his host devoutly. 'Go on. Where did he find the stuff?'

'In a woollen duck inside one of these White Elephant parcels,' said the chief unexpectedly. 'We've got the duck; home-made toy with little chamois pockets under its wings. The odd thing is that Swan swears the old lady gave the parcel to him herself, told him to post it, and made such a fuss about it that he became suspicious and opened it up.'

'Do you believe that?' Mr Campion was grinning and Oates frowned.

'I do,' he said slowly. 'Curiously enough I do, in the main. In the first place, this chap honestly wants to go straight. One dose of clink has put him in terror of it for life. Secondly, if he was in on the theft why give the whole game away? Why produce the duck? What I do think is that he recognized the address. He says he can't remember anything about it except that it was somewhere abroad, but that's just what he would say if he recognized it and thought it was dangerous and was keeping quiet for fear of reprisals. Anyway, I believed him sufficiently to go down and interview the old lady.'

'Did you, By Jove!' murmured Mr Campion with respect.

Stanislaus Oates smiled wryly and ran his finger round the inside of his collar.

'Not a homely woman,' he observed. 'Ever met someone who made you feel you wanted a haircut, Campion? I was very careful, of course. Kid gloves all the way. Had to. I tell you one funny thing, though: she was rattled.'

Mr Campion sat up. He knew his friend to be one of the soberest judges of humanity in the police force, where humanity is deeply studied.

'Sure?' he demanded incredulously.

'Take my dying oath on it,' said the chief. 'Scared blue, if you ask me.'

The young man in the horn-rimmed spectacles made polite but depreciating noises. The chief shook his head.

'It's the truth. I gave her the facts – well, most of them. I didn't explain how we came to open the parcel, since that part of the business wasn't strictly orthodox. But I gave her the rest of the story just as I've given it to you, and instead of being helpful she tried to send me about my business with a flea in my ear. She insisted that she had directed each outgoing parcel during the last four weeks herself and swore that the Matisse woman could never have had access to any of them. Also, which is significant, she would not give me a definite reply about the duck. She was not sure if she'd ever seen it before. I ask you – a badly made yellow duck in a blue pullover. Anyone'd know it again.'

Mr Campion grinned. 'What was the upshot of this embarrassing interview?' he enquired.

The chief coughed. 'When she started talking about her son in the Upper House I came away,' he said briefly. 'I thought I'd let it rest for a day or two. Meanwhile, we shall keep a wary eye on Swan and the Borringers, although if those three are working together I'll resign.'

He was silent for a moment.

'She certainly was rattled,' he repeated at last. 'I'd swear it. Under the magnificent manner of hers she was scared. She had that set look about the eyes. You can't mistake it. What d'you make of that, my lad?'

'I don't,' said Campion discreetly. 'It's absurd.'

Oates sighed. 'Of course it is,' he agreed. 'And so what?'

'Sleep on it,' his host suggested and the chief took the hint . . .

It was unfortunate for everyone concerned that Mr Campion should have gone into the country early the following morning on a purely personal matter concerning a horse which he was thinking of buying and should not have returned to his flat until the evening. When he did get back he found Juliet and the dark, good-looking Philip Graysby, with whom she had presumably made up her differences, waiting for him. To Mr Campion they both seemed very young and very distressed. Juliet appeared to have been crying and it was she who broke the news.

'It's Auntie Flo,' she said in a small tragic voice. 'She's bunked, Albert.'

It took Mr Campion some seconds to assimilate this interesting development, and by that time young Graysby had launched into hurried explanations.

'That's putting it very crudely,' he said. 'My aunt caught the Paris plane this morning. Certainly she travelled alone, which was unusual, but that may not mean anything. Unfortunately, she did not leave an address, and although we've got into touch with the Crillon she doesn't seem to have arrived there.'

He hesitated and his dark face became suddenly ingenuous.

'It's so ridiculously awkward, her going off like this without telling anyone just after Detective-Inspector Oates called on her last night. I don't know what the interview was about, of course – nobody does – but there's an absurd feeling in the household that it wasn't very pleasant. Anyway, the inspector was very interested to hear that she had gone away when he called round this afternoon. It was embarrassing not being able to give him any real information about her return, and precious little about her departure. You see, we shouldn't have known she'd taken the plane if the chauffeur hadn't driven her to Croydon. She simply walked out of the house this morning and ordered the car. She didn't even take a suit-case, which looks as though she meant to come back to-night, and, of course, there's every possibility that she will.'

Mr Campion perched himself on the table and his eyes were grave.

'Tell me,' he said quietly, 'had Lady Florence an appointment with her manicurist to-day?'

'Miss Matisse?' Juliet looked up. 'Why, yes, she had, as a matter of fact. I went round there quite early this morning. Swan phoned me and told me Aunt had left rather hurriedly, so I – er – I went to see him.'

She shot an appealing glance at Philip, who grimaced at her, and she hurried on.

'While I was there Miss Matisse arrived and Bennett – Aunt's maid – told her all the gossip before I could stop her. Oh my dear, you don't think . . .?'

Instead of replying Mr Campion reached for the telephone and dialled a famous Whitehall number. Chief Detective-Inspector Oates was glad to hear his voice. He said so. He was also interested to know if Mr Campion had heard of the recent developments in The Sparrow case.

'No,' he said in reply to Mr Campion's sharp question. 'The two Borringers are behaving just as usual. Blower's had the girl under his eye all day . . . No, she hasn't communicated with anyone . . . What? . . . Wait a minute. I've got notes on Blower's telephoned report here. Here we are. "On leaving the Dowager Countess of Marie's house Miss Matisse went to the Venetian Cinema in Regent Street for the luncheon programme." Nothing happened there except that she pulled Blower's leg again.'

'Did she shout to someone?' Mr Campion's tone was urgent.

'Yes. Called to a woman named Mattie, who she said she thought was in the circle. Same silly stunt as last time. What's the matter?'

Campion checked his exasperation. He was desperately in earnest and his face as he bent over the instrument was frighteningly grave.

'Oates,' he said quietly, 'I'm going to ring you again in ten minutes and then you've got to get busy. Remember our little talk about the Meyers? This may be life or death.'

'Good . . .' began the chief and was cut off.

Mr Campion hustled his visitors out of the flat

'We're going down to see Swan,' he said, 'and the quicker we get there the better.'

Henry Swan proved to be a small frightened man who was inclined to be more than diffident until he had had matters explained to him very thoroughly. Then he was almost pathetically anxious to help.

'The address on the duck parcel, sir?' he said, echoing Mr Campion's question nervously. 'I daren't tell the police that. It might have been more than my life was worth. But if you think her ladyship–"

'Let's have it,' cut in Graysby irritably.

'Please,' murmured Juliet.

Mr Swan came across. 'Nineteen A, Rue Robespierre, Lyons, France,' he blurted out. 'I've burned the label, but I remember the address. In fact, to tell you the truth, it was because of the address I opened the box in the first place. I never had such a fright in all my life, sir, really.'

'I see. Whom was the parcel sent to?' Mr Campion's manner was comfortingly reassuring.

Henry Swan hesitated. 'Maurice Bonnet,' he said at last, 'and I once met a man who called himself that.'

Mr Campion's eyes flickered. 'On those occasions when he wasn't calling himself Meyer, I suppose?' he remarked.

The small man turned a shade or so paler and dropped his eyes.

'I shouldn't like to say, sir,' he murmured.

'Very wise,' Campion agreed. 'But you've got nothing to worry about now. We've got the address and that's all that matters. You run along. Graysby, you and I have got to hurry. I'll just have a word with Oates on the phone and then we'll nip down to Croydon and charter a plane.'

Juliet caught his arm. 'You don't mean Philip's aunt might be in *danger*?' she said.

Mr Campion smiled down at her. 'Some people do resent interference so, my dear,' he said, 'especially when they have quite a considerable amount to lose . . .'

The Rue Robespierre is not in the most affluent quarter of Lyons and just before midnight on a warm spring evening it is not seen at its best. There silent figures loll in the dark doorways of houses which have come down in the world, and the night life has nothing to do with gaiety.

From Scotland Yard the wires had been busy and Campion and Graysby were not alone as they hurried down the centre of the wide street. A military little capitaine and four gendarmes accompanied them, but even so they were not overstaffed.

As their small company came to a stop before the crumbling façade of number nineteen A an upper window was thrown open and a shot spat down upon them. The capitaine drew his own gun and fired back, while the others put their shoulders to the door.

As they pitched into the dark musty hall a rain of fire met them from the staircase. A bullet took Mr Campion's hat from his head, and one of the gendarmes stepped back swearing, his left hand clasping a shattered right elbow.

The raiding party defended itself. For three minutes the darkness was streaked with fire, while the air became heavy with the smell of cordite.

The end came suddenly. There was a scream from the landing and a figure pitched over the balustrade on to the flags below, dragging another with it in its flight, while pattering footsteps flying up to the top storey testified to the presence of a fugitive.

Mr Campion plunged forward, the others at his heels. They found Florence, Dowager Countess of Marie, at last in a locked bedroom on the third floor. She had defended herself and had suffered for it. Her black silk was torn and dusty and her coiffure dishevelled. But her spirit was unbroken and the French police listened to her tirade with a respect all the more remarkable since they could not understand one word of it.

Graysby took his aunt back to her hotel in a police car and Mr Campion remained to assist in the cleaning up.

Bertrand Meyer himself actually succeeded in getting out on to the roof, but he was brought back finally and the little capitaine had the satisfaction of putting the handcuffs on him.

One of the gang had been killed outright when his head had met the flagstones of the hall, and the remaining member was hurried off to a prison hospital with a broken thigh.

Mr Campion looked at Meyer with interest. He was an oldish man, square and powerful, with strong sensitive hands and the hot angry eyes of a fanatic. His workroom revealed many treasures. A jeweller's bench, exquisitely fitted with all the latest appliances, contained also a drawer which revealed the dismembered fragments of the proceeds of the first three London burglaries, together with some French stones in particular request by the *Sûrelé*.

Campion looked round him. 'Ah,' he said with satisfaction, 'and there's the wireless set. I wondered when some of you fellows were going to make use of the outside broadcasting programmes. How did you work it? Had someone listening to the first part of the first programme to be broadcast from a London public place each day, I suppose? It really is amazing how clearly those asides come, her voice quite fearless and yet so natural that it wasn't until some time afterwards that I realized she had been standing just below the orchestra's live microphone.'

Meyer did not answer. His face was sullen and his eyes were fixed on the stones which the Frenchmen were turning out of little chamois leather bags on to the baize surface of the bench . . .

It was some days later, back in the flat in Bottle Street, when Chief Detective-Inspector Oates sipped a whisky and soda and beamed upon his friend.

'I take off my hat to the old girl,' he said disrespectfully. 'She's got courage and a great sense of justice. She says she'll go into the witness-box if we need her and she apologized handsomely to me for taking the law into her own hands.'

'Good,' said Mr Campion. 'You've got the Borringers, of course?'

The chief grinned. 'We've got 'em as safe as a couple of ferrets in a box,' he declared. 'The man's an expert, but the woman's a genius. The story she told the old lady, for instance. That was more than brains. After she'd got her ladyship interested in her she broke down one day and told a pretty little yarn about her cruel husband in France who had framed a divorce and got the custody of the kid. She told a harrowing story about the little presents she had made for it herself and had had sent back to her *pronto*. It didn't take her long to get the old woman to offer to send them as though they'd come from the White Elephant Society. Every woman has a streak of sentimentality in her somewhere. So all the Borringer – alias Matisse – girl had to do was to bring along the toys in her manicure case from time to time and have 'em despatched free, gratis, with a label which almost guaranteed 'em a free pass. Very nice, eh?'

'Very,' Campion agreed. 'Almost simple.'

The chief nodded. 'She did it well,' he said; 'so well that even after I'd given the old lady the facts she didn't trust me. She believed so strongly in this fictitious kid that she went roaring over to Lyons to find out the truth for herself before she gave the girl away. Unfortunately, the Borringers had that means of wireless communication with Meyer and so when she arrived the gang was ready for her. It's a good thing you got there, Campion. They're a hot lot. I wonder what they'd have done with her.'

'Neat,' muttered Mr Campion. 'That wireless stunt, I mean.'

'It was.' Oates was still impressed.' The use of the names made it sound so natural. What was the code exactly? Do you know?'

His host pulled a dictionary from a shelf at his side and turned over the leaves until he came to a small section at the end.

'It's childish,' he said. 'Funny how these people never do any inventing if they can help it. Look it all up.'

The chief took the book and read the heading aloud.

'*The More Common British Christian Names and Their Meanings.*'

He ran his eyes down the columns.

'*Gregory,*' he read. '*A watcher.* Good Lord, that was to tell 'em Blower was on their track, I suppose. And Mattie . . . what's Mattie?'

He paused. '"*Diminutive of Matilda*",' he said at last. '"*Mighty Battle Maid*". I don't get that.'

'Dangerous, indignant and female,' translated Mr Campion. 'It rather sums up Philip Graysby's Auntie Flo, don't you think?'

It was after the chief had gone and he was alone that Juliet phoned. She was jubilant and her clear voice bubbled over the wire.

'I can't thank you,' she said. 'I don't know what to say. Aunt Florence is perfectly marvellous about everything. And I say, Albert . . .'

'Yes?'

'Philip says we can keep Swan if we have him at the country house. We're going to be married quite soon, you know. Our reconciliation rather hurried things along . . . Oh, what did you say?'

Mr Campion smiled. 'I said I'll have to send you a wedding present, then,' he lied.

There was a fraction of silence at the other end of the wire.

'Well, darling . . . it would be just too terribly sweet if you really *wanted* to,' said Miss Fysher-Sprigge.

THE CASE OF THE OLD MAN IN THE WINDOW

Newly appointed Superintendent Stanislaus Oates was by no means intoxicated, but he was cheerful, as became a man celebrating an important advance in a distinguished career, and Mr Campion, who sat opposite him at the small table in the corner of the chop-house, surveyed the change in his usually taciturn friend with interest.

'This promotion puts me into the memoir class when I retire, you know,' observed the ex-Inspector suddenly with uncharacteristic ingenuousness. 'I could write a first-rate book if someone put it down for me. We professionals get to know all kinds of things, interesting stuff a lot of it, that you amateurs never come across; things you'd never consider worth noticing. I struck something very curious to-day. Big business is extraordinary, Campion. Amazing inducements to crime in it. Let me tell you something about company law.'

Mr Campion grinned. 'Tell the world as well,' he suggested affably, for the Superintendent's voice had risen. 'I thought you said this place was deserted in the evening,' he went on, stretching his long thin legs under the table and adjusting his horn-rimmed spectacles. 'It seems to me to be pretty well crowded with youth and – er – passion.'

The ex-Inspector's innate caution reasserted itself and as he glanced about him his long face took on its natural melancholy expression.

'Must have suddenly become fashionable,' he said gloomily. 'That's the trouble with these places. The word goes round that So-and-so's is good, quiet and cheap, and what happens? Before you know where you are a great bunch of goggle-eyed sweethearts swoop down on it and up go the prices while the food goes to pieces. There's a lad over there out with someone he doesn't intend to take home to meet the family.'

Mr Campion, glancing casually over his thin shoulder, caught a glimpse of a heavily jowled face beneath a domed head prematurely bald, and beyond it the dark curls and crimson lips of a girl in a grey hat. He looked away again hastily.

'The name is March,' said Oates, whose spirits were reviving. 'Member of the big theatrical machinery firm. Funny we should see him. It reminds me of what I was going to tell you. They're in low water again, you know.'

His voice promised to carry across the small print-hung room and Mr Campion protested.

'Does alcohol always make you shout?' he enquired gently. 'Don't bellow. I know the fellow quite well by sight. We're members of the same club.'

'Really? I heard the clubs were having a thin time,' said Oates more quietly but unabashed. 'Still, I didn't know they had to let anyone in.'

Mr Campion looked hurt. 'He's a valued and respected member as far as I know,' he said, 'and may very well be out with his wife.'

'Don't you believe it,' said Oates cheerfully. 'That little kid is on at the Frivolity, or was until the show closed last week. And what's more, my lad, Mr Arthur March is due to marry someone else in less than a month. A good policeman studies everything, even the gossip columns, and that bears out what I told you about you amateurs not being thorough. You don't collect sufficient out-of-the-way information. Take this company law, for instance . . .'

He broke off, a light of interest in his mournful grey eyes. From where they sat the view of the entrance was unobstructed and Campion, following his glance, saw two young people come in. Superintendent Stanislaus Oates grinned broadly.

'This is good,' he said. 'That's the girl March is engaged to – Denise Warren. She's out on the spree with a boy friend too. They've come here because they've heard it's quiet, I bet you. They haven't seen March yet.'

Mr Campion did not speak. He was looking at the girl. She was an unusual type, taller than the average and very fair, with wide-apart blue-grey eyes and a magnificent carriage.

Her companion was a square, solid young man only a few years her senior. He was not unhandsome and had an air of authority about him unusual in one of his age. They found a table and settled down in full view of Campion and his guest. Oates was frankly delighted.

'They'll see each other in a moment,' he said with schoolboy mischievousness. 'Who's the fellow with her? Do you know?'

Mr Campion was frowning. 'Yes, I do,' he said. 'That's Rupert Fielding, a surgeon. He's young but an absolute prodigy, they say. I hope he's not playing the fool. His is the one profession that still demands absolute conventionality.'

Oates grinned: 'Another member of the club?'

Campion echoed his smile. 'Yes, as it happens. Spends all his spare time there. Gives the older members a sense of security, I think.'

Oates glanced at the girl again. 'Oh well, she's keeping it in the family, isn't she? What is this famous club? Not Puffin's?'

'No. Quite as respectable if not so eminent. The Junior Greys, Pall Mall.'

Oates sat up with interest. 'Curiouser and curiouser,' he said. 'Isn't that the place where the old boy sits in the window all day?'

'Old Rosemary?'

'That's the man. One of the landmarks of London. Hasn't changed in fifty years. It's a funny thing, I was hearing of him to-day, as I was going to tell you. Is he as old as they say?'

'He's ninety some time this year.'

'Really?' The Superintendent was interested. 'I've seen him, of course, dozens of times. You can't very well miss him sitting there in that great window. He looks young enough from the street. Scraggy men like yourself wear well. What's he like close to?'

Mr Campion considered. He was eager to give serious attention to any subject which would divert his guest's embarrassing attention from his two fellow-members and their more intimate affairs.

'One doesn't get very close to him in the ordinary way,' he said at last. 'That bay window is his holy of holies. There's a draught screen round the back of his chair and a table between him and the rest of the room. I'm seldom there early enough to see him come in in the morning but I meet him tottering out at half-past six now and again.'

'He's frail then?' the Superintendent persisted.' Frail but

young-looking? I'm sorry to be so inquisitive,' he added, 'but I don't like freaks. How young does he actually look close to in a good light?'

Mr Campion hesitated. 'He's very well preserved,' he began at last. 'Had all kinds of things done to him.'

'Oh, facial stuff, rejuvenation, toupets, special teeth to take out the hollows – I know.' The Superintendent spoke with contempt. 'That accounts for it. I hate that sort of thing. It's bad enough in old women but in old men it's revolting.'

He paused and, evidently thinking that he might have expressed himself ungraciously, added handsomely: 'Of course, when you remember he was a famous actor it doesn't seem so bad. He was one of the first of the stage knights, wasn't he?'

'I believe so. Sir Charles Rosemary, one of the great figures of the eighties. I believe he was magnificent.'

'And now he spends his days sitting in a window trying to look sixty,' the Superintendent murmured. 'Is it true he does it all day and every day?'

'An unbroken record of twenty years, I believe,' said Mr Campion, who was growing weary of the catechism. 'It's quite a legend. He comes up to the club at eleven o'clock and sits there until six-thirty.'

'My God!' said Oates expressively and added abruptly: 'Hullo, he's seen her!'

Mr Campion gave up the hope of diverting him. The Super-intendent's round dull eyes were alight with amusement.

'Look at March,' he said. 'He's wild. Isn't that typical of that sort of chap? Doesn't seem to realize he's in the same boat. Can you see him?'

'Yes, in the mirror behind you,' Campion admitted grudgingly. 'Rather awkward for his guest, isn't it?'

'She's used to it, I'd say,' said the ex-Inspector cheerfully. 'Look at him.'

Arthur March was angry and appeared to be indifferent about showing it. He sat upright in his chair, staring at his fiancée and her companion with white-faced indignation. The girl opposite in the grey hat did her best to look faintly amused, but her eyes were angry.

Campion looked at Miss Warren and caught her at the moment when curious glances from other tables directed her attention to the furious man on the other side of the room. She met his eyes for a moment and grew slowly crimson. Then she murmured something to the stolid young man at her side.

Oates was very interested.

'March is going over,' he said suddenly. 'No, he's changed his mind. He's sending a note.'

The waiter who bore the hastily scribbled message on the half-sheet torn from a memorandum book looked considerably embarrassed and he handed it to Miss Warren with a word of apology. She glanced at it, blushed even more deeply than before, and passed it on to Fielding.

The young surgeon's square, immobile face became a shade darker and, leaning towards the girl, he said something abruptly. She hesitated, looked up at him and nodded.

A moment later the waiter was off across the room again, a faint smile on his face. The Superintendent frowned.

'What happened?' he demanded. 'I didn't see, did you? Wait a minute.'

Before Campion could stop him he had risen from his seat and sauntered off across the room, ostensibly to get a pipe out of the pocket of his overcoat which hung on a stand near the doorway. The somewhat circuitous route he chose led him directly behind March's chair at the moment when he received the return note from the waiter.

Oates came back smiling.

'I thought so,' he said triumphantly as he sat down. 'She wrapped her engagement ring in his own note and sent it back to him. Oh, very dignified and crushing, whatever he wrote! Look at him now . . . is he going to make a row?'

'I hope not,' said Mr Campion fervently.

'No, he's thought better of it. He's going.' The Superintendent seemed a little disappointed. 'He's livid, though. Look at his hands. He's shaking with fury. I say, Campion, I don't like the look of him; he's demented with rage.'

'Don't gawp at him then, poor chap,' his host protested. 'You were going to tell me something of unparalleled interest about company law.'

The Superintendent frowned, his eyes still on the retreating figures at the other side of the room.

'Was I? This little show has put it out of my head,' he said. 'Ah, they've gone and the other two are settling down again. Well, that's the end of that little romance. I enjoyed it.'

'Obviously,' said Mr Campion bitterly. 'It's probably cost me two perfectly good acquaintances, but what of that if you're happy? The whole incident would have been washed away with a few pretty tears in a day or so and might have been decently forgotten. Still, if you enjoyed it . . .'

The ex-Inspector regarded him owlishly.

'You're wrong,' he said. 'I'm not a man given to – er – sooth-saying . . . what's the word?'

'Prophecy?' suggested Campion, laughing.

'Prophecy,' echoed Oates with success. 'But I tell you, Campion, that the incident we have just witnessed is going to have far-reaching consequences.'

'You're tight,' said his companion.

He was, of course, but it was a remarkable thing, as he himself pointed out afterwards, that he was unequivocably right at the same time.

The engagement between Miss Denise Warren and Mr Rupert Fielding, F.R.C.S., was announced at the end of August, a decent six weeks after the intimation that her marriage to Mr Arthur March, son of the late Sir Joshua March, would not take place, and when Mr Campion walked down Pall Mall to the Junior Greys one morning in October the whole affair was ancient history.

It was a little before twelve and the sun was shining in at the great bay windows of the club, windows so large and frank that the decorous gentlemen within looked almost more like exhibits under glass than spectators of the procession of traffic in the street below.

As he approached the building Mr Campion was aware of a subtle sense of loss. It was not until he had stood for some seconds on the pavement surveying the broad façade of the left wing of the building that he realized where the difference lay. When he saw it he was shocked. The great chair in the centre window of the lounge was occupied not by the familiar aquiline

figure of old Rosemary but by a short fattish old gentleman
by the name of Briggs, a member of but ten or fifteen years'
standing, a truculent tasteless person of little popularity.

Mr Campion entered beneath the Adam porch with a premonition of disaster and was confirmed in his suspicions a few
moments later when he discovered Walters, the head steward,
in tears. Since Walters was a portly sixty-five and possessed a
dignity which was proverbial, the spectacle was both shocking
and embarrassing. He blew his nose hastily when Mr Campion
appeared and murmured a word of apology, after which he added
baldly: 'He's gone, sir.'

'Not old – I mean Sir Charles Rosemary?' Mr Campion was
shocked.

'Yes, sir.' Walters permitted himself a ghostly sniff. 'It happened this morning, sir. In his chair where he always sat, just as
he would have liked. Mr March and one or two other gentlemen
had a word with him when he first came in and then he dozed
off. I saw him sleeping heavily but didn't think anything of it,
him being so old, but when Mr Fielding came in about an hour
ago he noticed at once that something was wrong and called
me. We got the old gentleman into a taxi between us and Mr
Fielding took him home. He died in the taxi. Mr Fielding has
just come in and told us. He'd have been ninety in two days'
time. It's been a great shock. Like the end of an era, sir. I
remember the old Queen going but it didn't seem like this. I
remember him when I came here forty years ago, you see.'

Mr Campion was surprised to find that he was a trifle
shaken himself. There was a great deal in what Walters said.
Old Rosemary had been an institution.

As he came into the lounge he caught sight of Fielding standing by the eastern fireplace with a small crowd round him. Mr Campion joined it.

Fielding's professional calm was standing him in good stead. He was giving information quietly and seriously, without capitalizing or even seeming conscious of the undue prominence into which chance had forced him. He nodded to Campion and went on with his story.

'He was breathing so stertorously that I went and had a look at him,' he was saying. 'He wasn't conscious then and didn't recover before the end, which came in the taxi, as you know.'

'He had a flat in Dover Street, hadn't he?' said someone.

Fielding nodded. 'Yes. Walters got me the address. He'd gone before we arrived and I knew I couldn't do anything, so I got hold of his man, who seems a very capable chap. We put him on to his bed and the servant told me that his regular doctor was Philipson, so I rang Harley Street and came away.'

'Sir Edgar was upset, I bet,' said a man Campion did not know. 'They knew each other well. Still, he was very old. I don't suppose he was surprised. The very old often die suddenly and peacefully like that.'

The crowd split up into smaller groups, which grew again as other members came in to lunch. Mr Brigg's behaviour in commandeering the favourite seat came in for a good deal of comment and the secretary received several complaints. A half-excited gloom, as at a major disaster, settled over the smoking-room, and the newspapers, who had already been notified by one of Walter's underlings, received quite a number of calls.

The awkward incident occurred just before lunch, however. Mr Campion witnessed it and was shocked by it, in company with nine-tenths of his fellow-members present. Arthur March came in and made a scene.

It began in the hall when he heard the news from Scroop, the porter. His high thin tones protesting disbelief reached the lounge before he appeared himself, pale and excitable, in the doorway. He sank into a chair, snapped at the wine steward, and, after mopping his brow a trifle ostentatiously, rose to his feet again and came across the room to where Fielding stood with Campion.

'This is ghastly,' he said without preamble. 'I was with the old man only this morning, you know. He was in one of his black moods but otherwise he seemed perfectly all right. You found him, didn't you? Was – was it peaceful?'

'Perfectly,' said Fielding shortly. He was obviously embarrassed and Campion found himself wondering if the two men had ever spoken since the little scene in the City chop-house earlier in the year.

'Thank God!' said March with nauseating fervour. 'Oh, thank God!'

He did not move away and the surgeon hesitated.

'Relation of yours?' he enquired abruptly.

March coloured. 'Practically,' he said. 'My grandfather and he were like brothers.'

The explanation evidently sounded a little lame, even to himself, for he took refuge in wholly unwarrantable abuse.

'You wouldn't understand that sort of loyalty,' he muttered and turned on his heel.

Fielding stood looking after him, his eyebrows raised.

'That chap's in a funny mental state . . .' he was beginning when Mr Campion touched his sleeve.

'Lunch,' said Mr Campion.

It was after the meal, nearing the end of the hour of pleasant somnolence sacred to the gods of digestion, when the Junior Greys experienced its first real sensation since the suffragette outrage, of which no one ever speaks. Campion had been watching with lazy eyes the efforts of the bishop in the chair next to his own to keep his attention on the pamphlet on his knee when he saw that divine sit upright in his chair, the healthy colour draining rapidly from his plump cheeks.

At the same moment, on the other side of the room, Major-General Stukely Wivenhoe's cigar dropped from his mouth and rolled on the carpet.

A communal intake of breath, like the sigh of a great animal, sounded all over the room and in a far corner somebody knocked over a coffee-cup.

Mr Campion hoisted himself on one elbow and looked round. He remained arrested in that uncomfortable position for some seconds.

Old Rosemary, immaculate and jaunty as ever, was coming slowly across the room. There was a red carnation in his buttonhole, his flowing white hair glistened, and his curiously unwrinkled face wore its customary faint smile.

Behind him, portly and efficient, strode Sir Edgar Philipson, the Harley Street man.

It was a petrifying moment and one which demanded every ounce of the Junior Grey's celebrated aplomb.

Half-way across the room the newcomers were met by a page hurrying in with the early editions. Confronted by the spectacle of old Rosemary himself the boy lost his head completely. He thrust an *Evening Wire* at the old man.

'They – they say you're dead, sir,' he blurted out idiotically.

Rosemary took the paper and peered at it while the stupified room waited in silence.

'Greatly exaggerated,' he said in the unmistakable clipped tone they all knew so well. 'Take it away.'

He moved on to his chair. No one saw Briggs leave it. Some insist that he crawled out behind the screen on all fours; and others, more imaginative, that he dived out of the window and was afterwards found gibbering in the basement. But at all events, his departure was silent and immediate.

Old Rosemary sat down, and beckoning to a paralysed servant, ordered a whisky and soda.

Meanwhile, Sir Edgar Philipson stood looking round the room, and Fielding, pale and incredulous, rose to meet him. The elder man was not kind.

'That's the trouble with you younger men, Fielding,' he said in a rumbling undertone that was yet loud enough to be heard. 'Overhasty in your diagnosis. Make sure before you act, my boy. Make sure.'

He walked away, a handsome old man very pleased with himself.

Fielding glanced helplessly round the room, but no one met his eyes. Mr Campion, who alone was sympathetic, was looking at old Rosemary, noting the healthy brilliance of his eyes and the colour in his cheeks.

Fielding walked out of the room in silence.

Mr Campion dined alone that evening and was writing a brief report on his own share in the Case of the Yellow Shoes, which had just come to a satisfactory conclusion, when the young surgeon called. Fielding was embarrassed and said so. He stood awkwardly in the middle of the study in the flat in Bottle Street and made a hesitating apology.

'I'm terribly sorry to presume on an acquaintance like this, Campion,' he said, 'but I'm in such a devil of a mess. That chap Rosemary, you know, he was dead as mutton this morning.'

Mr Campion produced a decanter.

'I should sit down,' he said. 'It soothes the nerves and rests the feet. I suppose this affair is going to be – er – bad for business?'

Fielding looked relieved and a faint smile appeared for an instant on his square, solemn face.

'Frightfully,' he said, accepting the glass Campion handed him. 'It makes such a darned good story, you see. Rupert Fielding is such a brilliant surgeon that he doesn't know when he's beaten and the patient is dead – it's all over the place already. I shall be ruined. Incompetence is bad enough in any profession, but in mine it's unforgivable. And,' he added helplessly, 'he was dead, or at least I thought so. His heart had stopped and when I got him home I tried the mirror test. Of course, miracles do happen nowadays, but not under old Philipson. At least, I wouldn't have said so yesterday. It's funny, isn't it?'

'Odd, certainly,' Mr Campion agreed slowly. 'When you talk of these modern miracles, what are they exactly?'

'Oh, electrical treatment and that sort of thing.' Fielding

spoke vaguely. 'You see,' he added frankly, 'I'm not a physician; I'm a surgeon. I've done a certain amount of medicine, of course, but I don't set up to be a GP. Drugs are not in my line.'

Mr Campion glanced up and his pale eyes behind his spectacles were inquisitive.

'You're wondering if the old boy couldn't have taken something that produced a pretty good simulation of death?' he suggested.

The younger man regarded him steadily. 'It sounds far-fetched, I know,' he said, 'but it's the only explanation I can think of, although what on earth the stuff can have been I can't imagine. You see, the dreadful thing is that I didn't do anything. I just made up my mind he was dead and, realizing the whole was hopeless, I simply rang up Philipson in accordance with medical etiquette.'

'I see,' Mr Campion spoke gravely. 'What do you want me to do?'

Fielding hesitated. 'If you could find out what actually happened you'd save my reason, anyway,' he said so simply that the words were robbed of any hint of melodrama. 'Nothing can save my career – at least for a few years, I'm afraid. But I tell you, Campion, I must know if I'm losing my grip or if my mind's going. I must know how I came to make such an incredible mistake.'

Mr Campion glanced at the dignified youngster and noted that he betrayed no hint of the nervous strain he was undergoing. He felt his sympathy aroused and, at the same time, his curiosity. Before he could speak, however, Fielding went on.

'There are other complications too,' he said awkwardly. 'I'm engaged to old Rosemary's grandchild, you know, and when I tell you she's his principal heir you'll see how infernally awkward it all is.'

Mr Campion whistled. 'I say, that's very unfortunate.'

'It is,' said Fielding grimly. 'And it's not all. I'm afraid she broke off her engagement with Arthur March on my account and he had the impudence to phone her about this business almost as soon as it happened. I saw him this evening and frankly I don't understand the fellow. My mistake is an appalling one, I know. Old Rosemary's perfectly entitled to sue me. But March has taken the business as a personal insult. He blew me up as if I was a schoolboy, and, after all, he's only the grandson of a friend of the family. There's no blood tie at all. I couldn't say much to him; I'm so hopelessly in the wrong.'

Mr Campion considered. 'I noticed the old man when he came in this afternoon,' he said. 'He was looking remarkably well.'

Fielding smiled wryly. 'If you'd gone close to him you'd have been amazed,' he said. 'I was when I got him into the cab. It's vanity, I suppose, but the amount of time he must spend while his man gets him ready for the day must be considerable. It's gone on for so many years, I suppose, that the little additions and adjustments have mounted up, but what began presumably as a toupet is now damned nearly a wig, I can tell you. I don't think you'd have seen any ill effects of a drug, even if there were any. Still, I've talked too much. Will you have a shot at it?'

Mr Campion would not commit himself. 'I'll have a look round,' he said. 'I can't promise anything. It sounds like conjury to me.'

All the same, the following morning found him at the Junior Greys much earlier than usual. He sought out Walters and cornered him in the deserted smoking-room. The steward was in expansive mood.

'A dreadful thing, sir,' he agreed. 'Quite a scandal in its way. One gets to trust doctors, if I may say so. Still, I'd rather a dozen scandals than lose Sir Charles. Yes, he's here already, right on his usual time and in one of his good moods.'

Mr Campion smiled. 'His bad moods were pretty sensational, weren't they?'

'Well, he's old, sir.' Walters spoke indulgently. 'There are days when he snaps everybody's head off and sits sulking over his paper without speaking to a soul, but I don't take any notice because I know that to-morrow he'll be quite different, quite his old charming self with a nod and a smile to everyone. I always know which mood it's to be. As soon as he comes in he calls for a whisky. If it's a good day it's whisky and water and if he's upset it's whisky and soda, so I have plenty of warning, you see.'

Mr Campion thanked him and wandered away. He had suddenly become very grave and the expression in his eyes behind his horn-rimmed spectacles was one of alarm.

He went down to the telephone and called Oates. Less than twenty minutes later he and the Superintendent were in a taxi speeding towards Fleet Street. Stanislaus Oates was his customary sombre self. The somewhat elephantine gaiety which he had displayed at the chop-house was gone as if it had never been. This morning he was a trifle irritable.

'I hope this isn't a wild-goose chase, Campion,' he protested as the cab lurched down the Embankment 'I'm not an idle man, you know, and I've got no business careering off on a purely private jaunt like this.'

Campion turned to him and the elder man was surprised by the gravity of his expression.

'Somehow, I don't think even you could keep this business private if you wanted to,' said Mr Campion. 'Here we are. Wait for me.'

The cab had pulled up outside a dingy building in a narrow court and the Superintendent, peering out after his departing guide, saw him disappear into the offices of the *Curtain*, a well-known stage weekly, famous for its theatrical cards and intimate gossip.

He was gone for some little time, but seemed pleased with himself when he reappeared. He gave an address in Streatham to the man and clambered back beside his friend.

'I've got it,' he said briefly. 'We shan't be too late to interfere, although of course the main mischief is done. Why? That's what I don't understand. It couldn't have been merely to discredit Fielding; that was taking far too long a chance.'

'I wish you'd explain and not talk like the wrong end of a telephone,' said Oates testily. 'What have you got from the benighted hole we've just left?'

Campion looked at him as though he had only just remembered his existence.

'The address, of course,' he said briefly.

The cab drew up at last in a wide suburban street where each pair of houses was exactly like the next – red brick, white stucco and solid chocolate paint.

Mr Campion led the way up a short tiled path to a neat front door and Oates, who had taken one look at the windows with their drawn blinds, followed him hastily, his irritation vanishing.

A little woman in a dark overall, her grey hair scraped into a tight knot at the back of her head, opened the door to them. Her face was mottled and her eyes red.

'Mr Nowell?' she echoed in response to Campion's question, and then, fishing hastily for her handkerchief, she began to cry.

Mr Campion was very gentle with her.

'I'm sorry,' he said. 'I shouldn't have asked for him like that. He's dead, isn't he?'

She looked up at him sharply. 'Oh, you're from the police, are you?' she said unexpectedly. 'The doctor told me there'd have to be an inquest, as the death was so sudden. It's been such a shock. He lodged here so long.'

She made way for them and they crowded into the little hall. The Superintendent realized they were entering by false pretences, but there seemed to be no point in going into explanations just then.

'When did you find him?' Campion enquired cautiously.

'Not until this morning when I took up his tea.' The old woman was anxious to talk. 'He must have died last night, so the doctor says. He put me through it very carefully. "Well, he was alive at ten o'clock," I said, "because I spoke to him." I always go to bed at a quarter to ten and if Mr Nowell was later he didn't like me to sit up for him. He had his own key and there was always someone to help him up.'

She paused for breath and Campion nodded encouragingly.

'Well,' she went on, 'last night I had just turned out my bedroom light when I heard a motor stop and then the door went.

"Is that you, Mr Nowell?" I called. "Yes, Mrs Bell," he said. "Good night." A little while afterwards I heard the car drive away.'

Oates interrupted her. 'Did the chauffeur come in with him?'

Mrs Bell turned to him. 'I don't know if it was the chauffeur, sir, but somebody did. He was nearly eighty, you know, and it was nothing for the gentleman who brought him home to help him up to his room.'

'Can we see him, please?' said Mr Campion softly.

Mrs Bell began to weep again, but afterwards, when they stood bareheaded in the big front bedroom and looked down at the gaunt still figure on the bed, she began to speak quietly and with pride.

'You're not seeing him as he was at all,' she said. 'He was wonderfully handsome with his white hair, his cane and his buttonhole. He used to take a great pride in his appearance. Spend hours and hours and pounds and pounds over it, he would. There was something he used to do with his cheeks to make them stand out more; I don't know what it was.'

Campion bent towards her and murmured something. She shook her head dubiously.

'A photograph, sir?' she repeated. 'No, that's a thing I don't think I 'ave got. He was extraordinarily touchy about having his photograph took, which was funny when he thought so much of himself, if I can say such a thing without meaning to be unkind. Wait a minute, though. I do believe I've got a little snapshot I took of him in the garden one day when he didn't know. I'll go and get it.'

As soon as they were alone Campion bent over the man on the bed and raised an eyelid very gently.

'Yes, I think so,' he said softly. 'Fielding couldn't be blamed for not noticing that. It would look like a perfectly normal death to him, thinking he knew the fellow's age. If we can get your people on to this at once and get 'em to test for morphia sulphate I fancy they'll get results if they hurry.'

The Superintendent's question was cut short by the return of Mrs Bell with a faded snapshot and they adjourned to a little light room at the back of the house.

'There he is,' she said proudly. 'I was lucky to find him. That was taken last summer. He wasn't going up to town so often then.'

'What did he do in London?' inquired Mr Campion, holding the photograph down, to the annoyance of the Superintendent.

Mrs Bell looked uncomfortable. 'I hardly know,' she said. 'He used to tell me he spent his time in his nephew's office keeping an eye on things, but I think myself he was in a sort of high-class library and was one of those people who sit about making the place look respectable. "Dressing the house," we used to call it in my stage days.'

Oates smiled. 'That's a funny idea,' he said. 'I've never heard of it being done in a library.'

'Well, a very expensive tailor's, then,' she persisted. 'I know I thought I saw him sitting in a window in a West End street once. He wasn't doing anything; only sitting there and looking very nice. I asked him about it, of course, but he got very angry and made me promise never to speak of it again.'

The front-door bell interrupted her and she hurried out with a word of excuse.

Oates turned to Campion. 'I'm in a fog,' he said. 'You'll have to explain.'

The younger man gave him the snapshot and he stared at the little photograph of a tall, thin, distinguished figure walking down the gravelled path of the tiny garden.

'Old Rosemary!' ejaculated the Superintendent and raised a bewildered face to his friend's. 'Good Lord, Campion, who was that chap in the next room?'

'John Nowell, Sir Charles Rosemary's understudy at the Thespian Theatre thirty years ago – and ever since, apparently.'

Mr Campion spoke calmly.

'I admit the idea didn't seem credible when I first thought of it,' he went on, 'but afterwards, when I looked into it, it became obvious. Nowell got his job nearly sixty years ago because he resembled Rosemary; that was when he was twenty. Rosemary was nearly ten years older, but they were the same type and very much alike in feature. Since then Nowell has spent his life in imitating the greater actor. He copied his walk and his mannerisms, and as the two men grew older the simulation became easier. Rosemary resorted to artificial aids to keep young-looking, and Nowell, to the same aids to look like Rosemary.'

'Yes, yes, I get that,' said the Superintendent testily. 'But in the name of heaven, why?'

Mr Campion shrugged his shoulders.

'Vanity takes a lot of explaining,' he said. 'But Rosemary was a rich man and I think it was worth his while to employ a fellow, already a pensioner of his perhaps, to sit in the Greys and keep the legend of his perennial health alive. If ever Rosemary was prevented from going to the club Nowell took his place. When you think of it, Rosemary's record at the Greys, all day and every day for twenty years, is much more hard to swallow than this explanation of it.'

Oates continued to stare at the photograph.

'I grant the looks,' he said suddenly,' now that I've seen the chap in the next room, but what happened if he had to talk?'

'He didn't,' said Campion. 'At least, hardly at all. For the last few years Rosemary's been having moods. On his good days he was his old self. On his bad days he was very nearly speechless with sulkiness. It was these moods that put me on to Nowell, as a matter of fact. Walters told me this morning that on his good days Rosemary drank whisky and water and on his bad ones whisky and soda. I have met men who'd drink whisky and soup at a pinch, but never one who hadn't a definite preference in the water or soda controversy when he was in a position to choose. It occurred to me, therefore, that there must be two men, and an understudy naturally came into my mind because the imitation had to be so perfect. So I called at the *Curtain* offices and was lucky to catch Bellew, who does the old-timers' gossip. I asked him if Rosemary ever had a regular understudy and he coughed up the name and address immediately.'

'Neat,' admitted the Superintendent slowly. 'Very neat. But what are we doing here and where's the crime?'

'Well, it's murder, you know,' said Mr Campion diffidently. 'Yesterday morning someone gave that poor chap in there a shot of something in his whisky and soda under the impression that he was giving it to Rosemary. Nowell dropped into a coma at the club and young Fielding the surgeon, seeing that he was pretty far gone, took him home. In the cab he died. Morphia sulphate produces very much the same symptoms as the sudden cardiac collapse of the aged, and Fielding, thinking it was a clear case, left the body with Rosemary's man at the Dover Street flat, phoned Sir Edgar Philipson and went away like a polite little medico. When Philipson got there, of course, he saw Rosemary himself, who was perfectly fit. I imagine Nowell's body remained at Dover Street all day and in the evening, when Mrs Bell was thought likely to be in bed, the valet, probably aided by Rosemary's chauffeur, brought it down here. They took it up to his room, as they'd often done before, and went away.'

'But the voice?' protested the Superintendent. 'He spoke to the landlady; she said so.'

Campion glanced at him. 'I think,' he said slowly, 'old Rosemary must have come down here, too, just in case. After copying him so long, Nowell's voice was a replica of Rosemary's, you see.'

'At ninety?' exclaimed the Superintendent. 'A nerve like that at ninety?'

'I don't know,' said Mr Campion. 'It takes a bit of nerve to get to ninety, I should say.'

Oates glanced towards the door. 'She's a long time,' he said. 'I wonder if that was the coroner's officer . . .'

He went out on to the narrow landing with Campion behind him and appeared just as Mrs Bell opened the door of the front bedroom and showed a white-faced man out.

'I can't tell you any more, sir,' she was saying stiffly. 'Perhaps you'll ask the police gentlemen here?'

She got no further. With an inarticulate cry the stranger swung round and the light from the landing window fell upon his face. It was Arthur March. He stood staring at Campion, his eyes narrowed and the knotted veins standing out on his temples.

'You – you interfering swine!' he said suddenly and sprang.

Campion only just met the attack in time. As the man's fingers closed round his throat he jerked his knee upward and caught his opponent in the wind. March collapsed against the flimsy balustrade, which gave beneath the sudden weight and sent him sprawling on to the stairs below, Campion after him.

A vigorous pounding on the hall door announcing the arrival of the coroner's officer added to the general confusion, and the superintendent, with an energy surprising in one of his somewhat dyspeptic appearance, pounced down upon the two scuffling on the stairs.

It was nearly three hours later when Mr Campion sat in the Superintendent's office at Scotland Yard and expostulated mildly.

'It's all very well to arrest him on the assault charge,' he was saying, 'but you can't hold him. You cannot prove the attempted murder of Rosemary or the actual murder of Nowell.'

Stanislaus Oates sat at his desk, his hands crossed on his waistcoat. He was very pleased.

'Think not?' he enquired.

'Well,' said Mr Campion judicially, 'I hate to dampen your enthusiasm, but what have you got? Walters can swear that March met him in the lounge yesterday morning and persuaded him to let him take the old man's refresher over to him, as he wanted an excuse to have a word with the old boy, who was in a bad humour. There's opportunity there, I know, but that's not much in court. Then you can show that March spotted his error and, by much the same process of reasoning as mine, arrived at

Nowell's. And you can prove that he attacked me. But that's your whole case. He'll go scot-free. After all, why should March want to kill Rosemary? Because the old boy's granddaughter wouldn't marry him?'

'That's not so absurd as you think, my boy,' Oates was avuncular. 'As a matter of fact, if Denise Warren had married Arthur March, Rosemary would never have been attacked.'

Mr Campion stared at him and the Superintendent continued contentedly:

'Do you remember a meal we had together at Benjamin's chop-house to celebrate my promotion?'

'Perfectly. You were very tight and made an exhibition of us.'

'Not at all.' Oates was scandalized. 'I was observant and informative. I observed Miss Warren break off her engagement with the grandson of Rosemary's old friend, Sir Joshua March, and I tried to inform you of certain facts and you wouldn't listen to me. Do you remember me telling you that you amateurs don't collect enough data? Do you remember me telling you about company law?'

'It comes back to me,' admitted Mr Campion.

The Superintendent was mollified.

'Did you know it's a common practice among small companies to raise money on large life insurances taken out on behalf of a member of the firm for the express purpose of such money-raising?'

'Yes, I had heard of it. But it's usually a partner who insures his life, isn't it?'

'Not always. That's the point.' Oates was beaming. 'If the partners are none of them particularly good risks they often insure a junior member of the firm, or sometimes an outside person altogether who happens to be "a good risk", as they call it. Now look here, Campion . . .' Oates leant across the desk. 'When Allan March and Son – the first Sir Joshua was the son in those days – were in low water sixty-odd years ago they wanted to take out a sixty-thousand-pound policy in order to borrow upon it. Allan March was an old man and Joshua was a heart subject. They needed someone who was a good risk, you see, because the sum was so large that it was necessary to get the premium as low as possible. Rosemary and Joshua were friends and in those days Rosemary was something of a marvel. His constitution was wonderful, his habits were temperate, and also he had a strong publicity value.'

He paused and Campion nodded.

'Go on. I'm following.'

'Well, March and Son approached the Mutual Ordered Life Endowment, which was a young firm then, one of the first of the flashy, advertising insurance companies, and they agreed to take the risk at an extremely low premium because of the publicity and because, of course, the fellow was a pretty good life. Rosemary agreed to stand for his part in the business; that is, he agreed to have himself insured for friendship's sake and because the Marches were in a bad way. But as a sort of gesture he made a stipulation. "If I live to ninety," he said, "the policy reverts to me." It was a joke at the time, because the heavier Victorians didn't usually reach anywhere near that age, and, anyway, it was the immediate loan which interested everyone. However, they agreed to it and it was all duly signed and sealed.'

'Had March and Son kept up the insurance?'

'Oh yes.' The superintendent was watching Campion's face as he spoke. 'I don't suppose it's been convenient for them to repay the sum they'd borrowed on that policy, or that, since the premium was so low, they could have bought a loan more cheaply. But you see the situation now. I'd have told you all this back in the summer if you'd listened. It's a clear case, isn't it?'

Mr Campion blinked. 'If old Rosemary died before his ninetieth birthday, then,' he said at last, 'the residue of the sixty thousand went to March and Son; but if he lives until after to-morrow it will pass into his own estate and go to Denise Warren.'

'To-morrow's the ninetieth birthday, is it?' said Oates. 'March was cutting it pretty fine. I suppose he hoped the girl would come back to him and he'd get the cash through her. Well, my lad, what have you got to say now?'

'Nothing,' said Mr Campion affably. 'Nothing, except that it wasn't company law, was it? It sounds more like insurance to me.'

Oates shrugged his shoulders. 'You may be right,' he said airily. 'I'm not a dictionary and I didn't go to a night school. Still,' he added with a chuckle, 'we like to feel we do a little, you know, we professionals. You amateurs have your uses now and again, but when it comes to the groundwork we've got you licked every time.'

Mr Campion grinned at him.

'I really think you believe that, you old sinner,' he said.

THE CASE OF THE LATE PIG

CHAPTER I

The Invitations to the Funeral were Informal

The main thing to remember in autobiography, I have always thought, is not to let any damned modesty creep in to spoil the story. This adventure is mine, Albert Campion's, and I am fairly certain that I was pretty nearly brilliant in it in spite of the fact that I so nearly got myself and old Lugg killed that I hear a harp quintet whenever I consider it.

It begins with me eating in bed.

Lord Powne's valet took lessons in elocution and since then has read *The Times* to His Lordship while His Lordship eats his unattractive nut-and-milk breakfast.

Lugg, who in spite of magnificent qualities has elements of the Oaf about him, met His Lordship's valet in the May-fair mews pub where they cater for gentlemen in the service of gentlemen and was instantly inspired to imitation. Lugg has not taken lessons in elocution, at least not since he left Borstal in the reign of Edward the Seventh. When he came into my service he was a parole man with a stupendous record of misplaced bravery and ingenuity. Now he reads *The Times* to me when I eat, whether I like it or not.

Since his taste does not run towards the literary in journalism he reads to me the only columns in that paper which do appeal to him. He reads the Deaths.

'Peters . . .' he read, heaving his shirt-sleeved bulk between me and the light. 'Know anyone called Peters, cock?'

I was reading a letter which had interested me particularly because it was both flowery and unsigned and did not hear him, so presently he laid down the paper with gentle exasperation.

'Answer me, can't you?' he said plaintively. 'What's the good of me trying to give this place a bit of tone if you don't back me up? Mr Turke says 'Is Lordship is most attentive during the readings. He chews everything 'e eats forty times before 'e swallers and keeps 'is mind on everything that's being read to 'im.'

'So I should think,' I said absently. I was taken by the letter. It was not the ordinary anonymous filth by any means.

'PETERS – R. I. Peters, aged 37, on Thursday the 9th, at Tethering, after a short illness. Funeral, Tethering Church, 2.30 Saturday. No flowers. Friends will accept this as the only intimation.'

Lugg reads horribly and with effect.

The name attracted me.

'Peters?' I said, looking up from the letter with interest. 'R. I. Peters . . . Pig Peters. Is it in there?'

'Oh, my *gawd*!' Lugg threw down the paper in disgust. 'You're a philistine, that's what you are, a ruddy phylis. After a perishing short illness, I keep tellin' you. Know 'im?'

'No,' I said cautiously. 'Not exactly. Not now.'

Lugg's great white moon of a face took on an ignoble expression.

'I get you, Bert,' he said smugly, tucking his chins into his collarless neck. 'Not quite our class.'

Although I realize that he is not to be altered, there are things I dare not pass.

'Not at all,' I said with dignity. 'And don't call me "Bert".'

'All right.' He was magnanimous. 'Since you've asked me, cock, I won't. Mr Albert Campion to the world: Mr Albert to me. What about this bloke Peters we was discussin'?'

'We were boys together,' I said. 'Sweet, downy, blue-eyed little fellows at Botolph's Abbey. Pig Peters took three square inches of skin off my chest with a rusty penknife to show I was his branded slave. He made me weep till I was sick and I kicked him in the belly, whereupon he held me over an unlighted gas jet until I passed out.'

Lugg was shocked.

'There was no doings like that at our college,' he said virtuously.

'That's the evil of State control,' I said gently, not anxious to appear unkind. 'I haven't seen Peters since the day I went into the sicker with GO poisoning, but I promised him then I'd go to his funeral.'

He was interested at once.

'I'll get out your black suit,' he said obligingly. 'I like a funeral – when it's someone you know.'

I was not really listening to him. I had returned to the letter.

Why should he die? He was so young. There are thousands more fitting than he for the journey. 'Peters, Peters,' saith the angel. 'Peters, Pietro, Piero, come,' saith the angel. Why? Why should he follow him? He that

*was so strong, so unprepared, why should he die? The roots are red in
the earth and the century creepeth on its way. Why should the mole move
backwards? – it is not yet eleven.*

It was typewritten on ordinary thin quarto, as are all these things,
but it was not ill-spelt and the punctuation was meticulous,
which was an unusual feature in my experience. I showed it to
Lugg.

He read it through laboriously and delivered himself of his
judgement with engaging finality.

'Bit out of the Prayer Book,' he said. 'I remember learning it
when I was a nipper.'

'Don't be an ass,' I said mildly, but he coloured and his little
black eyes sank into my head.

'Call me a liar,' he said truculently. 'Go on, call me a liar and
then I'll do a bit of talking.'

I know him in these moods and I realized from experience
that it was impossible to shake him in a theory of this sort.

'All right,' I said. 'What does it mean?'

'Nothing,' he said with equal conviction.

I tried another tack.

'What's the machine?'

He was helpful at once.

'A *Royal* portable, new or newish, no peculiarities to speak
of. Even the E is as fresh as that bit of 'addock you've left. Paper's
the ordinary Plantag. – they sell reams of it everywhere. Let's
see the envelope. London, W. C. I,' he continued after a pause.
'That's the old central stamp. Clear, isn't it? The address is from
the telephone book. Chuck it in the fire.'

I still held the letter. Taken in conjunction with the announcement in *The Times* it had, it seemed to me, definite points of interest. Lugg sniffed at me.

'Blokes like you who are always getting their selves talked about are bound to get anonymous letters,' he observed, allowing the critical note in his tone to become apparent. 'While you remained strictly amateur you was fairly private, but now you keep runnin' round with the busies, sticking your nose into every bit of blood there is about, and you're gettin' talked of. We'll 'ave women sittin' on the stairs waitin' for you to sign their names on piller-cases so they can embroider it if you go on the way you are going. Why can't you take a quiet couple o' rooms in a good neighbour'ood and play poker while you wait for your titled relative to die? That's what a gentleman would do.'

'If you were female and could cook I'd marry you,' I said vulgarly. 'You nag like a stage wife.'

That silenced him. He got up and waddled out of the room, the embodiment of dignified disgust.

I read the letter through again after I had eaten and it sounded just as light-headed. Then I read *The Times* announcement.

R. I. Peters . . . It was Pig all right. The age fitted in. I remembered him booting us to persuade us to call him 'Rip'. I thought of us as we were then, Guffy Randall and I and Lofty and two or three others. I was a neat little squirt with sleek white hair and goggles; Guffy was a tough for his age, which was ten and a quarter; and Lofty, who is now holding down his seat in the Peers with a passionate determination more creditable than necessary, was a cross between a small tapir and a more ordinary porker.

Pig Peters was a major evil in our lives at that time. He ranked with Injustice, The Devil, and Latin Prose. When Pig Peters fed the junior study fire with my collection of skeleton leaves I earnestly wished him dead, and, remembering the incident that morning at breakfast, I was mildly surprised to find that I still did.

Apparently he was, too, according to *The Times*, and the discovery cheered me up. At twelve he was obese, red, and disgusting, with sandy lashes, and at thirty-seven I had no doubt he had been the same.

Meanwhile there was the sound of heavy breathing in the outer room and Lugg put his head round the door.

'Cock,' he said in a tone of diffident friendliness which showed that all was forgiven, 'I've had a squint at the map. See where Tethering is? Two miles west of Kepesake. Going down?'

I suppose it was that which decided me. At Highwaters, in the parish of Kepesake, there lives Colonel Sir Leo Pursuivant, Chief Constable of the county and an extremely nice old boy. He has a daughter, Janet Pursuivant, whom I like still in spite of everything.

'All right,' I said. 'We'll drop in at Highwaters on our way back.'

Lugg was in complete agreement. They had a nice piece of home-cured last time he was there, he said.

We went down in state. Lugg wore his flattest bowler, which makes him look like a thug disguised as a plain-clothes man, and I was remarkably neat myself.

Tethering was hardly *en fête*. If you consider three square miles of osier swamp surrounding a ploughed hill on which five cottages, a largish house and an ancient church crowd on each other's toes in order to keep out of a river's uncertain bed you have Tethering pretty accurately in your mind.

The churchyard is overgrown and pathetic and when we saw it in late winter it was a sodden mass of dead cowparsley. It was difficult not to feel sorry for Pig. He always had grand ideas, I remember, but there was nothing of pomp in his obsequies.

We arrived late – it is eighty miles from Town – and I felt a trifle loutish as I pushed open the mouldering lychgate and, followed by Lugg, stumbled over the ragged grass towards the little group by the grave.

The parson was old and I suspected that he had come on the bicycle I had seen outside the gate, for the skirts of his cassock were muddy.

The sexton was in corduroys and the bearers in dungarees.

The other members of the group I did not notice until afterwards. A funeral is an impressive business even among the marble angels and broken columns of civilization. Here, out of the world in the rain-soaked silence of a forgotten hillside, it was both grim and sad.

As we stood there in the light shower the letter I had received that morning faded out of my mind. Peters had been an ordinary unlovable sort of twirp, I supposed, and he was being buried in an ordinary unloved way. There was really nothing curious about it.

As the parson breathed the last words of the service, however, an odd thing happened. It startled me so much that I stepped back on Lugg and almost upset him.

Even at twelve and a half Pig had had several revolting

personal habits and one of them was a particularly vicious way of clearing his throat. It was a sort of hoarse rasping noise in the larynx, followed by a subdued whoop and a puff. I cannot describe it any more clearly but it was a distinctive sort of row and one I never heard made by anyone else. I had completely forgotten it, but just as we were turning away from the yawning grave into which the coffin had been lowered I heard it distinctly after what must have been twenty years. It brought Pig back to my mind with a vividness which was unnerving and I gaped round at the rest of us with my scalp rising.

Apart from the bearers, the parson, the sexton, Lugg, and myself there were only four other people present and they all looked completely innocent.

There was a pleasant solid-looking person on my left and a girl in rather flashy black beyond him. She was more sulky than tearful and appeared to be alone. She caught my eye and smiled at me as I glanced at her and I looked on past her at the old man in the topper who stood in a conventional attitude of grief which was rather horrible because it was so unconvincing. I don't know when I took such a dislike to a fellow. He had little grey curly moustaches which glittered in the rain.

My attention was distracted from him almost at once by the discovery that the fourth unaccountable was Gilbert Whippet. He had been standing at my elbow for ten minutes and I had not seen him, which was typical of him.

Whippet was my junior at Botolph's Abbey and he followed me to the same school. I had not seen him for twelve or fourteen years, but, save that he had grown, of course, he was unchanged.

It is about as easy to describe Whippet as it is to describe water or a sound in the night. Vagueness is not so much his characteristic as his entity. I don't know what he looks like, except that presumably he has a face, since it would be an omission that I should have been certain to observe. He had on some sort of grey-brown coat which merged with the dead cow-parsley and he looked at me with that vacancy which is yet recognition.

'Whippet!' I said. 'What are you doing here?'

He did not answer and unconsciously I raised my hand to clip him. He never did answer until he was clipped and the force of habit was too much for me. Fortunately I restrained myself in time, recollecting that the years which had elapsed between our meeting had presumably given him ordinary rights of citizenship. All the same I felt unreasonably angry with him and I spoke sharply.

'Whippet, why did you come to Pig's funeral?' I said.

He blinked at me and I was aware of round pale grey eyes.

'I – er – I was invited, I think,' he said in the husky diffident voice I remembered so well and which conveyed that he was not at all sure what he was talking about. 'I – I – had one this – this morning, don't you know . . .'

He fumbled in his coat and produced a sheet of paper. Before I read it I knew what it was. Its fellow was in my pocket.

'Odd,' said Whippet, 'about the mole, you know. Informal invitation. I – er – I came.'

His voice trailed away, as I knew it would, and he wandered off, not rudely but carelessly, as though there was nothing to keep him in place. He left the note in my hand by mistake, I was convinced.

I came out of the churchyard at the end of the straggling procession. As we emerged into the lane the stolid, pleasant-looking person I had noticed glanced at me with enquiry in his eyes and I went over to him. The question in my mind was not an easy one and I was feeling around for some fairly inoffensive way of putting it when he helped me out.

'A sad business,' he said. 'Quite young. Did you know him well?'

'I don't know,' I said, looking like an idiot, while he stared at me, his eyes twinkling.

He was a big chap, just over forty, with a square capable face.

'I mean,' I said, 'I was at school with an R. I. Peters and when I saw *The Times* this morning I realized I was coming down this way and I thought I might look in, don't you know.'

He remained smiling kindly at me as if he thought I was mental and I floundered on.

'When I got here I felt I couldn't have come to the right – I mean I felt it must be some other Peters,' I said.

'He was a big heavy man,' he observed thoughtfully. 'Deep-set eyes, too fat, light lashes, thirty-seven years old, went to a prep. school at Sheepsgate and then on to Totham.'

I was shocked. 'Yes,' I said. 'That's the man I knew.'

He nodded gloomily. 'A sad business,' he repeated. 'He came to me after an appendix operation. Shouldn't have had it: heart wouldn't stand it. Picked up a touch of pneumonia on the way down and – ' he shrugged his shoulders, ' – couldn't save him, poor chap. None of his people here.'

I was silent. There was very little to say.

'That's my place,' he remarked suddenly, nodding towards

the one big house. 'I take a few convalescents. Never had a death there before. I'm in practice here.'

I could sympathize with him and I did. It was on the tip of my tongue to ask him if Peters had let him in for a spot of cash. He had not hinted it but I guessed there was some such matter in his thoughts. However, I refrained; there seemed no point in it.

We stood there chatting aimlessly for some moments, as one does on these occasions, and then I went back to Town. I did not call in at Highwaters after all, much to Lugg's disgust. It was not that I did not want to see Leo or Janet, but I was inexplicably rattled by Pig's funeral and by the discovery that it actually was Pig's. It had been a melancholy little ceremony which had left a sort of 'half heard' echo in my ears.

The two letters were identical. I compared them when I got in. I supposed Whippet had seen *The Times* as I had. Still it was queer he should have put two and two together. And there had been that extraordinary cough and the revolting old fellow in the topper, not to mention the sly-eyed girl.

The worst thing about it was that the incident had recalled Pig to my mind. I turned up some old football groups and had a good look at him. He had a distinctive face. One could see even then what he was going to turn into.

I tried to put him out of my head. After all, I had nothing to get excited about. He was dead. I shouldn't see him again.

All this happened in January. By June I had forgotten the fellow. I had just come in from a session with Stanislaus Oates at the Yard, where we had been congratulating each other over the evidence in the Kingford shooting business which had just flowered into a choice bloom for the Judge's bouquet, when Janet rang up.

I had never known her hysterical before and it surprised me a little to hear her twittering away on the phone like a nest of sparrows.

'It's too filthy,' she said. 'Leo says you're to come at once. No, my dear, I can't say it over the phone, but Leo is afraid it's – Listen, Albert, it's M for mother, U for unicorn, R for rabbit, D for darling, E for – for egg, R for – '

'All right,' I said, 'I'll come.'

Leo was standing on the steps of Highwaters when Lugg and I drove up. The great white pillars of the house, which was built by an architect who had seen the B.M. and never forgotten it, rose up behind him. He looked magnificent in his ancient shootin' suit and green tweed flowerpot hat – a fine specimen for anybody's album.

He came steadily down the steps and grasped my hand.

'My dear boy,' he said, 'not a word . . . not a word.' He climbed in beside me and waved a hand towards the village. 'Police station,' he said. 'First thing.'

I've known Leo for some years and I know that the singleness of purpose which is the chief characteristic in a delightful personality is not to be diverted by anything less than a covey of Mad Mullahs. Leo had one thing in his mind and one thing only. He had been planning his campaign ever since he had heard that I was on my way, and, since I was part of that campaign, my only hope was to comply.

He would not open his mouth save to utter road directions until we stood together on the threshold of the shed behind the police station. First he dismissed the excited bobbies in charge and then paused and took me firmly by the lapel.

'Now, my boy,' he said, 'I want your opinion because I trust you. I haven't put a thought in your mind, I haven't told you a particle of the circumstances, I haven't influenced you in any way, have I?'

'No, sir,' I said truthfully.

He seemed satisfied, I thought, because he grunted.

'Good,' he said. 'Now, come in here.'

He led me into a room, bare save for the trestle table in the centre, and drew back the sheet from the face of the thing that lay upon it.

'Now,' he said triumphantly, 'now, Campion, what d'you think of this?'

I said nothing at all. Lying on the table was the body of Pig Peters, Pig Peters unmistakable as Leo himself, and I knew without touching his limp, podgy hand that he could not have been dead more than twelve hours at the outside.

Yet in January . . . and this was June.

CHAPTER 2

Decent Murder

Not unnaturally the whole thing was something of a shock to me and I suppose I stood staring at the corpse as though it were a beautiful view for some considerable time.

At last Leo grunted and cleared his throat.

'Dead, of course,' he said, no doubt to recall my attention. 'Poor feller. Damnable cad, though. Ought not to say it of a dead man, perhaps, but there you are. Truth must out.'

Leo really talks like this. I have often thought that his conversation, taken down verbatim, might be worth looking at. Just then I was more concerned with the matter than the form, however, and I said, 'You knew him, then?'

Leo grew red round the jawbone and his white moustache pricked up.

'I'd met the feller,' he murmured, conveying that he thought it a shameful admission. 'Had a most unpleasant interview with him only last night, I don't mind telling you. Extremely awkward in the circumstances. Still, can't be helped. There it is.'

Since there was a considerable spot of mystery in the business already I saw no point in overburdening Leo's mind by adding my little contribution to it just then.

'What was he calling himself?' I inquired with considerable guile.

Leo had very bright blue eyes which, like most soldiers', are of an almost startling innocence of expression.

'Masqueradin', eh?' he said. 'Upon my soul, very likely! Never thought of it. Untrustworthy customer.'

'I don't know anything,' I said hastily. 'Who is he, anyway?'

'Harris,' he said unexpectedly and with contempt. 'Oswald Harris. More money than was good for him and the manners of an enemy non-commissioned officer. Can't put it too strongly. Terrible feller.'

I looked at the dead man again. Of course it was Pig all right: I should have known him anywhere – and it struck me then as odd that the boy should really be so very much the father of the man. It's a serious thought when you look at some children.

Still, there was Pig and he was dead again, five months after his funeral, and Leo was growing impatient.

'See the wound?' he demanded.

He has a gift for the obvious. The top of the carrotty head was stove in, sickeningly, like a broken soccer ball, and the fact that the skin was practically unbroken made it somehow even more distressing. It was such a terrific smash that it seemed incredible that any human arm could have delivered the blow. It looked to me as if he had been kicked through a felt hat by a cart-horse and I said so to Leo.

He was gratified.

'Damn nearly right, my boy,' he said with comforting enthusiasm. 'Remarkable thing. Don't mind admitting don't follow this deducin' business myself, but substitute an urn for a cart-horse and you're absolutely right. Remind me to tell Janet.'

'An urn?'

'Geranium urn, stone,' he explained airily. 'Big so-called ornamental thing. Must have seen 'em, Campion. Sometimes have cherry pie in 'em. Madness to keep 'em on the parapet. Said so myself more than once.'

I was gradually getting the thing straight. Apparently Pig's second demise had been occasioned by a blow from a stone flower-pot falling on him from a parapet. It seemed pretty final this time.

I looked at Leo. We were both being very decent and noncommittal, I thought.

'Any suggestion of foul play, sir?' I asked.

He hunched his shoulders and became very despondent.

"Fraid so, my boy,' he said at last. 'No way out of it. Urn was one of several set all along the parapet. Been up to inspect 'em myself. All firm as the Rock of Gibraltar. Been there for years. Harris's urn couldn't have hopped off the ledge all by itself, don't you know. Must have been pushed by – er – human hands. Devilish situation in view of everything. Got to face it.'

I covered Pig's body. I was sorry for him in a way, of course, but he seemed to have retained his early propensities for making trouble.

Leo sighed. 'Thought you'd have to agree with me,' he said.

I hesitated. Leo is not one of the great brains of the earth, but I could hardly believe that he had dragged me down from London to confirm his suspicion that Pig had died from a bang on the head. I took it that there was more to come – and there was, of course; no end of it, as it turned out.

Leo stubbed a bony forefinger into my shoulder.

'Like to have a talk with you, my boy,' he said. 'One or two private matters to discuss. Have to come out some time. We ought to go down to Halt Knights and have a look at things.'

The light began to filter in.

'Was P – was Harris killed at Halt Knights?'

Leo nodded. 'Poor Poppy! Decent little woman, you know, Campion. Never a suspicion of – er – anything of this sort before.'

'I should hope not,' I said, scandalized, and he frowned at me.

'Some of these country clubs – ' he began darkly.

'Not murder,' I said firmly and he relapsed into despondency.

'Perhaps you're right,' he agreed. 'Let's go down there. Drop in for a drink before dinner.'

As we went out to the car I considered the business. To understand Halt Knights is to know Kepesake, and Kepesake is a sort of county paradise. It is a big village, just far enough from a town and a main road to remain exclusive without having to be silly about it. It has a Norman church, a village cricket green with elms, three magnificent pubs and a population of genuine country folk of proper independent views. It lies in a gentle valley on the shores of an estuary and is protected by a ring of modest little estates all owned by dear good fellers, so Leo says. The largest of these estates is Halt Knights.

At one period there was a nobleman at the Knights who owned the whole village, which had been left him by an ancestress who had had it, so the name would suggest, from a boy-friend off to the Crusades. Changing times and incomes drove out the nobleman and his heirs; hence the smaller estates.

The house and some nine hundred acres of meadow and salting remained a millstone round somebody's neck until Poppy Bellew retired from the stage and, buying it up, transformed that part of it which had not collapsed into the finest hotel and country pub in the kingdom.

Being a naturally expansive person of untiring energy, she did not let the nine hundred acres worry her but laid down an eighteen hole golf course and reserved the rest for anything anyone might think of. It occurred to some intelligent person that there was a very fine point-to-point course there somewhere and at the time Pig got the urn on his head there had been four meetings there in each of five consecutive springs.

It was all very lazy and homely and comfortable. If anyone who looked as if he might spoil the atmosphere came along somehow Poppy lost him. It was really very simple. She wanted to keep open house and the people round about were willing to pay their own expenses, or that was how it seemed to work out.

Leo's story was interesting. I could understand Pig getting himself killed at Halt Knights, but not how he managed to stay there long enough for it to happen.

Meanwhile Leo had reached the car and was looking at Lugg with mistrust. Leo's ideas of discipline are military and Lugg's are not. I foresaw an impasse.

'Ah, Lugg,' I said with forced heartiness, 'I'm going to drive Sir Leo on to Halt Knights. You'd better go back to Highwaters. Take a bus or something.'

Lugg stared at me and I saw rebellion in his eyes. His feet have been a constant source of conversation with him of late.

'A bus?' he echoed, adding 'sir' as a belated afterthought as Leo's eyes fell upon him.

'Yes,' I said foolishly. 'One of those big green things. You must have seen them about.'

He got out of the car heavily and with dignity and so far demeaned himself as to hold the door open for Leo, but me he regarded under fat white eyelids with a secret, contemplative expression.

'Extraordinary feller, your man,' said Leo as we drove off. 'Keep an eye on him, my dear boy. Save your life in the war?'

'Dear me, no!' I said in some astonishment. 'Why?'

He blew his nose. 'I don't know. Thought just crossed my mind. Now to this business, Campion. It's pretty serious and

I'll tell you why.' He paused and added so soberly that I started: 'There are at least half a dozen good fellers, including myself, who were in more than half a mind to put that feller out of the way last night. One of us must have lost his head, don't you know. I'm being very frank with you, of course.'

I pulled the car up by the side of the road. We were on the long straight stretch above the 'Dog and Owl'.

'I'd like to hear about it,' I said.

He came out with it quietly and damningly in his pleasant worried voice. It was an enlightening tale in view of the circumstances.

Two of the estates nearby had become vacant in the past year and each had been bought anonymously through a firm of London solicitors. No one thought much of it at the time but the blow had fallen about a week before our present conversation. Leo, going down to Halt Knights for a game of bridge and a drink, also had found the place in an uproar and Pig, of all people, installed. He was throwing his weight about and detailing his plans for the future of Kepesake, which included a hydro, a dog-racing track, and a cinema-dance-hall with special attractions to catch motorists from the none too far distant industrial town.

Taken on one side, Poppy had broken down and made a confession. Country ease and country hospitality had proven expensive, and she, not wishing to depress her clients, who were also her nearest and dearest friends, had accepted the generous mortgage terms which a delightful gentleman from London had arranged, only to find that his charming personality had been but the mask to cloak the odious Pig, who had decided to foreclose at the precise moment when a few outstanding bills had been paid with the greater part of the loan.

Leo, who justified his name if ever man did, had padded forth gallantly to the rescue. He roared round the district, collected a few good souls of his own kidney, held a meeting, formed a syndicate, and approached the entrenched Pig armed with money and scrupulously fair words.

From that point, however, he had met defeat. Pig was adamant. Pig had all the money he required. Pig wanted Kepesake – and a fine old silver stye he was going to make of it.

Leo's solicitor, summoned from Norwich, had confirmed his client's worst fears. Poppy had trusted the charming gentleman too well. Pig had an option to purchase.

Realizing that with money, Halt Knights, and the two adjoining estates Pig could lay waste Kepesake, and their hearts with it, Leo and his friends had tried other methods. As Leo pointed out, men will fight for their homes. There is a primitive love inspired by tree and field which can fire the most correct heart to flaming passion.

Two or three of Halt Knights' oldest guests were asked by Pig to leave. Leo and most of the others stolidly sat their ground, however, and talk was high but quiet, while plots abounded.

'And then this morning, don't you know,' Leo finished mildly, 'one of the urns on the parapet crashed down on the feller as he sat sleepin' in a deck-chair under the lounge window. Devilish awkward, Campion.'

I let in the clutch and drove on without speaking. I thought of Kepesake and its gracious shadowy trees, its sweet meadows and clear waters, and thought what a howling shame it was. It belonged to these old boys and their children. It was their sanctuary, their little place of peace. If Pig wanted to make more money, why in heaven's name should he rot up Kepesake to do it? There are ten thousand other villages in England. Well, they'd saved it from Pig at any rate, or at least one of them had. So much looked painfully apparent.

Neither of us spoke until we turned in under the red Norman arch which is the main drive gate to the Knights. There Leo snorted.

'Another bounder!' he said explosively.

I looked at the little figure mincing down the drive towards us and all but let the car swerve on to the turf. I recognized him immediately, principally by the extraordinary sensation of dislike he aroused in me. He was a thoroughly unpleasant old fellow, affected and conceited, and the last time I had seen him he had been weeping ostentatiously into a handkerchief with an inch-wide black border at Pig's first funeral. Now he was trotting out of Halt Knights as if he knew the place and was very much at home there.

CHAPTER 3

'That's Where He Died'

He looked at me with interest and I think he placed me, for I was aware of two beady bright eyes peering at me from beneath Cairn eyebrows.

Leo, on the other hand, received a full salute from him, a

wave of the panama delivered with one of those shrugs which attempt old-world grace and achieve the slightly sissy.

Leo gobbled and tugged perfunctorily at his own green tweed.

'More people know Tom Fool than Tom Fool knows,' he confided to me in an embarrassed rumble and hurried on so quickly that I took it he did not want the man discussed, which was curious.

'I want you to be careful with Poppy,' he said. 'Charmin' little woman. Had a lot to put up with the last day or two. Wouldn't like to see her browbeaten. Kid gloves, Campion: Kid gloves all the way.'

I was naturally aggrieved. I have never been considered brutal, having if anything a mild and affable temperament.

'It's ten years since I beat a woman, sir,' I said.

Leo cocked an eye at me. Facetiae are not his line.

'Hope you never have,' he said severely. 'Your mother – dear sweet lady – wouldn't have bred a son who could. I'm worried about Poppy, Campion. Poor charmin' little woman.'

I felt my eyebrows rise. The man who could visualize Poppy as a poor little woman must also, I felt, be able to think of her being actually ill-treated. I like Poppy. Charming she certainly is, but little – no. Leo was confusing the ideal with the conventional, and I might have told him so and mortally offended him had we not come through the trees at that moment to see the house awaiting us.

No English country house is worthy of the name if it is not breathtaking at half past six on a June evening, but Halt Knights is in a street by itself. It is long and low, with fine windows. Built of crushed strawberry brick, the Georgian front does not look out of place against the Norman ruins which rise up behind it and melt into the high chestnuts massed at the back.

As in many East Anglian houses the front door is at the side, so that the lawn can come right up to the house in front.

As we pulled up I was glad to see that the door was open as usual, though the place seemed deserted save for the embarrassed bobby in bicycle clips who stood on guard by the lintel.

I could not understand his acute discomfort until I caught the gleam of a pewter tankard among the candytuft at his feet. Poppy has a great understanding of the creature man.

I touched Leo on the shoulder and made a suggestion and he blinked at me.

'Oh all right, my boy. Make the examination first if you want to, by all means. This is where the feller was sittin'.'

He led me round to the front of the house where the deck-chairs, looking flimsy and oddly Japanese in their bright colours, straggled along under the windows.

'The urn,' he said.

I bent down and pulled aside the couple of sacks which had been spread over the exhibit. As soon as I saw it I understood his depression. It was a large stone basin about two and a half feet high and two feet across and was decorated with amorelli and pineapples. It must have weighed the best part of three hundredweight with the earth it contained, and while I could understand it killing Pig I was amazed that it had not smashed him to pulp. I said so to Leo and he explained.

'Would have done – would have done, my boy, but only the edge of the rim struck his head where it jutted over the back of the chair. He had a hat on, you know. There's the chair – nothing much to see.'

He kicked aside another sack and we looked down at a pathetic heap of splintered framework and torn canvas. Leo shrugged his shoulders helplessly.

I walked a little way down the lawn and looked up at the parapet. It is one of those long strips of plastered stone which finish off the flat fronts of Georgian houses and always remind me of the topping of marzipan icing on a very good fruit cake. The little windows of the second floor sit behind it in the sugarloaf roof.

There were seven other urns set along the parapet at equal distances, and one significant gap. There was obviously nothing dangerous about them; they looked as if they had been there for ever.

We went towards the house.

'There's one thing I don't understand,' I said. 'Our murderer pal seems to have taken a tremendous risk. What an extremely dangerous thing to do.'

Leo looked at me as though I had begun to gibber and I laboured on, trying to make myself clear.

'I mean,' I said, 'surely Harris wasn't sitting out here entirely alone? Someone might have come up to him to chat. The man who pushed the flowerpot over couldn't have made certain he was going to hit the right man unless he'd actually climbed out on the parapet to look first, which would have been lunatic.'

Leo grew very red. 'Harris was alone,' he said. 'He was sittin' out here when we turned up this mornin' and nobody felt like goin' to join him, don't you know. We left him where he was.

He ignored us and no one felt like speakin' to him, so we all went inside. I was playin' a game of cards in the lounge through this window here when the infernal thing crashed down on him. You may think it childish,' he added a little shamefacedly, 'but there you are. The feller was an unmitigated tick.'

I whistled. The clouds were blowing up.

'When you say "all of you", who do you mean?' I asked.

He looked wretched.

'About a dozen of us,' he said. 'All absolutely above suspicion. Let's go in.'

As soon as we set foot on the stone flags of the entrance hall and sniffed the sweet cool fragrance of old wood and flowers which is the true smell of your good country house, Poppy appeared, fat, gracious, and welcoming as always.

'Why, ducky,' she said as she took my hands, 'how very nice to see you. Leo, you're a lamb to send for him. Isn't it awful? Come and have a drink.'

She piloted us down the broad stone corridor to the big white-panelled lounge with the deep, comfortable, chintz-covered chairs, chattering the whole time.

It is not easy to describe Poppy. She is over fifty, I suppose, with tight grey curls all over her head, a wide mouth, and enormous blue eyes. That is the easy part. The rest is more difficult. She exudes friendliness, generosity, and a sort of naïve obstinacy. Her clothes are outrageous, vast flowery skirts and bodices embellished with sufficient frills to rig a frigate. However, they suit her personality if not her figure. You see her and you like her and that's all there is to it.

Leo was plainly batty about her.

'Such a horrid little man, Harris,' she said as she gave me my whisky. 'Has Leo told you all about him and me? How he tried to pinch the place . . . He has! Oh, well, that's all right. You see how it happened. Still, it's very wrong of someone, very wrong indeed – although, my dear, I'm sure they meant to be kind.'

Leo spluttered. 'Isn't she a *dear*?' he said.

'I'm not being silly, am I, Albert?' She looked at me appealingly. 'I did tell them it was dangerous last night. I said quite distinctly "This will lead to trouble" and of course it did.'

I intercepted a startled glance from Leo and sat up with interest. Poppy turned on him.

'Haven't you told him?' she said. 'Oh but you must. It's not fair.'

Leo avoided my eyes. 'I was comin' to that,' he said. 'I've only had Campion down here for half an hour.'

'You were trying to shield them,' said Poppy devastatingly, 'and that's no good. When we've got the truth,' she added naively, 'then we can decide how much we're going to tell.'

Leo looked scandalized and would have spoken but she forestalled him.

'It was like this,' she said confidingly, giving my arm a friendly but impersonal pat. 'Two or three of the more hearty old pets hatched up a plot last night. They were going to get Harris drunk and friendly first and then they were going to put the whole thing to him as man to man and in a burst of good fellowship he was going to sign a document they'd had prepared, relinquishing the option or whatever it is.'

She paused and eyed me dubiously, as well she might, I thought. As my face did not change she came a little nearer.

'I didn't approve,' she said earnestly. 'I told them it was silly and in a way not quite honest. But they said Harris hadn't been honest with us and of course that was right too, so they sat up in here with him last night. It might have been all right only instead of getting friendly he got truculent, as some people do, and while they were trying to get him beyond that stage he passed out altogether and they had to put him to bed. This morning he had a terrible hangover and went to sleep it off on the lawn. He hadn't moved all the morning when that beastly thing fell on him.'

'Awkward,' murmured Leo. 'Devilish awkward.'

Poppy gave me the names of the conspirators. They were all eminently respectable people who ought to have known a great deal better. It sounded to me as if everybody's uncle had gone undergraduate again and I might have said so in a perfectly friendly way had not Poppy interrupted me.

'Leo's Inspector – such a nice man; he's hoping to get promotion, he tells me – has been through the servants with a toothcomb and hasn't found anything, not even a brain, the poor ducks! I'm afraid there's going to be a dreadful scandal. It must be one of the visitors, you see, and I only have such dear people.'

I said nothing, for at that moment a pudding-faced maid, who certainly did not look as though she had sufficient intelligence to drop an urn or anything else on the right unwanted guest, came in to say that if there was a Mr Campion in the house he was wanted on the telephone.

I took it for granted it was Janet and I went along to the hall with a certain pleasurable anticipation.

As soon as I took up the receiver, however, the exchange said brightly: 'London call.'

Considering I had left the city unexpectedly two hours before with the intention of going to Highwaters, and no one in the world but Lugg and Leo knew that I had come to Halt Knights, I thought there must be some mistake and I echoed her.

'Yes, that's right. London call,' she repeated with gentle patience. 'Hold on. You're through . . .'

I held on for some considerable time.

'Hullo,' I said at last. 'Hullo. Campion here.'

Still there was no reply, only a faint sigh, and the someone at the other end hung up. That was all.

It was an odd little incident, rather disturbing.

Before going back to the others I wandered upstairs to the top floor to have a look at the parapet. No one was about and most of the doors stood open, so that I had very little difficulty in finding the spot where Pig's urn had once stood.

It had been arranged directly in front of a boxroom window and must, I thought, have obscured most of the light. When I came to look at the spot I saw that any hopeful theory I might have formed concerning a clumsy pigeon or a feather-brained cat was out of the question. The top of the parapet was covered with lichen save for the square space where the foot of the urn had stood. This was clear and brown save for the bodies of a few dead bugs of the kind one gets under stones, and in the centre of it there was a little slot, some three inches wide and two deep, designed to hold some sort of stone peg incorporated in the bottom of the urn all for safety's sake.

There was no question of the fall being accidental, therefore.

Someone both strong and determined must have lifted the heavy thing up before pushing it out.

There was nothing unusual about the vacant space, as far as I could see, save that the lichen at the edge of the parapet was slightly damp. How important that was I did not dream.

I went down again to the lounge. I am a naturally unobtrusive person and I suppose I came in quietly, because neither Leo nor Poppy seemed to hear me, and I caught his words, which were loud and excited.

'My dear lady, believe me, I don't want to butt into your private affairs – nothing's farther from my mind – but it was a natural question. Hang it all, Poppy, the feller was a bounder, and there he was striding out of this place as though it belonged to him. However, don't tell me who he was if you'd rather not.'

Poppy faced him. Her cheeks were pink and her eyes were bright with tears of annoyance.

'He came from the village to – to sell some tickets for a – a whist drive,' she said, all in one breath, and I, looking at her, wondered if she could have been such a very great actress after all, since she couldn't tell a lie better than that.

Then, of course, I realized who they were talking about.

CHAPTER 4

Among the Angels

I coughed discreetly, and Leo turned round to glance at me guiltily. He looked miserable.

'Ah!' he said absently, but with a valiant attempt to make normal conversation. 'Ah, Campion, not bad news, I hope?'

'No news at all,' I said truthfully.

'Oh, well, that's good. That's *good*, my boy,' he bellowed suddenly, getting up and clapping me on the shoulder with unnecessary fervour. 'No news is good news. We always say that, don't we? Well, Poppy, ought to go now, m'dear. People to dinner, you know. Good-bye. Come along, Campion. Glad you had good news.'

The old boy was frankly blethering, and I was sorry for him. Poppy was still annoyed. Her cheeks were very pink and her eyes were tearful.

Leo and I went out.

I made him come on to the lawn again where I had another look at the urn. The peg was intact. It protruded nearly two and a half inches from the flat surface of the stand.

Leo was very thoughtful when I pointed it out to him, but his mind could hardly have been on his work, for I had to explain the primitive arrangement to him twice before he saw any significance in it.

As we drove off under the trees he looked at me.

'Kittle-cattle,' he said sadly.

We drove back on to the main road in silence. I was glad of the spot of quiet because I took it that a little constructive thinking was overdue. I am not one of these intellectual sleuths, I am afraid. My mind does not work like an adding machine, taking the facts in neatly one by one and doing the work as it goes along. I am more like the bloke with the sack and spiked stick. I collect all the odds and ends I can see and turn out the bag at the lunch hour.

So far, I had netted one or two things. I had satisfied myself that Pig had been murdered; that is to say, whoever had killed him had done so intentionally, but not, I thought, with much premeditation. This seemed fairly obvious, since it was not reasonable to suppose that anyone could have insisted on him sitting just in that one spot, or made absolutely certain that he would stay there long enough to receive the urn when it came.

Considering the matter, I fancied some impulsive fellow had happened along to find the stage set, as it were; Pig sitting, porcine and undesirable, under the flower pot, and, not being able to curb the unworthy instinct, had trotted upstairs and done the necessary shoving all in the first fierce flush of inspiration.

Having arrived at this point, it struck me that the actual identification of the murderer must depend upon a process of elimination after an examination of alibis, and this, I thought, was definitely a job for the Inspector. After all, he was the young hopeful out for promotion.

The real trouble, I foresaw, would be the question of proof. Since finger-prints on the rough cast would be too much to hope for, and an eye-witness would have come forward before now, it was in pinning the crime down that I imagined the real snag would arise.

Perhaps I ought to mention here that at that moment I was absolutely wrong. I was wrong not only about the position of the snag but about everything else as well. However, I had no idea of it then. I leant back in the Lagonda with Leo at my side, and drove through the yellow evening light thinking of Pig and his two funerals, past and present.

At that time, and I was hopelessly mistaken, of course, I was inclined to think that Pig's murderer was extraneous to the general scheme. The clever young gentleman from London innocently looked forward to a nice stimulating civil mystery with the criminal already under lock and key in the mortuary, and this in spite of the telephone call and Poppy's unpleasant visitor. Which proves to me now that the balmy country air had gone to my head.

I was sorry for Leo and Poppy and the over-zealous old gentlemen who had come so disastrously to the aid of Halt Knights. I sympathized with them over the scandal and the general rumpus. But at that moment I did not think that the murder itself was by any means the most exciting part of the situation.

Of course, had I known of the other odds and ends that the gods had in the bag for us, had I realized that the unpleasant Old Person with the Scythe was just sitting up in the garden resting on his laurels and getting his breath for the next bit of gleaning, I should have taken myself in hand, but I honestly thought the fireworks were over and that I had come in at the end of the party and not, as it turned out, at the beginning.

As we drove down the narrow village street past 'The Swan', I asked Leo a question as casually as I could.

'D'you know Tethering, sir?' I said. 'There's a nursing home there, isn't there ?'

'Eh?' He roused himself with a jerk from his unhappy meditations. 'Tethering? Nursin' home? Oh, yes, excellent place – excellent. Run by young Brian Kingston. A good feller. Very small, though, very small – the nursin' home, not Kingston. You'll like him. Big feller. Dear chap. Comin' to dinner to-night.

Vicar's comin' too,' he added as an afterthought. 'Just the five of us. Informal, you know.'

Naturally, I was interested.

'Has Kingston had the place long?'

Leo blinked at me. He seemed to wish I wouldn't talk.

'Oh, several years. Father used to practise there years ago. Left the son a large house and he, bein' enterprisin' chap, made a goin' concern of it. Good doctor – wonderful doctor. Cured my catarrh.'

'You know him well, then?' I asked, feeling sorry to intrude upon his thoughts but anxious to get on with the inquiry.

Leo sighed. 'Fairly well,' he said. 'Well as one knows anyone, don't you know. Funny thing, I was playin' a hand with him and two other fellers this mornin' when that confounded urn fell on that bounder outside and made all this trouble. Came right down past the window where we were sittin'. Terrible thing.'

'What were you playing? Bridge?'

Leo looked scandalized. 'Before lunch? No, my dear boy. Poker. Wouldn't play bridge before lunch. Poker, that's what it was. Kingston had a queen-pot and we were settlin' up, thinkin' about lunch, when there was a sort of shadow past the window, and then a sort of thud that wasn't an ordinary thud. Damned unpleasant. I didn't like the look of him, did you? Looked a dangerous fellow, I thought, the sort of feller one'd set a dog on instinctively.'

'Who?' I said, feeling I was losing the thread of the argument.

Leo grunted. 'That feller we met in the drive at Poppy's place. Can't get him out of my mind.'

'I think I've seen him before,' I said.

'Oh?' Leo looked at me suspiciously. 'Where? Where was that?'

'Er – at a funeral somewhere,' I said, not wishing to be more explicit.

Leo blew his nose. 'Just where you'd expect to see him,' he said unreasonably, and we turned into the drive of Highwaters.

Janet came hurrying down the steps as we pulled up.

'Oh, darling, you're so late,' she murmured to Leo and, turning to me, held out her hand. 'Hello, Albert,' she said, a little coldly, I thought.

I can't describe Janet as I saw her then. She was, and is, very lovely.

I still like her.

'Hello,' I said flatly, and added idiotically because I felt I ought to say something else: 'Give us to drink, Ambrosia, and sweet Barm – '

She turned away from me and addressed Leo.

'You really must go and dress, pet. The Vicar's here, all of a twitter, poor boy. The whole village is seething with excitement, he says, and Miss Dusey sent up to say that "The Marquis" is full of newspaper men. She wants to know if it's all right. Has anything turned up?'

'No, no, m'dear.' Leo spoke absently and kissed her, unexpectedly, I felt sure.

He seemed to think the caress a little surprising himself, for he coughed as though to cover, or at least to excuse it, and hurried into the house, leaving her standing, darkhaired and attractive, on the step beside me.

'He's worried, isn't he?' she said under her breath, and then went on, as though she had suddenly remembered who I was, 'I'm afraid you must go and dress at once. You've only got ten minutes. Leave the car here and I'll send someone to take it round.'

I have known Janet, on and off, for twenty-three years. When I first saw her she was bald and pinkly horrible. I was almost sick at the sight of her, and was sent out into the garden until I had recovered my manners. Her formality both hurt and astonished me, therefore.

'All right,' I said, anxious to be accommodating at all costs. 'I won't wash.'

She looked at me critically. She has very fine eyes, like Leo's, only larger.

'I should,' she said gently. 'You show the dirt, don't you? – like a white fur.'

I took her hand. 'Friends, eh?' I said anxiously.

She laughed, but not very naturally.

'My dear, of course. Oh, by the way, your friend called at about half past six, but didn't stay. I said I expected you for dinner.'

'Lugg,' I said apprehensively, a great light dawning upon me. 'What's he done?'

'Oh, not *Lugg*.' She spoke with contempt. 'I *like* Lugg. Your girl-friend.'

The situation was getting out of hand.

'It's all a lie,' I said. 'There is no other woman. Did she leave a name?'

'She did.' There was grimness and I thought spite in Janet's tone. 'Miss Effie Rowlandson.'

'Never heard of her,' I said honestly. 'Was she a nice girl?'

'No,' said Janet explosively, and ran into the house.

I went into Highwaters alone. Old Pepper, pottering about in the hall doing the odd jobs that butlers do do, seemed pleased to see me, and I was glad of that. After a gracious though formal greeting, 'A letter for you, sir,' he said, in the same way as a man might say, 'I am happy to present you with a medal.' 'It came this morning, and I was about to readdress it and send it on to you, when Sir Leo informed me that we were to expect you this evening.'

He retired to his private cubby-hole at the back of the hall and returned with an envelope.

'You are in your usual room, sir, in the east wing,' he said, as he came up. 'I will send George with your cases immediately. It wants but seven minutes before the gong.'

I glanced at the envelope in my hand as he was sauntering off, and I suppose I hiccuped or something, for he glanced round at me with kindly concern.

'I beg your pardon, sir?'

'Nothing, Pepper,' I said, confirming his worst fears, and, tearing open the envelope, I read the second anonymous letter as I went up to my room. It was as neatly typed and precisely punctuated as the first had been, quite a pleasure to read.

'*O,*' *saith the owl.* '*Oho,*' *sobbeth the frog.* '*O-oh,*' *mourneth the worm.* '*Where is Peters that was promised us?*'

The Angel weepeth behind golden bars. His wings cover his face. '*Piero,*' *weepeth the Angel.*

Why should these things be? Who was he to disturb the heavens?

Consider, o consider the lowly mole. His small hands are sore and his snout bleedeth.

CHAPTER 5

Nice People

It's the nature-note *motif* I find confusing,' I confided to Lugg as I dressed. 'See any point in it at all?'

He threw the letter aside and smiled at me with unexpected sheepishness. Sentiment glistened all over his face.

'Pore little mole,' he said.

I gaped at him, and he had the grace to look abashed. He recovered his truculence almost at once, however.

'That walk,' he began darkly. 'I'm glad you've come in. I've bin waitin' to talk to you. What do you think I am? A perishin' centipede? Green bus, my old sock!'

'You're getting old,' I said offensively. 'See if your mental faculties have failed as far as your physique has deteriorated. I have four minutes to get down to the dining-room. Does that letter convey anything to you or not? It was sent here. It arrived this morning.'

The dig touched him and his great white face was reproachful as he reread the note, his lips moving soundlessly.

'A owl, a frog, a worm and a angel are all upset because they can't find this 'ere Peters,' he said at last. 'That's clear, ain't it?'

'Dazzlingly,' I agreed. 'And it would suggest that the writer knew Peters was not dead, which is interesting, because he is. The fellow I've been to see in the mortuary is – or rather was – Peters himself. He died this morning.'

Lugg eyed me. ''Avin' a game?' he inquired coldly.

I considered him with disgust as I struggled with my collar, and presently he continued without help, making an obvious effort to get his mind working.

'This mornin'? Reelly?' he said. 'Died, did he? What of?'

'Flower pot on the head, with intent.'

'Done in? Reelly?' Lugg returned to the note. 'Oh, well then, this is clear, ain't it? The bloke 'oo wrote this knew you was always anxious to snuff round a bit of blood, doin' the rozzers out of their rightful, and 'e kindly give you the tip to come along 'ere as fast as you could so's you wouldn't miss nothink.'

'Yes, well, you're offensive, muddle-headed, and vulgar,' I said with dignity.

'Vulgar?' he echoed in sudden concern. 'Not vulgar, cock. I may say what I mean, but I'm never vulgar.'

He considered a moment.

'Rozzers,' he announced with triumph. 'You're right, rozzers is common. P'lice officers.'

'You make me sick,' I said truthfully. 'The point you seem to have missed is that Peters died this morning, and that letter was posted to me at this address from central London some time before seven o'clock last night.'

He took in the facts and surprised me by getting up.

"Ere,' he said, 'see what this means? The bloke 'oo wrote you last night *knoo* Peters was goin' to die to-day.'

I hesitated. It was the first time I had felt the genuine trickle up the spine. Meanwhile he went on complaining.

'You've done it again,' he mourned. 'In spite of all I've done for you, here you are mixed up in the first bit of cheap mud that comes along. Lumme! You don't 'ave to whistle for it, even. It flies to you.'

I looked at him. 'Lugg,' I said, 'these words are in the nature of a prophecy. The puff paste has a sausage inside it, after all.'

The gong forestalled him, but his comment followed me as I hurried to the door.

'Botulistic, most likely,' he said.

I arrived in the dining-room with half a second to spare, and Pepper regarded me with affection, which was more than Janet did, I was sorry to see.

Leo was talking to a slim black back in a clerical dinner jacket, and I sat down to find myself beside the pleasant looking person with whom I had chatted at Pig's Tethering funeral.

He recognized me with a pleasing show of warmth, and laughed at me with deep lazy grey eyes.

'Always in at the death?' he murmured.

We introduced ourselves, and I liked his manner. He was a big fellow, older than I was, with a certain shyness which was attractive. We chatted for some moments, and Janet joined us, and it was not until some minutes later that I became aware of someone hating me.

It is one of those odd but unmistakable sensations one experiences sometimes on buses or at private dinners, and I looked across the table to observe a young cleric whom I had never seen before regarding me with honest hostility. He was one of those tall, bony ascetics with high-red cheek and wrist bones, and the humourless round black eyes of the indignant-hearted.

I was so taken aback that I smiled at him foolishly, and Leo introduced us.

He turned out to be the Reverend Philip Smedley Bathwick, newly appointed to the parish of Kepesake. I could not understand his unconcealed hatred, and was rather hurt by it until I saw him glance at Janet. Then I began to follow him. He positively goggled at her, and I might have felt sorry for him had it not been for something personal that there is no need to go into here.

He was doubly unfortunate, as it happened, because Leo monopolized him. As soon as we were safely embarked on the fish the old man bellowed, as he always does when he fancies the subject needs finesse: 'That fellow we were talking about before dinner; where d'you say he's staying?'

'At Mrs Thatcher's, sir. Do you know the woman? She has a little cottage below "The Swan".'

Bathwick had a good voice, but there was a tremor in it which I put down to his suppressed anxiety to listen to the conversation at our end of the table.

Leo was not giving him any respite.

'Oh, I know old Mrs Thatcher,' he said. 'One of the Jepson family on Blucher's Hill. A good woman. What's she doin' with a feller like that in the house? Can't understand it, Bathwick.'

'She lets rooms, sir.' Bathwick's eyes wandered to Janet and away again, as if the sight hurt him. 'This Mr Hayhoe has only been in the village a little under a week.'

'Heigh-ho?' said Leo. 'Idiotic name. Probably false.'

As usual when he is irritated he blared at the unfortunate young man, who gaped at him.

'Hayhoe is a fairly common name, sir,' Bathwick ventured.

'Heigh-ho?' repeated Leo, looking at him as if he were demented. 'I don't believe it. When you're as old as I am, Bathwick, you'll give up trying to be funny. This is a serious time, my dear feller, a serious time.'

Bathwick grew crimson about the ears at the injustice, but he controlled himself and glowered silently. It was a ridiculous incident, but it constituted, I submit, the whole reason why Leo considers Bathwick a facetious ass to this day, which is a pity, of course, for a more serious-minded cove was never born.

At the time I was more interested in the information than the man, however, and I turned to Kingston.

'D'you remember a fantastic old man in a top hat weeping into an immense mourning handkerchief at that funeral at your place last winter?' I said. 'That was Hayhoe.'

He blinked at me. 'Peters' funeral? No, I don't think I remember him. There was an odd sort of girl there, I know, and – '

He paused, and I saw a kind of excitement come into his eyes.

' – I say!' he said.

We were all looking at him, and he became embarrassed, and struggled to change the subject. As soon as the others were talking again, however, he turned to me.

'I've just thought of something,' he said, his voice as eager as a boy's. 'It may be useful. We'll have a chat after dinner, if you don't mind. You didn't know that fellow Peters well, did you?'

'Not intimately,' I said guardedly.

'He wasn't a nice chap,' he said and added, lowering his voice, 'I believe I'm on to something. Can't tell you here.'

He met my eyes, and my heart warmed to him. I like enthusiasm for the chase, or it's an inhuman business.

We did not have an opportunity to talk immediately we broke

up, however, because the Inspector in charge of the case came to see Leo while the port was still in circulation, and he excused himself.

Left with Bathwick, Kingston and I had our hands full. He was a red-hot innovator, we discovered. He spoke with passion of the insanitary condition of the thatched cottages and the necessity of bringing culture into the life of the average villager, betraying, I thought, a lack of acquaintance with either the thatched cottage or, of course, the villager in question, who, as every countryman knows, does not exist.

Kingston and I were trying to convince him that the whole point of a village is that it is a sufficiently scattered community for a man to call his soul his own in it without seriously inconveniencing his neighbour, when Pepper arrived to ask me if I would join Sir Leo in the gun-room.

I went into the fine old chamber on the first floor, where Leo does both his writing and his gun cleaning with impartial enthusiasm, to find him sitting at his desk. In front of him was an extremely attractive soul enjoying a glass of whisky. Leo introduced him.

'Inspector Pussey, Campion, my boy. Able feller. Been workin' like a slave all day.'

I liked Pussey on sight; anyone would.

He was lank and loose-jointed, and had one of those slightly comic faces which are both disarming and endearing, and it was evident that he regarded Leo with that amused affection and admiration which is the bedrock of the co-operation between man and master in rural England.

When I arrived they were both perturbed. I took it that the

affair touched them both nearly. It was murder in the home meadow, so to speak. But there was more to it even than that, I found.

'Extraordinary thing, Campion,' Leo said when Pepper had closed the door behind me. 'Don't know what to make of it at all. Pussey here assures me of the facts, and he's a good man. Every reason to trust him every time.'

I glanced at the Inspector. He looked proudly puzzled, I thought, like a spaniel which has unexpectedly retrieved a dodo. I waited, and Leo waved to Pussey to proceed. He smiled at me disarmingly.

'It's a king wonder, sir,' he said, and his accent was soft and broad. 'Seems like we've made a mistake somewhere, but where that is I can't tell you, nor I can't now. We spent the whole day, my man and I, questioning of people, and this evening we got 'em all complete, as you'd say.'

'And no one but Sir Leo has a decent alibi?' I said sympathetically. 'I know . . .'

'No, sir.' Pussey did not resent my interruption; rather he welcomed it. He had a natural flair for the dramatic. 'No, sir. Everyone has their alibi, and a good one, sir. The kitchen was eating of its dinner at the time of the – accident, and everyone was present, even the garden boy. Everyone else in the house was in the lounge or in the bar that leads out of it, and has two or three other gentlemen's word to prove it. There was no strangers in the place, if you see what I mean, sir. All the gentlemen who called on Miss Bellew this morning came for a purpose, as you might say. They all knew each other well. One of 'em couldn't have gone off and done it unless . . .'

He paused, getting very red.

'Unless what?' said Leo anxiously. 'Go on, my man. Don't stand on ceremony. We're in lodge here. Unless what?'

Pussey swallowed.

'Unless *all the other gentlemen knew*, sir,' he said, and hung his head.

CHAPTER 6

Departed Pig

There was an awkward pause for a moment, not unnaturally. Pussey remained dumb-stricken by his own temerity, I observed a customary diffidence, and Leo appeared to be struggling for comprehension.

'Eh!' he said at last. 'Conspiracy, eh?'

Pussey was sweating. 'Don't hardly seem that could be so, sir,' he mumbled unhappily.

'I don't know . . .' Leo spoke judicially. 'I don't know, Pussey. It's an idea. It's an idea. And yet, don't you know, it couldn't have been so in this case. They would all have had to be in it, don't you see, and *I was there.*'

It was a sublime moment. Leo spoke simply and with that magnificent innocence which is as devastating as it is blind. Pussey and I sighed with relief. The old boy had swept away the slender supports of fact and left us with a miracle, but it was worth it.

Leo continued to consider the case.

'No,' he said at last. 'No. Impossible. Quite impossible. We'll have to think of something else, Pussey. We'll go over the alibis together. Maybe there's a loophole somewhere; you never know.'

They settled down to work and I, not wishing to interfere in the Inspector's province, drifted off to find Kingston. I discovered him in the drawing-room with Janet and Bathwick, who stiffened and bristled as I came in. I wished he wouldn't. I am not over-sensitive, I hope, but his violent dislike embarrassed me, and I offered him a cigarette on the gift principle. He refused it.

Kingston was as keen to chat as I was, and he suggested a cigar on the terrace. In any other drawing-room, with the possible exception of Great-aunt Caroline's at Cambridge, such a remark might have sounded stilted or at least consciously period, but Highwaters is that sort of house. The late Lady Pursuivant liked her furniture gilt and her porcelain by the ton.

I saw Bathwick shoot him a glance of dog-like gratitude which enhanced my sense of injustice, while Janet smouldered at me across the hearthrug.

We went out through the french windows on to as fine a marble terrace as any you'd find in Hollywood to-day, and Kingston took my arm.

'I say,' he began, 'that chap Peters . . .'

It took me back years to the little patch of grass behind the chapel at school and old Guffy taking me by the arm, with the same words uttered in exactly the same tone of mingled excitement and outrage.

'That chap Peters . . .'

'Yes?' I said encouragingly.

Kingston hesitated. 'This is in the nature of a confession,' he began unexpectedly, and I fancy I stared at him, for he coloured and laughed. 'Oh, I didn't rob the blighter,' he said. 'But I took down his will for him. That's what I wanted to talk to you about. He came down to my place to recuperate after appendicitis, you know. He made the arrangements himself by letter, and on the way down he picked up a chill and developed roaring pneumonia and died in spite of everything. He came to me because I was fairly inexpensive, you know. Someone in the district recommended him, he said, and mentioned a chap I knew slightly. Well, when he was very ill he had a lucid period, and he sent for me and said he wanted to make a will. I wrote it down, and he signed it.'

Kingston paused and fidgeted.

'I'm telling you this because I know about you,' he went on at last. 'I've heard about you from Janet, and I know Sir Leo called you down on this Harris business. Well, Campion, as a matter of fact, I altered the will a bit.'

'Did you though?' I said foolishly.

He nodded. 'Not in substance, of course,' he said, 'but in form. I had to. As he dictated it it ran something like this: "To that unspeakable bounder and unjailed crook, my brother, born Henry Richard Peters – whatever he may be calling himself now – I leave all I possess at the time of my death, including everything that may accrue to my estate after I die. I do this not because I like him, am sorry for him, or sympathize in any way with any nefarious business in which he may be engaged, but simply because he is the son of my mother, and I know of no one else." '

Kingston hesitated, and regarded me solemnly in the moon-light.

'I didn't think it was decent,' he said. 'A thing like that can cause a lot of trouble. So I cleaned up the wording a bit, I simply made it clear that Mr Peters wanted everything to go to his brother, and left it at that. He signed it and died.'

He smoked for a moment or so in silence, and I waited for him to continue.

'As soon as I saw Harris he reminded me of someone,' he said, 'and to-night at dinner, when you reminded me of that funeral, I realized who it was. Peters and Harris had a great deal in common. They were made of the same sort of material, if you see what I mean, and had the same colouring. Peters was larger and had more fat on him, but the more I think about it the stronger the likeness becomes. You see what I'm driving at, Campion? This man Harris may well be the legatee's brother.'

He laughed apologetically.

'Now I've said it it doesn't sound so very exciting,' he said.

I did not answer him at once. I knew perfectly well that the Peters in the mortuary was my Peters, and if there was a brother in the business, I took it that it was he who had been Kingston's patient. It confirmed my earlier suspicions that Pig had been up to something characteristically fishy before retribution in the flower-pot had overtaken him.

'I sent the will along to his solicitors,' Kingston continued. 'I took all instructions about the funeral and so on from them, and they paid my account. I've got their name at home; I'll let you have it. To-morrow morning do?'

I assured him it would, and he went on:

'I was down at the Knights this morning when it happened,' he said, not without a certain pride. 'We were playing poker. I'd just netted a queen-pot when I heard the thud and we all rushed out. There was nothing to be done, of course. Have you seen the body?'

'Yes,' I said. 'I haven't examined it yet. Was that the first time you'd seen Harris?'

'Oh, Lord, no! He's been there all the week. I've had to go along there every day to see Flossie Gage, one of the maids. She's had jaundice. I didn't talk to Harris much because – well, none of us did, you know. He was an offensive type. That incident with Bathwick showed you the type he was.'

'Bathwick?'

'Oh, didn't you hear about that?' Kingston warmed to me. Like most country doctors he relished a spot of gossip. 'It had its humorous side in a way. Bathwick is an earnest soul, as you may have noticed.'

I agreed, and he chuckled and hurried on:

'Harris talked about a dance hall and a bathing beach he was going to build on that bit of land which runs down to the creek on the far side of the cricket pitch. Bathwick heard the gossip and was appalled by it. It didn't fit into his own scheme for Kepesake's development, which is more on welfare lines – communal kitchens and superintended creches, and so on. He rushed down to see Harris in a panic, and I believe there was a grand scene. Harris had a sort of sense of humour and took a delight in teasing old Bathwick, who has none. They were in the lounge at the Knights, and Bill Duchesney and one or two other people were there, so Harris had an audience and let himself go. Bill told me Bathwick went off at last with his eyes bulging. Harris had promised him dancing houris, secret casinos, and God knows what else, until the poor chap saw his dream yokel walking straight out of the church clinic on one side of the road into the jaws of hell on the other. Bill tried to soothe the Vicar, I believe, but he said he was scared out of his wits and shocked to the marrow. You see the sort of fellow Harris was. He liked to show off. There was no need for him to tease old Bathwick, who'd be quite a good chap if he wasn't so solemn. However, that's not the point. The question is, who killed Harris? I'll bring down that solicitor's name, and any papers I can find first thing in the morning, shall I?'

'I wish you would,' I said trying not to sound too eager. 'Thanks for telling me.'

'Not at all. I wish I could be really helpful. It's so seldom anything happens down here.' He laughed awkwardly. 'That's a bit naïve, isn't it?' he murmured. 'But you've no idea how dull the country is for a fairly intelligent man, Campion.'

We went back to the drawing-room. Janet and Bathwick were listening to the wireless, but she got up and switched it off as we appeared, and Bathwick sighed audibly at the sight of me.

Leo looked in after a bit, but he was plainly preoccupied, and he excused himself soon after. Not unnaturally the party broke up early. Kingston went home, taking the reluctant and smouldering cleric with him, and Janet and I wandered out on the terrace. It was warm and moonlit and rather exotic, what with night-scented stocks in the garden below and nightingales in the ilex.

'Albert . . .' said Janet.

'Yes?'

'You've some very peculiar friends, haven't you?'

'Oh, you meet all kinds of people at school,' I said defensively, my mind still clinging to Peters. 'It's like knowing a lot of eggs. You can't tell which one is going to grow into something definitely offensive.'

She drew a long breath and her eyes glinted in the faint light.

'I didn't know you went to a co-ed,' she said witheringly. 'That accounts for you, I suppose.'

'In a way,' I agreed mildly. 'I remember Miss Marshall. What a topping Head she was, to be sure. Such a real little sport on the hockey field. Such a demon for impositions. Such a regular little whirlwind with the birch.'

'Shut up,' said Janet unreasonably. 'How d'you like Bathwick?'

'A dear fellow,' I said dutifully. 'Where does he live?'

'At the Vicarage, just behind the Knights. Why?'

'Has he a nice garden?'

'Quite good. Why?'

'Does his garden adjoin the Knights garden?'

'The vicarage garden runs up to the chestnut copse at the back of Poppy's place. Why?'

'I like to know a man's background,' I said. 'He's rather keen on you, isn't he?'

She did not answer me, and I fancied she considered the

question to be in bad taste. To my astonishment I felt her shiver at my side.

'Albert,' she said in a very small voice, 'do you know who did this beastly murder?'

'No, not yet.'

'You think you'll find out?' She was almost whispering.

'Yes,' I said. 'I'll find out.'

She put her hand in mine. 'Leo's very fond of Poppy,' she murmured.

I held her hand closely. 'Leo has no more idea who killed Harris than a babe unborn,' I said.

She shivered again. 'That makes it worse, doesn't it? It'll be such a dreadful shock for him when he – he has to know.'

'Poppy?' I said.

Janet clung to my arm. 'They'd all shield her, wouldn't they?' she said unsteadily. 'After all, she had most to lose. Go back to Town, Albert. Give it up. Don't find out.'

'Forget it,' I said. 'Forget it for now.'

We walked on in silence for a little. Janet wore a blue dress and I said I liked it. She also wore her hair in a knot low on her neck, and I said I liked that, too.

After a while she paid me a compliment. She said I was an eminently truthful person, and she was sorry to have doubted my word in a certain matter of the afternoon.

I forgave her readily, not to say eagerly. We turned back towards the french windows and had just decided not to go in after all, when something as unforeseen as it was unfortunate occurred. Pepper came out, blowing gently. He begged our pardons, he said, but a Miss Effie Rowlandson had called to see Mr Campion and he had put her in the breakfast-room.

CHAPTER 7

The Girl Friend

As I followed Pepper through the house, I ventured to question him.

'What's she like, Pepper?'

He turned and eyed me with a glance which conveyed clearly that he was an old man, an experienced man, and that dust did not affect his eyesight.

'The young woman informed me that she was a great friend of yours, sir, which was why she took the liberty of calling on you so late.' He spoke sadly, intimating that the rebuke hurt him as much as it did me. He opened the breakfast-room door.

'Yoo-hoo!' said someone inside.

Pepper withdrew and Miss Effie Rowlandson rose to meet me.

'O-oh!' she said, glancing up at me under fluttering lashes, 'you're not really, truly cross, are you?'

I am afraid I looked at her blankly. She was *petite*, blonde, and girlish, with starry eyes and the teeth of toothpaste advertisement. Her costume was entirely black save for a long white quill in her hat, and the general effect lay somewhere between Hamlet and Aladdin.

'O-oh, you don't remember me,' she said. 'O-oh, how awful

of me to have come! I made sure you'd remember me. I am a silly little fool, aren't I?'

She conveyed that I was a bit of a brute, but that she did not blame me, and life was like that.

'Perhaps you've got hold of the wrong man?' I suggested helpfully.

'O-oh no . . . ' Again her lashes fluttered at me. 'I remember you – at the funeral, you know.' She lowered her voice modestly on the last words.

Suddenly she came back to me with a rush. She was the girl at Peters' funeral. Why I should have forgotten her and remembered the old man, I do not know, save that I recollect feeling that she was not the right person to stare at.

'Ah, yes,' I said slowly. 'I do remember now.'

She clapped her hands and squealed delightedly.

'I knew you would. Don't ask me why, but I just knew it. I'm like that sometimes. I just know things.'

At this point the conversation came to an abrupt deadlock. I was not at my best, and she stood looking at me, a surprisingly shrewd expression in her light grey eyes.

'I knew you'd help me,' she added at last.

I was more than ever convinced that I was not her man, and was debating how to put it when she made a surprising statement.

'He trampled on me,' she said. 'I don't know when I've been so mistaken in a man. Still, a girl does make mistakes, doesn't she, Mr Campion? I see I made a mistake in saying I was such an old friend of yours when we'd only met once – or really only just looked at each other. I know that now. I wouldn't do it again.'

'Miss Rowlandson,' I said, 'why have you come? I – er – I have a right to know,' I added stalwartly, trying to keep in the picture.

She peered at me. 'O-oh, you're *hard*, aren't you?' she said. 'All men are hard, aren't they? They're not all like him, though. O-oh, he was hard! Still,' she added, with a wholly unconvincing attempt at gallant restraint, 'I ought not to talk about him like that, did I, when he's dead – if he *is* dead. Is he?'

'Who?'

She giggled. 'You're cautious, aren't you? Are all detectives cautious? I like a man to be cautious. Roly Peters, of course. I use to call him Roly-Poly. That used to make him cross. You'd never guess how cross that used to make him. Poor Roly-Poly! It's wrong to laugh when he's dead – if he *is* dead. Do you know?'

'My dear girl,' I said. 'We went to his funeral, didn't we?'

I suppose I spoke sharply, for her manner changed. She assumed a spurious dignity and sat down, arranging her short black skirts about her thin legs with great care.

'I've come to consult you, Mr Campion,' she said. 'I'm putting all my cards on the table. I want to know if you're satisfied about that funeral?'

'It wasn't much to do with me,' I countered, temporarily taken aback.

'Oh, wasn't it? Well, why was you there? That's pinked you, hasn't it? I'm a straightforward girl, Mr Campion, and I want a straight answer. There was something funny about that funeral, and you know it.'

'Look here,' I said, 'I'm perfectly willing to help you. Suppose you tell me why you think I can.'

She looked at me steadily. 'You've been to a good school,

haven't you?' she said. 'I always think it helps a man to have gone to a good school. Then you *know* he's a gentleman; I always say that. Well, I'll trust you. I don't often. And if you let me down, well, I've been silly again, that's all. I was engaged to marry Roly Peters, Mr Campion, and then he went and died in a hole-and-corner nursing home and left all his money to his brother. If you don't think that's suspicious, I do.'

I hesitated. 'You think it's odd because he left his brother everything?' I began.

Effie Rowlandson interrupted me.

'I think it's funny he died at all, if you ask me,' she said. 'I'd threatened him with a lawyer, I had really. I had the letters and everything.'

I said nothing, and she grew very pink.

'Think what you like about me, Mr Campion,' she said, 'but I've got feelings and I've worked very hard to get married. I think he's done the dirty on me. If he's hiding I'll find him, if it's the last thing I do.'

She sat looking at me like a suddenly militant sparrow.

'I came to you,' she said, 'because I heard you were a detective and I liked your face.'

'Splendid! But why come here?' I demanded. 'Why come to Kepesake, of all places?'

Effie Rowlandson drew a deep breath. 'I'll tell you the truth, Mr Campion,' she said.

Once again her lashes flickered, and I felt that our brief period of plain dealing was at an end.

'I've got a friend in this village, and he's seen my photographs of Roly Peters. He's an old man, known me for years.'

She paused, and eyed me to see if I was with her or against her, and apparently she was reassured, for she went on breathlessly:

'A few days ago he wrote me, this friend of mine did. "There's a gentleman in the village very like a friend of yours," he wrote. "If I were you I'd come and have a look at him. It might be worth your while." I came as soon as I could, and when I got here I found this man I'd come to see had got himself killed only this morning. I heard you were in the village, so I came along.'

I began to follow her. 'You want to identify him?' I said.

She nodded resolutely.

'Why come to me? Why not go to the authorities?'

Her reply was disarming. 'Well, you see, I felt I knew you,' she said.

I considered. The advantages of a witness at this juncture were inestimable.

'When can you be down at the police station?'

'I'd like to go now.'

It was late for the country, and I said so, but she was adamant.

'I've made up my mind to it and I shan't sleep if I've got it hanging over me till to-morrow. Take me down now in your car. Go on, you know you can. I am being a nuisance, aren't I? But I'm like that. If I make up my mind to a thing, I fret till I've done it. I should be quite ill by the morning, I should really.'

There was nothing else for it. I knew from experience that it is safest to catch a witness as soon as he appears on the scene.

I rang the bell, and told the girl who answered it to send Lugg round with the car. Then, leaving Miss Rowlandson in the breakfast-room, I went to find Janet.

It was not a very pleasant interview. Janet is a dear girl, but she can be most obtuse. When she went to bed, which she did with some dignity a few minutes after I had located her, I went back to the breakfast-room.

Lugg seemed a little surprised when I appeared with Miss Rowlandson. I tucked her into the back of the car, and climbed into the front seat beside him. He let in the clutch, and as we roared down the drive in fourth he leant towards me.

'Ever see a cat come out of a dawg-kennel?' he murmured, and added when I stared at him: 'Gives you a bit of a turn. That's all.'

We drove on in silence. I began to feel that my friend, Miss Effie Rowlandson, was going to be a responsibility.

It was a strange night with a great moon sailing in an infinite sky. Small odd-shaped banks of cumulus clouds swam over it from time to time, but for the most part it remained bland and bald as the knob on a brass bedstead.

Kepesake, which is a frankly picturesque village by day, was mysterious in the false light. The high trees were deep and shadowy and hid the small houses, while the square tower of the church looked squat and menacing against the transparent sky. It was a secret village through which we sped on what I for one felt was our rather ghastly errand.

When we pulled up outside the cottage which is also the Police Station, there was only a single light in an upstairs room, and I leant over the back of my seat.

'Are you sure you wouldn't rather leave it until the morning?' I ventured.

She answered me through clenched teeth. 'No, thank you,

Mr Campion. I've made up my mind to go through with it. I've got to know.'

I left them in the car and went down the path to rouse someone. Pussey himself came out almost at once, and was wonderfully obliging considering he had been on the point of going to bed. We conferred in whispers out of deference to the darkness.

'That's all right, sir,' he said in reply to my apologies. 'Us wants a bit o' help in this business, and that's the truth now, so it is. If the lady can tell us anything about the deceased it's more than the landlord of his flat in London can. We'll go round the side, sir, if you don't mind.'

I fetched the others, and together we formed a grim little procession on the gravel path leading round to the yard behind the cottage. Pussey unlocked the gates, and we crossed the tidy little square to the slate-roofed shed which looked like a small village schoolroom, and was not.

I took Effie Rowlandson's arm. She was shivering and her teeth were chattering, but she was not a figure of negligible courage.

Pussey was tact itself. 'There's a light switch just inside the door,' he said. 'Now, Miss, there ain't nothin' to shock you. Just a moment, sir; I'll go first.'

He unlocked the door, and we stood huddled together on the stone step. Pussey turned over the light switch.

'Now,' he said, and a moment later swallowed with a sound in which incredulity was mixed with dismay. The room remained as I had seen it that afternoon, save for one startling innovation.

The table in the middle of the floor was dismantled. The cotton sheet lay upon the ground, spread out as though a careless riser had flung it aside.

Pig Peters had gone.

CHAPTER 8

The Wheels Go Round

There was a long uncomfortable pause. A moment before I had seen Pig's outline under the cotton clearly in my mind's eye. Now the image was dispelled so ruthlessly that I felt mentally stranded. The room was very cold and quiet. Lugg stepped ponderously forward.

'Lost the perishin' corpse now?' he demanded, and he spoke so truculently that I knew he was rattled. 'Lumme, Inspector, I 'ope your 'elmet's under lock and key.'

Pussey stood looking down at the dismantled table, and his pleasant yokel face was pale.

'That's a wonderful funny thing,' he began, and looked round the ill-lit barren little room as though he expected to find an explanation for the mystery on its blank walls.

It was a moment of alarm, the night so silent, the place so empty and the bedraggled cotton pall on the ground.

Pussey would have spoken again had it not been for Effie Rowlandson's exhibition. Her nerve deserted her utterly and she drew away from me, her head strained back as she began to scream, her mouth twisted into an O of terror. It was nerve-racking, and I seized her by the shoulders and shook her so violently that her teeth rattled.

It silenced her, of course. Her final shriek was cut off in the middle, and she looked up at me angrily.

'Stop it!' I said. 'Do you want to rouse the village?'

She put up her hands to push me away.

'I'm frightened,' she said. 'I don't know what I'm doing. What's happened to him? You told me he was here. I was going to look at him, and now he's gone.'

She began to cry noisily. Pussey glanced at her and then at me.

'Perhaps that'd be best if the young lady went home,' he suggested reasonably.

Miss Rowlandson clung to me. 'Don't leave me,' she said. 'I'm not going down to "The Feathers" in the dark. I won't, I tell you, I won't! Not while he's about, *alive*.'

'It's all right,' I began soothingly. 'Lugg'll drive you down. There's nothing to be alarmed about. There's been a mistake. The body's been moved. Perhaps the undertaker –'

Pussey raised his head as he heard the last word.

'No,' he said. 'That was in here an hour ago, because I looked.'

Effie began to cry again. 'I won't go with him,' she said. 'I won't go with anyone but you. I'm frightened. You got me into this. You must get me out of it. Take me home! Take me home!'

She made an astounding amount of noise, and Pussey looked at me beseechingly.

'Perhaps if you would drive the young lady down, sir,' he suggested diffidently, 'that would ease matters up here, in a manner of speaking. I better get on the telephone to Sir Leo right away.'

I glanced at Lugg appealingly, but he avoided my eyes, and Miss Rowlandson laid her head on my shoulder in an ecstasy of tears.

The situation had all the unreality and acute discomfort of a nightmare. Outside the shed the yard was ghostly in the false light. It was hot, and there was not a breath of wind anywhere. Effie was trembling so violently that I thought she might collapse.

'I'll be back in a minute,' I said to Pussey, and hurried her down the gravel path to the waiting car.

'The Feathers Inn' is at the far end of the village. It stands by itself at the top of a hill, and is reputed to have the best beer, if not the best accommodation, in the neighbourhood.

Effie Rowlandson scrambled into the front seat, and when I climbed in beside her she drew close to me, still weeping.

'I've had a shock,' she snivelled. 'I'd prepared myself and then it wasn't necessary. That was one thing. Then I realized Roly got out by himself. You didn't know Roly Peters as well as I did, Mr Campion. When I heard he'd been killed I didn't really believe it. He was clever, and he was cruel. He's about somewhere, hiding.'

'He was dead this afternoon,' I said brutally. 'Very dead. And since miracles don't happen nowadays he's probably dead still. There's nothing to get so excited about. I'm sorry you should have had a rotten experience, but there's probably some very ordinary explanation for the disappearance of the body.'

I was rather shocked to hear myself talking so querulously.

There had been something very disturbing in the incident. The elusiveness of Pig dead was becoming illogical and alarming.

As we came out of the village on to the strip of heath which lay silent and deserted in the cold secretive light, she shuddered.

'I'm not an imaginative girl, Mr Campion,' she said, 'but you read of funny things happening, don't you? Suppose he was to rise up behind one of these banks of stones by the side of the road and come out towards us . . .'

'Shut up,' I said, even more violently than I had intended. 'You'll frighten yourself into a fit, my child. I assure you there's some perfectly reasonable explanation for all this. When you get into "The Feathers" make them give you a hot drink and go to bed. You'll find the mystery's been cleared up by the morning.'

She drew away from me. 'Oh, you're hard,' she said with a return of her old manner. 'I said you were hard. I like hard people, I do reelly.'

Her lightning changes of mood disconcerted me, and I was glad when we pulled up outside the pub. The fine old lath and plaster front was in darkness, which was not astonishing, for it was nearly midnight.

'Which door is it?' I inquired.

'The one marked Club Room. I expect it'll be locked.'

I left her in the car while I tapped on the door she indicated. For a time there was no response, and I was getting restive at the delay when I heard a furtive movement on the inside. I tapped again, and this time the door was opened.

'I say, you're fearfully late,' said the last voice I expected, and Gilbert Whippet of all people thrust a pale face out into the moonlight.

I gaped at him, and he had the grace to seem vaguely disturbed to see me.

'Oh . . . er . . . Campion,' he said. 'Hello! Terribly late, isn't it?'

He was backing into the dark pit of the doorway when I pulled myself together.

'Hey,' I said, catching him by the sleeve. 'Here, Whippet, where are you going?'

He did not resist me, but made no attempt to come out into the light. Moreover, I felt that once I let him go he would fade quietly into the background.

'I was going to bed,' he murmured, no doubt in reply to my question. 'I heard you knock, so I opened the door.'

'You stay and talk to me,' I commanded. 'What are you doing here, anyway?'

In spite of myself I heard the old censorious note creeping into my tone. Whippet is so very vague that he forces one into an unusual directness.

He did not answer me, and I repeated the question.

'Here?' he said, looking up at the pub. 'Oh yes, I'm staying here. Only for a day or two.'

He was infuriating, and I quite forgot the girl until I heard her step behind me.

'Mr Whippet,' she began breathlessly, 'he's gone! The body's gone! What shall we do?'

Whippet turned his pale eyes towards her, and I thought I detected a warning in the glance.

'Ah, Miss Rowlandson,' he said. 'You've been out? You're late, aren't you?'

I was glad to see she wasn't playing, either.

'The body's gone,' she repeated. 'Roly Peters' body is gone.'

The information seemed to sink in. For a moment he looked positively intelligent.

'Lost it?' he said. 'Oh! . . . Awkward. Holds things up so.'

His voice trailed away into silence, and he suddenly shook hands with me.

'Glad to have seen you, Campion. I'll look you up some time. Er – good night.'

He stepped back into the doorway, and Effie followed him. With great presence of mind I put my foot in the jamb.

'Look here, Whippet,' I said, 'if you can do anything to help us in this matter, or if you know anything, you'd better come out with it. What do you know about Peters, anyway?'

He blinked at me.

'Oh . . . nothing. I'm just staying here. I've heard the talk, of course . . .'

I caught his sleeve again just as he was disappearing.

'You had one of those letters,' I said. 'Have you had any more?'

'About the mole? Yes. Yes, as a matter of fact, I have, Campion. I've got it somewhere. I showed it to Miss Rowlandson. I say, it's terribly awkward you losing the body. Have you looked in the river?'

It was such an unexpected question that it irritated me unreasonably.

'Why on earth in the river?' I said. 'D'you know anything?'

In my excitement I must have held him a little more tightly than I had intended, for he suddenly shook himself free.

'I should look in the river,' he said. 'I mean, it's so obvious, isn't it?'

He stepped back and closed the door with himself and Miss Rowlandson inside. I still had my foot there, however, and he opened it again. He seemed embarrassed.

'It's fearfully late,' he said. 'I don't mean to be rude, Campion. I'll look you up to-morrow, if I may, but there's no point in your doing anything at all until you've found the body, is there?'

I hesitated. There was a great deal in what Whippet said. I was itching to get back, and yet there was evidently much he could explain. What on earth was he doing there with Effie Rowlandson, for one thing?

In that moment of hesitation I was lost. He moved forwards, and as I stepped backward involuntarily the door was gently, almost politely, closed in my face.

I cursed him, but decided he could wait. I hurried back to the car and turned her. As I raced down to the Police Station I tried to reconcile Whippet's reappearance with the whole mysterious business.

I covered the half mile in something under a minute, and pulled up outside Pussey's cottage at the same moment that another car arrived from the opposite direction. As I climbed out I recognized Leo's respectable Humber. Pepper Junior was driving, and Leo hailed me from the tonneau.

'Is that you, Campion? Most extraordinary business! Pussey told me over the phone.'

I went up to the car and opened the door.

'Are you coming, sir?' I said.

'Yes, my boy, yes. Should have been here before, but I stopped to pick up Bathwick here. Seems to have had a little accident on the way home from our place to-night.'

He put up his hand and turned on the light as he spoke, and I stared down into the pale, embarrassed face of the Reverend Smedley Philip Bathwick, who smiled at me with uncharacteristic friendliness. He was wringing wet. HIs dinner-jacket clung to him, and his dog-collar was a sodden rag.

'Been in the river, he tells me,' said Leo.

CHAPTER 9

'And a Very Good Day to You, Sir'

'The river?' I echoed, Whippet's idiotic remark returning to me. 'Really?'

Bathwick giggled. It was a purely nervous sound, but Leo scowled at him.

'Well, hardly,' he said. 'I was taking a short cut home across the saltings and I stumbled into one of the dykes. I'd come out without my torch. I made my way back to the road, and Sir Leo very kindly picked me up and gave me a lift.'

It was a fantastic story in view of the moonlight, which was so bright that colours were almost distinguishable, and I thought Leo must notice it. He had a one-track mind, however. His one desire was to get back to the scene of the disappearance.

'Never mind, never mind. Soon get you home now,' he said. 'Pepper'll take you along. Make yourself a hot toddy. Wrap yourself in a blanket and you'll come to no harm.'

'Er – thank you, thank you very much,' said Bathwick. 'I should like nothing better. I feel I must express –'

We heard no more, for Pepper Junior, who doubtless shared his employer's anxiety to get to the scene of the excitement in the shortest possible time, let in the clutch and Bathwick was whisked away.

I was sorry to lose him. His astonishing friendliness towards me was not the least fishy circumstance of his brief appearance.

'Where did you find him?' I asked Leo.

'On the lower road. Nearly ran him down. He's all right – just a duckin'.' Leo was fighting with the catch of the police-station gate as he spoke and appeared profoundly uninterested.

'Yes, I know,' I said. 'But he left Highwaters at about a quarter to ten. I thought Kingston was going to run him home?'

'So he did, so he did,' said Leo, sighing with relief as we got the wicket open. 'Kingston put him down at the White Barn corner, and he said he'd strike his way home across the marshes. Can't be more than five hundred yards. But the silly feller stumbled into a dyke, lost his nerve, and made his way back to the road. Perfectly simple, Campion. No mystery there. Come on, my boy, come on. We're wastin' time.'

'But it's now midnight,' I objected. 'It couldn't have taken him a couple of hours to scramble out of a dyke.'

'Might have done,' said Leo irritably. 'Backboneless feller. Anyway, we can't bother about him now. Got somethin' serious to think about. I don't like monkey-business with a corpse. It's not a bit like my district. It's indecent. I tell you I feel it, Campion. Ah, here's Pussey. Anythin' to report, my man?'

Pussey and Lugg came up together. I could see their faces quite plainly, and I wondered how Bathwick could possibly have avoided seeing a rabbit-hole, much less a dyke.

Pussey, I saw at once, was well over his first superstitious alarm. At the moment he was less mystified than shocked.

'That's a proper nasty thing, sir,' he said, 'so that is, now.'

He led us into the shed and, with Lugg remaining mercifully silent in the background, gave us a fairly concise account of his investigations.

'All these windows were bolted on the inside, sir, the same as you see them now, and the door was locked. At a quarter to eleven I went round the station just to see everything was all right for the night, and the body was here then. After that I went in to the front of the house, and I stayed there for some little time until I went up to my bedroom. I was just thinking about bed when Mr Campion here arrived with the young lady and Mr Lugg, and we come round here and made the discovery, sir.'

He paused, took a deep breath, and Leo spluttered.

'Did the key leave your possession?'

'No, sir.'

Leo's natural reaction to the story of a miracle is to take it as read that someone is lying. I could hear him boiling quietly at my side.

'Pussey, I've always found you a very efficient officer,' he began with dangerous calm, 'but you're askin' me to believe in a fairy story. If the body didn't go through the windows it must have gone through the door, and if you had the only key –'

Pussey coughed. 'Excuse me, sir,' he began, 'but Mr Lugg and me we made a kind of discovery, like. This building was put up by Mr Henry Royle, the builder in the Street, and Mr Lugg and me we noticed that several other buildings in this yard, sir, which were put up at the same time, all have the same locks, like.'

Leo's rage subsided and he became interested.

'Any of the other keys here missin'?'

'No, sir; but as Mr Royle has done a lot of work hereabouts lately, it doesn't seem unlikely –?'

He broke off on the question.

Leo swore, and it seemed to relieve him.

'Oh, well, we shan't get any help there,' he rumbled. 'Wonder you trouble to lock the place at all, Pussey. Damned inefficient. Typical of the whole county,' he added to me under his breath.

But Pussey had more to offer. With considerable pride he led us over the rough grass by the side of the shed to the tarred fence which marked the boundary line of police property. Three boards had been kicked down and there was a clear way into the narrow lane beyond.

'That's new,' he said. 'That's been done to-night.'

A cursory search of the lane revealed nothing. The ground was hard and the surface was baked mud interspersed with tufts of grass. It was Pussey who put the general thought into words.

'Whoever moved him must' a done it between quarter to eleven and twenty-five minutes past. Seems very likely that was done with a car, or a cart. He was a heavy fellow. If you'll excuse me, sir, I think the best thing is for us to wait till the morning and then question all those as live nearby. Seems like we can't do nothing while that's dark.'

In the end we left it at that. Pepper Junior collected Leo and I sent Lugg back with the Lagonda. Pussey went to bed and I walked off down the grassy lane behind the shed. The moon was sinking and already there were faint streaks of light in the east. It was colder and I was in the mood to walk home.

The lane went on for some distance between high hedges. Pussey had given me clear directions how to get on to the road again, and I sauntered on, my mind on the business.

Leo and Pussey, I saw, were outraged. The murder had shaken them up, but this apparently wanton disturbance of the dead shocked them both deeply.

As I thought of it, it seemed to me that this element was perhaps the most enlightening thing I had noticed so far, because, although I knew I had no proof of it, it seemed to me that it constituted a complete let-out for Leo's particular band of friends who had gathered round Poppy in her trouble. Whereas any one of them might quite easily have staged the slightly ludicrous accident which had killed Pig, I could not see any of them dragging his body about afterwards in this extraordinarily pointless fashion.

I was considering those who were left, and Bathwick was figuring largely in my mind, when I turned out of the lane on to a grass field which rose up to form a considerable hill, circular against the skyline. I knew I had to skirt this field and pass through another before I came to the road, if I was to avoid an unnecessary couple of miles.

It was almost dark at the bottom of the hill, and as I plodded on, lost in my thoughts, there came to me suddenly over the brow of the hill a sound at once so human and so terrifying that I felt the hair on my scalp rising.

It was Pig's cough.

The night was very still, and I heard the rattle in the larynx, the whoop, and even the puff at the end of it.

For a moment I stood still, a prey to all the ridiculous fears of childhood. Then I set off up the hill at a double. The wind whistled in my ears and my heart was thumping.

Suddenly, as I reached the brow, I saw something silhouetted against the grey sky. This was so unexpected that I paused to gape at it. It was a tripod with something else which I at first took to be a small machine-gun, and which turned out to be an old-fashioned telescope mounted upon it.

I approached this cautiously, and had almost reached it when a figure rose up out of the earth beside it and stood waiting for me. He was against what light there was and I could only see his small silhouette. I stopped, and for want of something better, said what must have been the silliest thing in the world in the circumstances. I said 'Good-day.'

'And a very good day to you, sir,' answered one of the most unpleasant voices I have ever heard in all my life.

He came towards me and I recognized him with relief by his peculiar mincing walk.

'Perhaps I have the advantage of you, sir,' he began. 'You are Mr Campion?'

'Yes,' I said. 'And you're Mr Hayhoe.'

He laughed, a little affected sound.

'It will serve,' he murmured. 'It will serve. I was looking forward to an interview with you to-day, sir. I was wondering how I could manage it with a certain amount of privacy. This is a most unexpected pleasure. I didn't expect to find a man of your age wandering about in the dawn. Most young men nowadays prefer to spend the best part of their day in their beds.'

'You're up early yourself,' I said, glancing at the telescope. 'Waiting to see the sunrise?'

'Yes,' he said, and laughed again. 'That and other things.'

It was a mad conversation up there on the hill at two o'clock in the morning, and it went through my mind that he must be one of those fashionable nature-lovers who rush round the country identifying birds. He soon disabused me of that idea, however.

'I take it you are making investigations concerning the death of that unfortunate fellow Harris?' he said. 'Now, Mr Campion, I can be very useful to you. I wish to make you a proposition. For a reasonable sum, the amount to be settled between us, I will undertake to give you certain very interesting information, information which it would take you a very long time to collect alone and which should lead you to a very successful conclusion of the case. Your professional reputation will be enhanced, and I shall, of course, take none of the kudos. Now, suppose we come to terms . . .'

I am afraid I laughed at him. This is the kind of offer which I have had so often. I thought of the cough I had heard.

'Harris was a relation of yours, I suppose?' I observed.

He stiffened a little and shrugged his shoulders.

'A nephew,' he said, 'and not a very dutiful one. He was quite a wealthy young man, you see, and I – well as you can imagine, I am not the sort of man who normally spends his holidays in a wretched workman's hovel or his evenings traipsing about the barren countryside.'

He was rather a terrible old man, but I was glad I had cleared up the mystery of the cough.

It was then that I remembered something. After all, so far, I myself was the only person to connect Roly Peters with Oswald Harris, with the possible exception of Effie Rowlandson, who merely had her suspicions.

'Let me see,' I murmured, 'that was your nephew Rowland Peters, wasn't it?'

To my intense regret he brushed the inference aside.

'I have several nephews, Mr Campion, or, rather, I had,' he said with spurious dignity. 'I hate to press the point, but I regard this as a business interview. Terms first, if you please. Shall we say five hundred guineas for a complete and private explanation of the whole business? Or, of course, I might split up the lots, as it were.'

While he was rambling on I was thinking, and at this point I had an inspiration.

'Mr Hayhoe,' I said, 'what about the mole?'

A little shrill sound escaped him, but he bit it off instantly.

'Oh!' he said, and there was cautiousness and respect in his voice, 'you know about the mole, do you?'

CHAPTER 10

The Parson's Dram

I did not reply. In the circumstances of my extreme ignorance there was very little I could say. I remained silent, therefore, and, I hope, enigmatic. However, he was not to be drawn.

'I hadn't thought of the creature myself,' he said unexpectedly, 'but there may be something there. It's a valuable contribution. You seem to be unexpectedly intelligent, if I may say so without offence.'

He sighed and sat down on the grass.

'Yes,' he continued, clasping his knees. 'Thinking it over we ought to go far, you and I, once we can come to an understanding. Now, about this question of terms . . . I hate to insist upon the subject, but at the moment my financial affairs are in considerable disorder. How far would you be prepared to meet me?'

'Not to a pound,' I said flatly, but with politeness. 'If you know anything about the death of your nephew it's your obvious duty to go to the police with it.'

Mr Hayhoe shrugged his shoulders. 'Oh, well,' he said regretfully, 'I gave you the opportunity. You can't deny that.'

I turned away expecting him to call me back, which he did.

'My dear young man,' he protested when I had taken a few steps down the hill, 'don't be precipitate. Let us talk this thing over reasonably. I have certain information which is of value to you. Why should we quarrel?'

'If you knew anything of importance,' I said over my shoulder, 'you'd hardly dare to talk about it.'

'Ah, you don't understand.' He seemed greatly relieved. 'My own situation is perfectly safe. I have nothing to lose, everything to gain. My position is simple. I happen to possess an asset which I intend to realize. There are two likely purchasers: one is yourself, and the other is a certain person I need not name. Naturally, I shall dispose to the highest bidder.'

I was growing weary of him. 'Mr Hayhoe,' I said, 'I am tired.

I want to go to bed. You are wasting my time. You are also making a fool of yourself. I'm sorry to be so explicit, but there it is.'

He got up. 'Look here, Campion,' he said with a complete change of tone, his artificiality dropping from him and a wheedling note taking its place, 'I could tell you something interesting if I wanted to. The police can pull me in and bullyrag me, but they can't hold me because they've nothing on me. I shan't talk to them and they can't make me. I can put you on to the right track for a consideration. What's it worth to you?'

'At this stage, very little,' I said. 'Half a crown, perhaps.'

He laughed. 'I think I can get more than that,' he said softly. 'Very much more. However, I'm not a rich man. Between ourselves, at the moment I'm very short indeed. Suppose we meet to-morrow morning, not quite as early as this? Say, seven o'clock. That gives me a clear twenty-four hours. If I can't get satisfaction in other quarters, well, I may bate my price a little. What do you say?'

He was an unpleasant piece of work, but I liked him better in this mood.

'We might have a chat about the mole,' I conceded ungraciously.

He cocked an eye at me. 'Very well,' he agreed. 'About the mole and – other things. I'll meet you here, then, at seven o'clock to-morrow morning – '

As I turned away an idea occurred to me.

'About your other purchaser,' I said. 'I shouldn't approach Sir Leo if I were you.'

This time his laugh was spontaneous.

'You're not quite so clever as I thought you were,' he said, and I went off down the hill with something to think about. Quite frankly, until that moment I had not seen him as a possible blackmailer.

At the time I thought I was justified in letting him cook for twenty-four hours, but at that time, as I have said, I did not know the type of person we were up against. Whenever I am apt to get over-pleased with myself, I remembered that little chat on the hill-side.

As I came wearily up the drive at Highwaters it was full dawn. The air was magnificent, the sky a translucent blue, and the birds were roaring at one another in undisturbed abandonment.

I suspected the french windows in the dining-room had been left unlatched, and as I went round to them a rather unfortunate thing happened. Janet, who had no business to be awake at such an hour, came out on her balcony and caught me. I looked up to see her staring down at my slinking dinner-jacketed figure with mingled surprise and contempt.

'Good morning,' I said innocently.

Two bright spots of colour appeared on her cheeks.

'I hope you saw Miss Rowlandson home safely,' she said, and went back to her room before I could explain.

I had a tepid bath and slept for a couple of hours, but I was waiting for Leo when he appeared round about eight o'clock. We went for a stroll round the garden before breakfast, and I put my request to him.

'Have the feller watched?' he said. 'Good idea. I'll phone

down to Pussey. Extraordinary name, Heigh-ho. Must be fictitious. Any reason above general suspicion?'

I told him about the conversation on the hill-top, and at first he wanted to have the man pulled in immediately.

'I don't think I would, sir,' I objected. 'I don't see how he can be involved himself, unless he's playing an incredibly dangerous game. Leave him loose, and he'll lead us to someone more interesting.'

'As you like,' he said. 'As you like. Prefer the straightforward method myself.'

As it happened, of course, he was perfectly right, but none of us knew that then.

Janet did not appear to breakfast, but I had no time to think about her, for Kingston arrived before the meal was over. He was bubbling with excitement, and looked very young for his forty years as he came striding in, his coarse fair hair dishevelled and his rather lazy eyes unwontedly bright.

'I've found it,' he announced, before he was well in the room. 'I've been up half the night turning over papers, but I tracked it down in the end. The firm I dealt with in Peters' affairs was Skinn, Sutain and Skinn, of Lincoln's Inn Fields. Any good?'

I took the name down, and he looked at me expectantly.

'I could take the day off and go up and see them for you, if you like,' he said. 'Or perhaps you'll go yourself?'

I didn't like to damp his enthusiasm, though it occurred to me that his life must be incredibly dull, since he was so anxious to play the detective.

'Well, no,' I said. 'I think it'll have to wait for the time being. The body's disappeared, you see.'

'Really? I say!' He seemed delighted, and chattered on when I explained. 'Things are moving, aren't they? I suppose you'll have to leave the solicitors for a day or two. Anything I can do? I've got to run down to Halt Knights to see my young patient, and there are one or two other people I ought to see, but after that I can be at your service entirely.'

'I've got to go down to Poppy's,' I said. 'I'll come with you, if I may.'

Leo had left us and was on the telephone in the gunroom, talking to Pussey, when I disturbed him a minute or so later. He listened to my rather hurried story with unexpected intelligence.

'Wait a minute,' he said, when I had finished. 'You think there may be some connexion between this feller Peters you knew and Harris, and you want me to get the London people to interview these solicitors with a view to their identifying the body. That right?'

'Yes,' I said. 'There may not be anything in it, but they might make general inquiries there about the two men, Peters and Harris. What I particularly want to know is where Harris got his money – if he was insured or anything. It's rather a shot in the dark, I know, but there's just a chance these people may be useful. I think they'll have to be handled delicately. I mean, I don't think it could be done by phone.'

He nodded. 'All right, my boy. Anything that helps us to get any nearer to this terrible thing, don't you know . . . Pussey's going to put a man on to that feller, Heigh-ho.'

He paused abruptly, and stood looking at me.

'Let's hope he doesn't lead us to anyone . . . '

He broke off helplessly.

'I'm coming down to Halt Knights now,' I murmured.

He coughed. 'I'll follow you down. Don't alarm her, my boy; don't alarm her. Can't bring myself to believe that she's anything to do with it, poor little woman.'

Kingston was waiting for me in the drive. He was exuberant. The turn affairs were taking seemed to stimulate him.

'I suppose it's all in the day's work for you?' he said a little enviously, as I climbed in beside him. 'But nothing ever happens down here, and I should be inhuman if I wasn't interested. It's rather shocking how the human mind reacts to someone else's tragedy, isn't it? I didn't know Harris, of course, but what I did see of him didn't attract me. I should say the world's a better place without him. I saw him just before he died, you know, or at least an hour or so before, and I remember thinking at the time that he constituted a waste of space.'

I was busy with my own problems, but I did not wish to be impolite.

'When was this?' I said absently.

He was anxious to tell me.

'On the stairs at Halt Knights. I was going up to see my little patient with jaundice, and he came staggering down. I never saw a fellow with such a hangover. He brushed past me, his eyes glazed and his tongue hanging out. Didn't say good morning or anything – you know the type.'

'That patient of yours,' I said. 'She must have been upstairs all through the incident. . .?'

He turned to me in surprise. 'Flossie?' he said. 'Yes, she was; but you're on the wrong tack there. She's away at the back of the house in a little top attic. Besides, you must have a look at her. The poor little beast is a bit better now, but a couple of days ago she couldn't stand, poor kid. However, she may have heard something. I'll ask her.'

I told him not to bother, and he went on chattering happily, making all sorts of useless suggestions. When I listened to him at all, he had my sympathy. A life that needs a murder to make it interesting must, I thought, be very slow indeed.

When we arrived he went straight up to see his patient, but I sought out Poppy in the lounge. It was early, and we were alone. She seemed delighted to see me and, as usual, insisted on getting me a drink at once. I followed her into the bar while she mixed it, and hurried to put the question that was on my mind before Kingston should return.

'You say you remember yesterday morning very clearly?' I said. 'Did you have a visitor who left here some little time before the accident? Someone who wasn't in the house at the time, but who wandered off within half an hour or so of the trouble?'

She paused in the act of scooping little blocks of ice out of the refrigerator tray.

'No, there was no one,' she said, 'unless you count the parson.'

I took off my spectacles.

'Bathwick?'

'Yes. He always comes in round about twelve o'clock. He likes his highballs American fashion, like this thing I'm mixing for you. He never has more than one. Drops in about twelve o'clock, drinks it, and trots out again. I saw him to the door myself yesterday morning. He goes off through the kitchen garden to the stile leading into the Vicarage meadow. Why?'

I stood looking down at the glass in my hand, twirling the

ice round and round in the amber liquid, and it was then that I had the whole case under my nose.

Unfortunately, I only saw half of it.

CHAPTER II

'Why Drown Him?'

I was still working it out when Poppy laid her hand upon my arm. I turned to find her plump face flushed and anxious.

'Albert,' she murmured confidentially, 'I can't talk now because Kingston's just coming down, but there's something I want to say to you. Ssh! There he is.'

She turned back to the bar and began to bustle among the glasses. Kingston came in, cheerfully superior.

'She's all right now,' he said, grinning at Poppy, 'or will be in a day or two. Don't let her eat too much grease. Like to come up and see her, Campion?'

Poppy raised her eyebrows at him, and he explained. She began to laugh at us.

'The child hasn't the strength, and she hasn't the wits,' she said. 'And if she had she wouldn't do it. She's a good little girl, our Flossie. Flossie, indeed! I've never heard of anything so futile.'

Kingston was very insistent, however, and his anxiety to keep in the picture might easily have been exasperating if there had been anything pressing to be done. As it was, I went upstairs with him through a maze of corridors and unexpected staircases until we found the little attic under the roof at the far end of the house from the box-room.

As soon as I met Flossie I saw they were right. Her little yellow face was pathetic and disinterested. Kingston asked her questions – Had she heard anything? Had she been out of the room? Had anything unusual happened on the day before? – and she answered 'No, sir' to them all with the weary patience of the really ill.

We left her and went along to have another look at the box-room. It was just as I had left it. Kingston was tremendously knowing and important. Evidently he fancied himself in his new rôle.

'There's a scratch there,' he said, pointing to the one I had already noticed. 'Does that tell you anything, Campion? It looks fairly new, doesn't it? How about getting some finger-prints?'

I looked at the rough cast sadly, and led him away.

We got rid of him at last. He offered to drive me down to the Police Station, but I refused, explaining that Leo was coming to pick me up. I caught sight of Poppy as I spoke, and saw her turn colour.

We stood in the window together and watched Kingston's car disappear down the drive. She sighed.

'They're *bored*,' she said. 'They're all bored, poor darlings. He's a nice boy, he doesn't want to be a ghoul; but it'll all give him something to talk about when he goes to see his patients. It must be terrible going to see people every day if you haven't got anything to tell them, don't you think?'

'Yes,' I said dubiously. 'I suppose it is. What have you got to tell *me*, by the way?'

She did not answer me immediately, but the colour came into her face, and she looked like some large guilty baby faced with confession.

'I had a few words with Leo yesterday,' she began at last. 'Not that I mind, of course, although it does do to keep in with one's clients, and – er – friends. I can see that I've annoyed him. I told him a silly lie, and then I didn't like to explain. You can see that happening, can't you?'

She paused and eyed me.

'I can,' I said cheerfully.

'The stupid thing is that it doesn't matter,' she went on, playing with her rings. 'People down here are terrible snobs, Albert.'

I didn't quite follow her, and I said so.

'Oh well it's Hayhoe,' she said explosively. 'An awful little bounder, Albert, but probably quite human, and he's got to live, like anybody else, hasn't he?'

'Wait a minute,' I said. 'I've got to get this straight. Is Hayhoe a friend of yours?'

'Oh no, not a *friend*.' She brushed the term away irritably. 'But he came to me for help last week.'

I was inspired.

'Did he borrow money?'

'Oh no!' She was shocked. 'He was very hard up, poor man. He told me his story, and I may have lent him a pound or two. But you wouldn't say he'd borrowed *money*. You see, Ducky, it was like this – he came to me about two days after that wretched man Harris settled here. I was just beginning to find out the sort of man Harris was when this poor old chap came along, asked

176 MY FRIEND MR CAMPION AND OTHER MYSTERIES

to see me privately, and told me the whole thing. Harris was his nephew, you see, and there'd been a lot of jiggery-pokery going on, and somehow – I forget quite how – this little tick Harris had done the old man out of all his money. He wanted to see him on the quiet to get it back, and he wanted me to help him. I let him into Harris's room – '

'You what?' I said aghast.

'Well, I showed him where it was, and let him go upstairs. That was some days ago. There was an awful row, and poor little Hayhoe came running out with a flea in his ear, since when he's never been near the place – until last night, when Leo happened to see him. I didn't want to explain the whole story – because there's no point in that man getting into a row when he wasn't even near the house yesterday morning – and so I was short with Leo, and he is cross. Put it all straight for me, Albert. Have another drink.'

I refused the one and promised to do my best with the other.

'How do you know Hayhoe wasn't about yesterday morning?' I said.

She looked at me as though I was an imbecile.

'Well, I know what goes on in my own house, I hope,' she said. 'I know it's the fashion round here to think I'm a dear silly old fool, but I'm not completely demented. Besides, everybody's been questioned. That doesn't come into it.'

'Why did Hayhoe come down here yesterday?'

'In the evening? Well' – she was hesitant again – 'it's difficult to explain. He came to tell me that he knew how I felt being surrounded by snobby, county people in a trouble like this, and he offered his help as a man of the world.'

She was thoughtful for a moment or two.

'I really think he came to get a drink, if you ask me,' she added with that touch of the practical which always redeems her.

'Did you lend him any more money?' I murmured diffidently.

'Only half a crown,' she said. 'Don't tell Leo. He thinks I'm such a fool.'

My mind went back to Bathwick, and in the end she took me out and showed me the little path through the kitchen garden which led down to the Vicarage stile. It was a quiet little path, almost entirely hidden by the foliage of the fruit trees. As we came back, I turned to her.

'Look here,' I said, 'I know the police have badgered your staff about the events of yesterday morning, and I don't want to rattle them again, but do you think you could find out by un-obtrusive, gossipy questioning if there was anybody pottering about the upper storeys some little time before the accident? Bathwick could have come back, you see, quite easily.'

'A parson!' said Poppy. 'Well. . .! You don't think. . .? Oh Albert, you can't!'

'Of course not,' I said hastily. 'I only wondered if he could have got upstairs. It'd be interesting, that's all.'

'I'll find out,' she said with decision.

I thanked her and added a warning note about the law of slander.

'Don't tell *me*,' she said, and added, brightening, 'Is that the car?'

We hurried down to meet it, Poppy patting her tight grey curls as she went. But it was Lugg in the Lagonda and not Leo who pulled up outside the front door. He beckoned to me mysteriously, and as I hurried up I saw that his great moon of a face betrayed unusual excitement.

' 'Op in,' he commanded. 'The General wants you down at the station. Got something there for you.'

'Have they found the body?'

He seemed disappointed. 'Got your second-sight outfit workin' again, I see,' he said. 'Morning, ma'am.' He leered at Poppy over my shoulder as he spoke, out of deference, I felt sure, to the memory of myriad past beers.

'I'm awfully sorry,' I explained to her. 'I've got to go. Leo's waiting for me down at the police station. Something's turned up. I'll send him along when the excitement's over.'

She patted my arm. 'Do,' she said earnestly. 'Do. He's a pet, Albert. One of the very best. Tell him I've been silly and I'm sorry, but – but he's not to mention it when he sees me.

I climbed in beside Lugg. 'Where was it?' I demanded as we raced off.

'In the river. Calm as you please. Bloke in a fishin' boat picked it up. If we 'ad your magic sea-shell 'ere p'raps that could tell us somethin'.'

I was not listening to him. I was thinking of Whippet. Whippet and the anonymous letters, Whippet and Effie Rowlandson, and now Whippet and his extraordinary guess – if it was a guess. I couldn't imagine where he fitted into the picture. He upset all my calculations. I decided I must have a chat with him.

Lugg was sulking. 'It seems to be a funny place we've come to,' he said. 'First they bang a chap on 'is 'ead and then they chuck 'im in the river . . . some persons aren't never satisfied, reelly.'

I sat up. That was the point that had been bothering me all along. Why the river, where the corpse was almost certain to be found, sooner or later?

By the time we arrived at the little mortuary the obvious had sunk in. Leo was there and Pussey, and with them the two excited fisherman, who had made the discovery. I took Leo on one side, but he would not listen to me immediately. He was bubbling.

'It's an outrage,' he said. 'It's a disgraceful thing. It shocks me, Campion. In my own village! There was no point in it. Wanton mischief.'

'D'you think so?' I said, and I made a certain suggestion.

He stood looking at me and his blue eyes were incredulous. For a policeman, Leo has an amazing faith in the innate decency of his fellow men.

'We want an old man,' I said. 'Someone with the necessary skill, of course, but someone you can trust to hold his tongue. Anyone locally do?'

He considered. 'There's old Professor Farringdon over at Rushberry,' he said at last. 'He did something of the sort for us some time ago. But you can see for yourself that the cause of death is obvious. Are we justified in having an autopsy?'

'In the case of violent death one's always justified in having an autopsy,' I pointed out.

He nodded. 'When you saw the body yesterday, did you notice anything then to put such an idea in your head?'

'No,' I said truthfully. 'No, I didn't. But this makes all the difference. Water has a peculiar property, hasn't it?'

He put his head on one side.

'How d'you mean?'

'Well, it washes things,' I said, and I went off to find Whippet.

CHAPTER 12

The Disturbing Element

I had almost reached the car when I remembered something which had slipped my mind in the excitement of the moment. I hurried back and sought out Pussey.

'Don't you worry, sir. We've put a man on him,' he said reassuringly in reply to my question.

I still hesitated. 'Hayhoe is slippery,' I ventured, 'and also it's important that he's not alarmed.'

Pussey was not offended, but he seemed to think that I was a little fussy.

'Young Birkin'll follow him and he won't know it no more than if he was being trailed by a ferret,' he said. 'You can set your mind at rest.'

All this was very comforting, and I was going off again when Leo buttonholed me. He was still dubious about the necessity of an autopsy, and in the end I had to go back and take another look at Pig's pathetic body. There were one or two interesting signs when we looked for them, and in the end I left him convinced.

By this time it was comparatively late, and I arrived at 'The Feathers' just before two o'clock. The landlady, a typical East-

Anglian, gaunt of body and reticent of speech, was not helpful. It took me some time to get it into her head that it was Whippet I wanted to see.

'Oh,' she said at last, 'a fair young gentleman, soft-spoken like, almost a natural, as you might say. Well, he's not here.'

'But he slept here last night,' I persisted.

'Yes, yes, so he did, and that's the truth now,' she agreed, 'but he's not here now.'

'Is he coming back?'

'I couldn't say.'

It occurred to me that Whippet must have told her to keep quiet, and this was extremely unlike him. My interest in him grew.

There was no sign of Miss Rowlandson, either. She, too, appeared to have gone out. But whether they went together or separately the landlady was not prepared to tell me.

In the end I had to go back to Highwaters unsatisfied. I was late for lunch, of course, and Pepper served me alone in the dining-room, sorrow and disappointment apparent in every line of his sleek body.

What with one thing and another I was falling headlong in his estimation.

When the meal was over he turned to me.

'Miss Janet is in the rose garden, sir,' he said, conveying clearly that, murder or no murder, he thought a guest owed a certain deference to his hostess.

I took the rebuke meekly and went out to make amends. It was one of those vivid summer days which are hot without being uncomfortable. The garden was ablaze with flowers and the air serene and peaceful.

As I walked down the grass path between the lavender hedges I heard the sound of voices, and something familiar about them caught my attention. Two deck-chairs were placed side by side on the rose lawn with their backs to me, and I heard Janet laugh.

At the sound of my approach her companion rose, and as I saw his head and shoulders appearing over the back of the chair I experienced an odd sensation which was half relief and half an unwarrantable exasperation. It was Whippet himself. Very cool and comfortable he looked, too, in his neat white flannels. His opening words were not endearing.

'Campion! Found you at last,' he said. 'Er – good. I've been searching for you, my dear fellow, searching all over the place. Here and there.'

He moved a languid hand about a foot in either direction.

'I've been busy,' I said gracelessly. 'Hello, Janet.'

She smiled up at me. 'This is a nice friend of yours,' she said with slightly unnecessary accent on the first word. 'Do sit down.'

'That's right, do,' Whippet agreed. 'There's a chair over there,' he added, pointing to a pile on the other end of the lawn.

I fetched it, opened it, and sat down opposite them. Whippet watched me put it up with interest.

'Complicated things,' he observed.

I waited for him to go on, but he seemed quite content to lie basking in the sun, with Janet, looking very lovely in white furbelows at his side.

I began boldly. 'It's been found, you know – in the river.'

He nodded. 'So I heard in the village. The whole place is

terribly shaken by the tragedy, don't you think? Extraordinary restless spirit pervades the place – have you noticed it?'

He was infuriating, and again I experienced that desire to cuff him which I had felt so strongly on our first adult meeting.

'You've got rather a lot to explain yourself,' I said, wishing that Janet would go away.

To my surprise he answered me intelligently.

'I know,' he said. 'I know. That's why I've been looking for you. There's Miss Rowlandson, for one thing. She's terribly upset. She's gone down to the Vicarage now. I didn't know what to advise.'

'The Vicarage?' I echoed. 'What on earth for?' Janet, I noticed, was sitting up with interest.

'Oh, help, you know,' said Whippet vaguely. 'When in doubt in a village one always goes to the parson, doesn't one? Good works and that sort of thing. Oh, yes – and that reminds me, what about this? It came this morning. As soon as I saw it, I thought "Campion ought to have a look at this; this'll interest Campion". Have you had one?'

He took a folded sheet of typing-paper out of his wallet as he spoke, and handed it to me.

'The same postmark as the other,' he said. 'Funny, isn't it? I didn't know anyone knew I was staying at "The Feathers", except you, and – well, I mean you'd hardly have the time, would you, even if you – '

His voice trailed away into silence, and I read the third anonymous letter. This one was very short, typed on the same typewriter and with the same meticulous accuracy:

'Although the skinner is at hand his ease is in the earth.

'He waiteth patiently. Peace and hope are in his warm heart.

'He foldeth his hands upon his belly.

'Faith is his that can remove the mountain or his little hill.'

And that was all.

'Do you make anything of it?' I inquired at last.

'No,' said Whippet. 'No.'

I read it through again.

'Who's the "he"?' I asked.

Whippet blinked at me. 'One can't really say, can one? I took it to be the mole. "His little hill", you know.'

Janet laughed. 'I suppose you both know what you're talking about?' she said.

Whippet rose. 'I fancy I ought to go, now that I've found Campion and cleared all this up. Thank you for allowing me to inflict myself upon you, Miss Pursuivant. You've been most kind.'

I let him say good-bye, and then insisted on escorting him to the gates myself.

'Look here, Whippet,' I said, as soon as we were out of earshot, 'you'll have to explain. What are you doing in this business at all? Why are you here?'

He looked profoundly uncomfortable. 'It's that girl, Effie, Campion,' he said. 'She's got a strong personality, you know. I met her at Pig's funeral, and she sort of collected me. When she wanted me to drive her down here yesterday I came.'

It was an unlikely story from anybody but Whippet, but in his case I was rather inclined to accept it.

'Well, what about the letters?' I persisted.

He shrugged his shoulders. 'One's supposed to tear up anonymous letters, isn't one?' he said. 'Tear 'em up or keep 'em as mementoes, or frame 'em. Anything but take them seriously. And yet, you know, when they go on and on one seems to come to a point where one says to oneself, "Who the hell is writing these things?" It's very disturbing, but I like the mole. I shall be at "The Feathers", Campion. I give you my word I shall remain there. Look me up when you can spare the time, and we'll go into it. Good-bye.'

I let him go. Talking to him, it seemed impossible that he should have the energy to involve himself very deeply in anything so disturbing as our case.

Walking back to the rose garden, I thought about the mole seriously for the first time. A great deal of what Whippet had said about anonymous letters was true. Hayhoe was an educated man, and so was Bathwick, but, even so, why should either of them send both to me and Whippet? It seemed inexplicable.

Janet came to meet me. She was not pleased.

'I don't want to interfere,' she said, using the tone and the phrase to mean its exact opposite, 'but I don't think you ought to allow her to annoy poor Bathwick.'

'Who?' I said, momentarily off my guard.

Janet flared. 'Oh, how you irritate me,' she said. 'You know perfectly well who I mean . . . that wretched, stupid little girl, Effie Rowlandson. It's bad enough to bring her down here to our village, without letting her get her claws into people who couldn't possibly look after themselves. I hate to have to talk to you like this, Albert, but really you know it is rather disgusting of you.'

I was not going to be dragged into a defence of Effie Rowlandson, but I was tired and resented Bathwick being held up to me as an example of an innocent lamb.

'My dear girl,' I said, 'you heard about Bathwick getting wet last night. He told Leo an absurd story about falling into a dyke on his way home. However, it took him nearly two hours to get out and on to the main road again, and I'm afraid he'll have to explain himself now that Harris's body has turned up – er – where it has.'

I was not looking at her as I spoke, and her little cry brought me round to face her. Her cheeks were crimson and her eyes wide and alarmed.

'Oh!' she said. 'Oh! Oh! How terrible!'

And then before I could stop her she had taken to her heels and fled back to the house. I followed her, of course, but she had shut herself in the bedroom, and once more I was given furiously to think.

I went to the library, which is a large, old-fashioned room hardly ever used by the Pursuivants. It was cool and the air was aromatic with the smell of paper. I sat down in a big leather armchair to think things out, and I am afraid that my lack of sleep the night before was too much for me. I woke up to find Janet standing before me. She was pale but determined.

'I thought you'd gone out,' she said breathlessly. 'It's late, you know. Look here, Albert, I've got to tell you something. I can't let Bathwick get into trouble for something he didn't do, and I know he'd rather die than tell you himself. If you laugh, I'll never speak to you again.'

I got up and shook off the remnants of sleep. She looked very charming in her white dress, her eyes defiant.

'I've never felt less like laughing in my life,' I said truthfully. 'What's all this about Bathwick?'

She took a deep breath. 'Mr Bathwick didn't fall in a dyke,' she said. 'He fell in our lily-pool.'

'Really? How do you know?'

'I pushed him,' said Janet in a small voice.

Pressed to continue, she explained:

'Last night, after you took Miss Rowlandson home, I didn't go to bed immediately. I went out on the balcony leading from my room. It was a very bright night, as you know, and I saw someone wandering about in the rose garden. I thought it was Daddy mooching about, worrying over the case, and I went out to talk to him. When I got there it was Bathwick. We walked round the garden together, and when we were quite near the lily-pool he – er – '

She paused.

'Offered you his hand and heart in a slightly too forthright manner?' I suggested.

She nodded gratefully. 'I pushed him away, and unfortunately he overbalanced and fell in the pool. As soon as I saw he was safe on land again I went back to the house. It seemed the nicest thing to do. I don't have to tell anybody else, do I?'

'No,' I murmured. 'No, I don't think so.'

She smiled at me. 'You're all right really, Albert,' she said.

And then, of course, I was called to the telephone. It was Poppy on the end of the wire. She has never grown quite used to the instrument, and I had to hold the receiver some inches away from my ear before I could get her message.

'I've made those inquiries,' she boomed. 'I don't think the V. came back; anyway, no one saw him. But who do you think was seen roaming about the top storey yesterday morning? My dear, I wouldn't have thought it of him. He seemed so *genuine*. Who? Oh, didn't I tell you? Why, the uncle, *Hayhoe*, of course. Trotting round as though the place belonged to him. The girl who saw him naturally thought I'd given him permission. You never can tell with people, can you?'

CHAPTER 13

Scarecrow in June

Janet was at my side when I hung up the receiver. 'What is it?' she said anxiously. 'That was Poppy's voice, wasn't it? Oh, Albert, I'm afraid! Something else terrible has happened.'

'Good lord, no!' I said, with an assurance I did not feel. 'There's nothing to be frightened of. At least, I don't think so.'

She stood looking up at me.

'You know it's all right about Bathwick now, don't you?'

'Of course,' I assured her cheerfully. 'I'd better go, though. There's something rather important to be fixed, something that's got to be done pretty quickly.'

Lugg brought round the car and we went down to the Police Station together. Leo was still there in consultation with Pussey and I was sorry to see him so drawn and haggard. The affair was getting him down. There were deep lines in his face, and his bright eyes were darker than usual in their anxiety. I stated my case.

'Arrest Heigh-ho?' he said. 'Really? I don't think we can arrest him, don't you know. We can bring him in and question him – wanted to in the beginnin' – but we can't hold him. There's not a tittle of solid evidence against the feller.'

I didn't like to annoy him but I was desperately anxious.

'You must hold him, sir,' I said. 'That's the whole point. Pull him in for something else.'

Leo looked aghast. 'Trump up a charge?' he said. 'Monstrous!'

There was not time to explain, and I had no proof anyway.

'At least keep him here for twenty-four hours,' I pleaded.

Leo frowned at me. 'What's got on your mind, my boy?' he enquired. 'Sound apprehensive. Anythin' in the wind?'

'I don't know,' I said, trying not to appear as rattled as I felt. 'Let's go and get him anyway.'

Leaving Leo to ponder over the question of arrest, Pussey and I went down in the Lagonda to Mrs Thatcher's cottage. We picked up young Birkin leaning against a fence on the opposite side of the road. He was a pleasant, shy youth in dilapidated khaki and he made his report in a stage whisper.

'He's been in all the day,' he said. 'That's 'is room where the light is. You can see 'im if you look.'

He pointed to a blurred shadow on the faded chintz curtains and my heart sank. Birkin, I saw, was destined to confine his attentions to dog licences for some time to come. It was a coat and a bolster over the back of a chair, of course.

Pussey stood looking at it when we got into the stuffy little

attic bedroom and his language was restrained and almost dignified.

The unfortunate Birkin rather enjoyed it, I fancy. In his
private opinion it was a wonderful clever trick and something
to tell the lads of the village.

Mrs Thatcher, a poor old woman who had been too busy
all her life to have had time to develop an intelligence, was
obstinately mystified. She had told Johnny Birkin that her lodger
was in his room, and she honestly thought he was. He must have
come downstairs in his stockinged feet, she reckoned. That was
all we had to help us.

My scalp was rising. 'We've got to find him,' I said. 'Don't
you see it's desperately important?'

Pussey came out of his trance with alacrity.

'Well, he can't have gone far,' he said. 'This ain't a busy place.
Someone will have seen him, bound to.'

From Birkin's evidence the curtains had been drawn just after
dusk and he had sat there peacefully watching the light ever
since. It gave Hayhoe about an hour, and my spirits rose a little.

To do Pussey justice, he mobilized his small force with speed
and efficiency. Leo and I had a meal at 'The Swan' while they
got busy. There were not many methods of exit from Kepesake
and, since Mr Hayhoe did not possess a car, it seemed certain
that we should get news of him within an hour or two.

I confess I was jumpy. I felt helpless. My own use in the
search was practically nil. I was a comparative stranger, and as
such did not inspire the confidence of the suspicious East-
Anglian.

We went down to 'The Feathers' to interview Whippet and

found him dining in the company of Effie Rowlandson and Bathwick. Leo was flabbergasted, and I was surprised myself – they were an odd trio.

When judiciously questioned, it became evident that they knew nothing about Hayhoe, but they looked so much like conspirators that I could have borne to stay and chat with them, had I not been so beset by the fear in my mind.

Round about eleven, Leo, Pussey, and I had a conference. We sat round the stuffy little charge-room at the Station and Pussey put the case before us.

'He didn't leave by a bus and he didn't hire a car, and if he went on foot by any of the main roads he moves a deal faster than any ordinary animal.' He paused and eyed us. 'Seems like that's unnatural he ain't been seen at all,' he said. 'It isn't as though any strange car 'as been seen goin' through the village. We ain't on the road to anywhere here. It's been a quiet evening, everyone sittin' out on their doorsteps. Can't understand it, unless 'e's took to the fields.'

I thought of the warm leafy darkness which surrounded us, of the deep meadows and grass-grown ditches, and I was afraid.

Leo was inclined to be relieved. 'Seems to pin it on to him, this boltin',' he said. 'Extraordinary thing! Took a dislike to the feller the moment I set eyes on him. Must have been skulkin' in the house all yesterday mornin'. Amazin'.'

I didn't know whether to relieve his mind or enhance his fears and I kept silent. Pussey seemed to catch his superior officer's mood.

'Ah well, we'll get him sure enough,' he said. 'Now we know as who we're lookin' for we won't let 'im go. The whole village is on the look-out for 'im and none of us 'ere won't rest to-night. You go back to your bed, sir. You can leave 'im to us.'

It seemed the only thing to do, but I was loth to go.

'You've searched that hill-top?' I said.

'Every inch of it, sir. There's 'is telescope up there but nothin' else. Besides, 'e couldn't get there without bein' seen. 'E's got to come right through the village street with every man on the look-out for 'im. No no, you won't find 'im on that hill-top – 'lest 'e's a mowle.'

I started, and I suppose my face betrayed me, for he explained in deference to my city training.

'They mowles, they travel underground,' he said, and I felt suddenly sick.

Before we left he brought up a matter which had gone clean out of my mind.

'That young lady,' he began, 'if she could identify . . .?'

'In the morning,' I said hastily. 'There'll be a lot to do in the morning.'

'Ah ha, you're right, sir,' he agreed. 'There'll be plenty if we catch un.'

'There'll be more if you don't,' I said and I went home with Leo.

I was climbing into bed for the first time for forty-eight hours when Pepper appeared with a telephone, which he plugged in by my bed.

'Doctor Kingston,' he said, and added, half in commiseration, half in reproach, 'at *this* hour, sir. . . . '

Kingston was not only awake but aggressively bright and eager.

'Hope I didn't disturb you,' he said. 'I've been ringing up all the evening. I was down in the village on a case just after dinner and found the whole place seething. I hear you've got your man on the run. There's nothing I can do, I suppose?'

'I'm afraid not,' I said, trying to keep polite.

'Oh, I see.' He seemed genuinely disappointed. 'I must apologize for being so inquisitive, but you know how it is. I feel I've got a sort of natural interest. You will let me know if anything happens or if I can possibly be of any use, won't you?'

'I will,' I said, but he did not ring off.

'You sound tired. Don't overdo it. Oh I say, there's some funny people staying at "The Feathers". Strangers. The village doesn't know if it's just a case of ordinary immorality or if there's more to it. The fellow's name is Greyhound, or something. Like 'em looked into?'

I cursed him for his dull life.

'They're spies of mine,' I said.

'What? I didn't quite catch you . . .'

'Spies,' I said. 'Mine. I've got 'em everywhere. Good night.'

I was awake at six. Lugg called me, protestingly.

'Conscientious, aren't you?' he said derisively.' 'Ayhoe's running away from a pack of narks who want to jug 'im for murder, but he's not going to pass up the little appointment 'e's made with you – Oh dear me no! I don't think.'

'All the same I think I'll go,' I said. 'You never know.'

He stood before me, disconsolate, in an outrageous dressing-gown.

'I'll come with you if you like,' he offered magnanimously. 'There's nothing I like better than a long country walk before the dew's off the grass – cools me feet.'

I sent him back to bed, dressed, and went out. It was one of those fine, clear mornings which promise great heat in the day to come. The sky was opal and the grass was soft and springy underfoot.

I went round by the field path and passed down the village street where I caught a glimpse of the ingenuous Birkin. He gave me the news, or rather, the smiling information that there was none.

'We'll be able to get 'im sure enough now the sun's up,' he said. 'We'll bring 'im back kicking.'

I shivered although the morning was warm.

'I hope so,' I said and went on.

The little sunken lane was deserted and it was a pleasant morning for walking, but I found my feet lagging and I entered the hill meadow with the deepest foreboding.

It was a longer climb to the top than I had thought and when I reached the summit I was momentarily relieved. It was clear and bare and I disturbed nothing but a brace of larks resting in the short grass. The old brass telescope was still mounted on its tripod. There was dew on the lenses and I wiped them with my handkerchief.

From where I stood I had a stupendous view of the surrounding country. I could see Halt Knights lying rose-red and gracious on the grey saltings, the river mouth, dazzling in the morning sun, and around it, the little pocket handkerchief fields and meadows, the corn high and green, the pasture browned a little by the hot weather. It was a lovely county.

Here and there little farms were dotted and among them the white ribbons of the roads twirled and turned.

I stood there for a long time looking at the scene. It was so peaceful, so quiet, and so charming. There was nothing out of place, nothing frightening or remarkable.

And then I saw it. About half a mile away, in the midst of a field waist high in green corn, there was a dilapidated scarecrow, a grotesque, unnatural creature set up to terrify the not-quite-so-clever rooks.

But about this particular effigy there was a difference. Far from being frightened, the rooks were swarming upon it.

I looked through the telescope and straightened myself a moment or so later, sick and giddy, my worst fears realized. Mr Hayhoe had been found.

CHAPTER 14

The Man They Knew

He had a wound in his neck, a strong deep thrust over the collar-bone which had severed the jugular, and when we found him he was not pretty to look at.

Pussey and Leo and I stood round the terrible thing hoisted on a piece of broken paling, and the green corn whispered around us.

After the usual preliminaries, the police brought Hayhoe down on a tumbril to the little mortuary behind the Station, and yet another trestle table was prepared there to receive him.

Leo looked pale and shaken, and Pussey, who had been

turned up physically by the first sight of my discovery, presented a mottled ghost of his former cherubic self.

When we were alone together in the mortuary shed, standing between the two white-covered things which had come to upset so violently the time-honoured peace of Kepesake, Leo turned to me.

'This is what you were afraid of?' he said, accusingly.

I looked at him helplessly. 'It did go through my mind that something like this might happen. He conveyed that he had definite information, you see.'

He passed his hand over his sparse grey hair.

'But who? Who's done it, Campion?' he exploded. 'Don't you see, my boy, a terrible thing is happening. It's the *strangers* who are getting killed off. The field's narrowing down to our own people. Good God! What's to be done now?'

'There's not much to go on,' I pointed out. 'The cornfield was bordered by the road, so the murderer would not have far to carry him even if he had to, although of course there's a chance he was killed on the spot. There was a great deal of blood about.'

Leo avoided my eyes. 'I know,' he murmured. 'I know. But what was the feller doing out in the middle of a cornfield with a murderer?'

'Having a very quiet private interview,' I said. 'I should like an opinion on this wound.'

'You shall have it, my boy, you shall have it. The best in the world. Professor Farringdon will be along this morning to see the – ah – other body. This is frightful, Campion – I'm sorry I couldn't get someone at work on him yesterday, but Farringdon was unobtainable, and I didn't want to drag the Home Office into it if I could help it. This makes all the difference, though. 'Pon my soul, I don't know what I ought to do.'

Any helpful suggestion I might have made was cut short by the return of Pussey, who had Kingston in tow. The doctor was excited and ashamed of himself for showing it. My opinion of him as a medical man went down a little as he made a cursory examination of Hayhoe. He was anxious to help and yet loth to commit himself by giving a definite opinion.

'I don't know what it was done with,' he said at last. 'Something narrow and sharp. A dagger, perhaps. One of those old-fashioned things – a trophy.'

I glanced at Leo, and from the expression on his face I knew he was thinking of the fearsome array of native weapons on the walls of the billiard-room at Halt Knights. All the same, I didn't see Poppy in the middle of the night in a cornfield with a dagger; that idea seemed to me farfetched and absurd.

Pussey seemed to find Kingston's guesses unsatisfactory, and he got rid of him in the end, but with considerable tact.

'It seems like we'd better leave that to the Professor,' he murmured to me. 'Wonderful clever old man, the Professor. I reckon he'll be over in half an hour or so. I don't know what he'll think on us – two on 'em instead of one,' he added naïvely.

Leo turned away, his hands thrust deep into his pockets and his chin on his breast. We followed him into the station and Pussey made all the necessary arrangements for taking statements, making a search of the place where the body was found, and the important inquiries into Mr Hayhoe's past history.

The routine work seemed to soothe Leo.

'I suppose we ought not to have moved him from the spot,'

he said, 'until Farringdon arrived. But there seemed no point in leavin' the feller out in the sun hitched up on a spike like that. It was indecent. There's a brutal obviousness about these crimes, Campion. 'Pon my soul, I can't conceive the mind that arranged 'em – anyway, not among my own friends.'

'Ah-h, there's still strangers about,' said Pussey, with the intention of comforting him. 'Likely there'll be *someone* who's had blood on's clothes. We'll find un. Don't you worry, sir.'

Leo swung away from him and walked over to the window. 'Eh!' he said suddenly, 'who's this?'

Looking over his shoulder, I saw a sleek chauffeur-driven Daimler pull up outside the cottage gate. A tall thin grey-faced man descended and came hesitantly up to our door. A moment or so later we made the acquaintance of Mr Robert Wellington Skinn, junior partner of the ancient and respectable firm of solicitors whose name Kingston had given me.

He was a stiff, dignified personage, and he and Leo took to each other immediately, which was fortunate, or the subsequent interview would certainly have taken much longer and been doubly confusing. As it was, Mr Skinn came to the point in what was for him, I felt sure, record time.

'In view of everything, I thought I'd better come down myself,' he murmured. 'An affair of this sort in connexion with one of our clients is, I can assure you, most unusual. I received your inquiries yesterday; I read the papers last night; I connected the two names immediately – Peters and Harris. In the circumstances I thought I had better come down myself.'

Pussey and I exchanged glances. We were getting somewhere.

'The two men knew each other, then?' I asked.

He looked at me dubiously as though he wondered if I could be trusted.

'They were brothers,' he said. 'Mr Harris changed his name for – ah – no doubt very good reasons of his own, and he is comparatively new to our books. Our principal client was his elder brother, Mr Rowland Isidore Peters, who died in this district last January.'

After a certain amount of delay he went with Leo to view the body, and came back a little green. He was also flustered.

'I wouldn't like to commit myself,' he murmured. 'I saw Mr Peters once twelve years ago, and I saw Mr Harris in London this spring. Those were the only two occasions on which I met either. The – ah – dead man I have just seen resembles both. Do you think I could have a glass of water?'

Pussey pressed him to be more exact, and would have taken him back again, but he refused to go.

'Really, I see no point in it,' he said. 'I think you can take it that, in my opinion, the dead man is Mr Harris. After all, there's no reason to suppose that it shouldn't be. He called himself Harris down here, did he not?'

We let him cool down, and when he was more at ease I asked him cautiously about the dead man's estate.

'I really couldn't say, without reference to my books,' he protested. 'I know Mr Harris received a considerable sum of money under his brother's will. I can let you know the figures to-night. There was personal property, and of course, the insurance, as far as I remember. It all seemed perfectly in order to me at the time.'

Pussey was relieved. 'Anyway, we've cleared up his identity, that's one thing,' he said. 'No doubt on it; can get on with the P.M.'

Leo and I escorted the solicitor back to his car. The unfortunate man was shaken by his experience, as well he might be, but he was an obliging soul and before he left, he promised to let us know full details of the two estates.

'There's just one thing,' I said, as he got into the car. 'Who was Mr Peters insured with? Do you know?'

He shook his head. 'I'm afraid I couldn't tell you offhand. I think it was the Mutual Ordered Life. I'll look it up.'

As soon as he had gone I made a suggestion to Leo, and, having got his consent, sent Lugg and a constable down in the car to fetch Miss Effie Rowlandson. They were gone some little time, and when at last they reappeared they brought not only the girl herself but Bathwick also, which was surprising. There was a considerable delay at the gate, and I went out. The vicar had got over his unexpected friendliness towards me of the night before, and I was aware that all his old antagonism had returned.

'I'm only doing what I'm told, sir,' I heard the constable protesting as I came up. 'Besides, the young lady suggested it 'erself only the night before last.'

Bathwick ignored him and turned to me.

'This is an outrage,' he said. 'A young girl subjected to a disgusting sight just to satisfy a few inefficient policemen . . . I must protest against it; I really must!'

Effie smiled at him wanly. 'It's very nice of you, I'm sure,' she said, 'but I've made up my mind to it; I have, really. You wait here for me,' she added.

However he was not to be soothed. He protested so much and so vigorously that my interest in him revived, and I wondered what conceivable purpose he could have in making such a fuss.

In the end we left him in the car, and I took the girl into the little mortuary once more. I was never exactly attracted by Effie Rowlandson, but on that occasion I admired her pluck. She was not callous, and the shock must have been considerable, but she kept her head and played her part with dignity.

'Yes,' she said huskily, as I drew the sheet over the limp form once more. 'Yes, it is Roly. I wasn't in love with him, but I'm sorry he's dead. I –'

Her voice broke, and she began to cry. She controlled herself within a moment or so, however, and when I took her back to the bewildered Pussey she made her statement.

'I met him a little over a year ago,' she said. 'He had a flat in Knightsbridge, and he used to take me out a lot. We got engaged, or nearly engaged, and then – oh, Mr Campion, you know the rest. I've told you.'

Between us we got the story down on paper, and I took her back to the car. Bathwick had climbed out and was waiting for her at the gate. I suppose he saw that she had identified Harris from our faces, for he did not speak to me but, taking her arm, hurried her down the road towards 'The Feathers'.

Lugg looked after him. 'Funny bloke,' he said. 'Now, where 'ave you got to?'

'An impasse,' I said truthfully, and went back to Pussey.

We worked it out while we waited for Professor Farringdon. Pussey put his deductions in a reasonable if not too tidy nutshell.

'There's impersonation been going on,' he said judicially.

'Sounds like the old story – the good brother and the bad brother. We'll call 'em Peters and Harris for the sake of simplicity. Peters had the money, and on occasions Harris used to impersonate him; well, that's been done before. Harris carried on with this little bird under the name of Peters so that if she should look him up or make inquiries she'd find out he was a man of substance. As for the solicitor, he was in a proper muddle, poor gentleman. The two brothers doubtless looked powerful alike to begin with, and of course that poor bloke in there doesn't look like anything now. What would you say, sir?'

I hesitated. It is never safe to identify a man after twenty-five years, and Kingston had told me that his patient resembled Harris considerably. On the whole, I was inclined to back the Inspector's theory, with one exception. When he talked of the 'good brother' and the 'bad brother' as Peters and Harris, I thought he should have reversed the names.

I told him so, and he eyed me. 'Very likely,' he said, 'but that doesn't get us any nearer, does it? Who's done they murders? That's what I'd like to know.'

We stood for a moment in silence looking at one another, and the Professor's arrival took us by surprise. He came bustling in, a vigorous little Scotsman with short tufty grey hair and the shrewdest grey-blue eyes I have ever seen.

'Good morning, Inspector,' he said. 'You've got a remarkable amount of bodies, I hear.'

His cheerfulness was disconcerting, and we escorted him to the shed in the yard in silence. As he pored over the man who had called himself Harris, however, his good humour changed, and he turned to me with a very grave face.

'I heard from Sir Leo what you were suggesting, and I take ma hat off to you,' he said. 'It's a diabolical thing – a diabolical thing.'

'Then you think – ?' I began.

He waved me silent.

'I wouldn't dare to give an opeenion without a very careful autopsy,' he said, 'but I wouldn't be at all surprised if you were right; I wouldn't at all.'

I walked over to the other side of the room while he was very busy. At last he straightened his back.

'Have it sent round to me,' he said, 'and I'll let you know for certain in a day or two. But I think I dare express an opinion – a very tentative one, you understand – that he met his death some little time before he had yon crack over the head.'

I put a question and he nodded to me.

'Oh aye,' he said, 'it was poison. Chloral hydrate, I wouldn't wonder. That' – he indicated the terrible indentation of the skull – 'that was in the nature of a blind. You've got a clever man up against you, Mr Campion. Now let's have a look at the other puir feller.'

CHAPTER 15

Lugg Gives Notice

For two days things hung fire; that is to say, for two days we were left in peace – Leo to struggle up from beneath the blow, and Pussey and I to collect what useful scraps of information we could.

The village was bright-eyed and uncommunicative. People went to bed early behind locked doors, and sightseers who came to gape at the corner of the field where the wretched Hayhoe had been found were sent hastily on their way by outraged country folk.

Janet developed a strained expression, Poppy took to her bed, and even Whippet was more solicitous than I had supposed possible. He drifted up to see me at odd hours of the day, and sat looking at me in inquiring silence until I packed him off to talk to Janet, who was kind enough to put up with him.

Kingston, of course, was very much in the foreground, and I even found him useful. He was an inveterate gossip, and the laws of libel and slander had no terrors for him.

The first piece of concrete information came from Mr Skinn, the solicitor. The Peters who had died in the Tethering nursing home, it transpired, had not been a poor man, and had also had the perspicacity to insure himself for twenty thousand pounds with the Mutual Ordered Life Endowment. His intention, so Mr Skinn said, had been to borrow upon this policy in order to further some business scheme which he had on hand. As it happened, it had turned out very well indeed for brother Harris.

Concerning Harris we found out very little. He had rented a flat in Knightsbridge under the name of Peters, but he had never been a wealthy man. Our difficulties were enhanced by the confusion in the actual identities of the two men: which was Harris and which was Peters?

In the end I went to Leo. He was sitting in his gun-room, staring mournfully at his magnificent collection of sporting trophies, a mass of papers lying disregarded on his desk.

'We've got ten days, my dear feller,' he said at last. 'The two inquests have been adjourned to give us a breathing space, don't y'know, but that means we've got to get results. There's a lot of talk already. I don't mind telling you, my boy, the feeling round about is that I ought to have called in Scotland Yard at the first. It seemed simple at the beginning, but now, 'pon my soul, I don't know where things are leading. Every morning I wake up wondering what the day's going to bring forth. We've got a killer at large in the village. God knows where he's going to strike next.'

He paused, and when I did not speak he looked at me sharply.

'I've known you since you were a child,' he said, 'and I know there's somethin' on your mind. If you know anythin' and you're waitin' for proof, don't hesitate to tell me your suspicions. I think I could bear anythin' rather than this uncertainty. Can you make any sense out of this puzzle?'

After working with Leo I knew that he was the most eminently trustworthy man in the world, but I hesitated to commit myself just then. It was too dangerous.

'Look here, Leo,' I said, 'I know how the first murder was done, and I think I know who did it, but at this stage proof is absolutely impossible, and without proof we can do nothing. Give me a day or two longer.'

He was inclined to be annoyed at first, and I thought he was going to exercise his authority and force my confidence, but he quietened down at last, and I made my next request.

'Can you get a Home Office order for the exhumation of R. I. Peters, who was buried in the Tethering churchyard last January?'

He looked very grave. 'I could try,' he said at last. 'But, my dear fellow, identification after all this time . . .' He grimaced and threw out his hands.

'I don't know,' I persisted. 'There are certain circumstances which make rather a lot of difference in that sort of thing.'

He frowned at me. 'Antimony in the body?' he suggested.

'Not necessarily,' I said. 'It's a question of the soil, mostly.' In the end I got my own way, and afterwards I went out to find Kingston.

He was at home, I discovered by telephone, and Lugg and I went up. He received us in his uncomfortable consulting-room with frank delight.

'Lord! you must be having an off day if you come up and see me,' he said reproachfully. 'Can I get you a drink?'

'No,' I said. 'Not now. This is hardly a social call, I want a bit of help.'

His round pink face flushed with pleasure.

'Really?' he said. 'That's very flattering. I had rather begun to feel that I was in the way down there, don't you know. As a matter of fact, I've been conducting a little private inquiry on my own. That's a most mysterious fellow staying down at "The Feathers". Do you know anything about him?'

'Not much,' I said truthfully. 'I knew him a long while ago – we were at school together, as a matter of fact – but I haven't seen him much since.'

'Ah . . . !' He wagged his head mysteriously. 'Mrs Thatcher says he used to come to see Hayhoe in the early part of the week. Did you know that?'

I hadn't, of course, and I thanked him.

'I'll look into it,' I said. 'Meanwhile, you wouldn't like to take me round your churchyard?'

He was only too anxious, and we left the great barrack of a house, which seemed servantless and neglected. He seemed conscious of its deficiencies, and explained in a shame-faced fashion.

'I manage with a man from the village when I haven't any patients,' he said. 'He's a good fellow, a sort of general odd job man, the son of the local builder, for whom he works when he's not being sexton or my charwoman. When I do get a patient, of course, I have to import a nurse and housekeeper.'

We had wandered on ahead of Lugg, and he turned and grimaced at me.

'It's not much of a practice,' he said, 'otherwise, I suppose, I shouldn't find time for things to be so terribly dull.'

As we passed the Lagonda, which was practically new, he looked at it a little wistfully, and I was sorry for him. There was something half childish in his unspoken envy. He had a genius for wasting time, and we spent some moments looking at it. He admired the engine, the gadgets, and the polish on the bodywork, and quite won Lugg's heart.

In fact we all got on very well together and, being in the mood for a confidant at the time, I took the risk and transferred the honour which I had been reserving for Whippet to himself. We talked about the soil of the churchyard. He was interesting and helpful.

'Yes,' he said, 'it's dry and it's hard, or there's some sort of preservative in it, I think, because I know old Witton, the grave-digger, dragged me out one morning to see a most extraordinary thing. He had opened a three-year-old grave to put in a relation of the dead woman, and somehow or other the coffin lid had become dislodged, and yet there was the body practically in a perfect state of preservation. How did you guess?'

'It's the cow-parsley,' I said. 'You often find it growing in soil like that.'

We went on talking about the soil for some time, and he suddenly saw the drift of my questioning.

'An exhumation?' he said. 'Really? I say! That'll be rather –'

He stopped, suppressing the word 'jolly', I felt sure.

'– exciting,' he added, after a pause. 'I've never been present at an exhumation. Nothing so startling ever happens down here.'

'I can't promise,' I protested. 'Nothing's fixed, and for heaven's sake shut up about it. The one thing that's really dangerous at this stage is gossip.'

'It's a question of identification, I suppose?' he said eagerly. 'I say, Campion, you've got a very good chance. What a miracle he chose this particular place to die in! In ninety-nine cemeteries out of a hundred, you know . . .'

'Yes, but be quiet,' I said. 'Don't talk about it, for heaven's sake.'

'I won't,' he promised. 'My dear old man, you can rely on me. Besides, I don't see a soul to talk to.'

We got away from him eventually, having discovered what we wanted to know, and he stood watching us until we disappeared down the hill. Lugg sighed.

'Lonely life,' he observed. 'When you see a bloke like that it makes you feel you'd like to take him on a pub-crawl, don't it?'

'Does it?' I said.

He frowned. 'You're getting so lah-di-dah and don't-speak-to-me-I'm-clever, you make me tired,' he complained. 'If I was in your position I wouldn't waste me time muckin' round with corpses. I'd ask a fellow like that up to Town for a week and show 'im the sights.'

'My God,' I said, 'I believe you would.'

He chose to be offended, and we drove home in silence.

The following day, which was the third since Hayhoe had been found, I woke up with a sensation that was half exhilaration and half apprehension. I had a premonition that things were going to move, although had I known in what direction I don't think I should have dared to go on.

It began with Professor Farringdon's report. He came over while I was at the station with Pussey, and made it verbally.

'Aye, it was chloral hydrate,' he said, 'as I told you. It was verra deeficult to decide just how much the man had taken before his death. So there is no way of knowing, you see, whether when yon stone crashed down on his head he was already dead, or if he was merely under the influence of the drug.'

Pussey and I both knew the peculiar properties of chloral hydrate; it is a very favourite dope among con-men, but we let him tell us all over again.

'It'd make him very sleepy, you understand. That's why it's so diabolically useful. If ye came upon a man suffering from a slight attack of this poison, ye'd simply think he was in a deep natural sleep.'

Pussey looked at me. 'All the time he was sitting in that chair, I reckon he was just waiting for the thing to fall upon him, helpless, unable to move. Ah! that's a terrible thing, Mr Campion.'

The Professor went on to dilate upon the fate of Mr Hayhoe.

'Yon was an interesting wound,' he said. 'Remarkably lucky, or delivered by someone who was no fool. It caught him just over the collar-bone, and went straight down into his neck. He must have died at once.'

He went on to describe the knife that had been used, and even drew it for us, or at least he drew the blade. Pussey didn't know what to make of it at all, but it fitted in to my theory all right.

I left them together and went on to find Whippet. Neither he nor Effie Rowlandson were at 'The Feathers' when I arrived, but presently he came up alone in his little A.G.

'I've been house-hunting,' he said. 'There's a little villa down the road that interests me. It's empty. I like empty houses. Do you? Whenever I'm in a district I go and look at empty houses.'

I let him ramble on for some time, and when I thought he must have tired of the subject I put my question to him suddenly. If I hoped to surprise him I was disappointed.

'Hayhoe?' he said. 'Oh yes. Oh yes, Campion, I had several conversations with him. Not a nice fellow; he tried to touch me.'

'Very likely,' I said. 'But what did you talk to him about?'

Whippet raised his head, and I looked into his vague pale blue eyes.

'Natural history I think, mostly,' he said. 'Flora and fauna, you know.'

At that moment another great wedge of the jigsaw slipped into place.

'Some are born blind,' I said bitterly. 'Some achieve blindness.

And some have blindness thrust upon them. Moles come into the first category, don't they?'

He said nothing, but remained quite still, looking out of the window.

I went back to Highwaters, and there the thing I had not foreseen, the thing for which I shall never forgive myself, awaited me.

Lugg had gone.

His suitcase, containing his few travelling things, had vanished, and on my dressing-table, weighted down by an ash-tray, was a crisp new pound note.

CHAPTER 16

The Red Hair

At first I did not believe it. It was the one contingency which had never entered my mind, and for a moment I was completely thrown off my balance. I heard myself blethering around like a hysterical woman. Pepper did his best to help me.

'A telephone call came through to you, sir,' he said. 'I didn't take much notice of it, but I understood it was a London call. Mr Lugg took it, and some time afterwards he came down the back stairs with a suitcase in his hand. He went down to the village by the field path.'

And that was all there was to it. That was all anybody could tell me. The exchange was not helpful. There had been a great many incoming calls. The girl at the Post Office had been run off her feet all day. No, she hadn't listened. Of course not! She never did.

I was beside myself. The question of time was so terribly important, and every now and again a variation of the ghastly vision which I had seen through the brass telescope rose up before my eyes.

The search began immediately.

Leo was sympathetic, and Janet did her best to be soothing. I had to explain to them all that the pound note meant nothing at all. Doubtless there are men-servants who go off at a moment's notice, leaving a week's wages in lieu of warning, but Lugg is not of them. Besides, he had not been seen in the village, nor at the bus stop. He had disappeared as mysteriously as Hayhoe had done; had wandered off into the fields and had vanished in precisely the same way.

I rang up Kingston. He listened to my excited story with disarming interest.

'I say, Campion!' His voice sounded young over the wire. 'I've got an idea. I don't know if you remember it, but I said something to you yesterday. You didn't think much of it at the time – I saw that in your face – but I believe it's going to come in useful now. I'll be over right away.'

He was. In less than twenty minutes, he came panting up the drive in second gear, his face pink and his eyes burning with delighted enthusiasm. If it had been anybody but Lugg I could have forgiven him.

We held a consultation on the front lawn.

'It's that chap Whippet,' he said. 'I've been keeping an eye on him. I know how you feel – old school friends and that sort of thing – but you don't really know him at all, and things have been happening, haven't they? Someone must be behind them.'

'Yes, well,' I said, impatiently, 'go on.'

He was a little overwhelmed to find me so receptive, I think, but he hurried on eagerly enough.

'There's a house,' he said, 'an empty villa which stands all by itself at the end of a partly made-up road. It was the beginning of a building scheme which got stopped when the parish council found out what was happening. Whippet's been down there once or twice. I don't say anything definite, but didn't it occur to you that that fellow Hayhoe must have been killed somewhere other than out in the open field? It's a lonely little place. Just the place for a spot of bother. Let's go down.'

There was a great deal in what he said, and I did not want to waste time arguing. I moved over towards his car. He looked a little shamefaced.

'I'm afraid we'd better take yours,' he said. 'Mine's not very young, you know, and she developed a spot of her usual trouble coming along just now. The oil gets in somewhere and rots up the ignition. That is, unless you can wait while I clean a plug or two?'

I was not in the mood to wait, and I got out the Lagonda. He settled beside me with a little sigh of sheer pleasure at its comfort.

'Straight down the hill,' he said, 'and first on the left.'

We turned out of the village and took the long lonely road which winds up through Tethering and on to Rushberry. Presently we turned again. There was a little beer-house, 'The Dog and

Fowl', sitting coyly under a bank of elms about half a mile farther on, and as we neared it he touched my arm.

'You're rotting yourself up,' he said. 'You haven't been sleeping, and now this shock on top of it is getting you down. You'd better stop and have one.'

I cursed at the delay, but he insisted and we went in.

It was an unattractive little place, old and incredibly dirty. The bar was a mass of cheap advertising trophies, and the only other customer at the time we entered was a toothless old person with a Newgate fringe.

Kingston insisted on beer. There was nothing like old beer for steadying one, he said, and while the half-wit landlady shambled off to fill our tankards, Kingston interrogated the old man concerning Lugg. He did it very well, all things considered, using the idiom of the county.

The old gentleman could not help us, however. He was short of sight and hard of hearing, so he said, and never took much count of strangers, anyway.

It was after the two greasy tankards had been pushed towards us that Kingston showed me the cottage we were going to investigate. It was just visible from the tiny window of the bar. I could see its hideously new red roof peering out amid a mass of foliage about half a mile away.

'Yes, well, let's get on,' I said, for I had no great hopes of finding my unfortunate old friend there and time was getting short.

Kingston rose to the occasion.

'All right,' he said. 'We won't wait for another.'

He drained his tankard and so did I. As I turned away from

the bar I stumbled and inadvertently caught the old man's pewter mug with my elbow. Its contents were splattered all over the floor and there was another few minutes' delay while we apologized and bought him another drink.

When I got out to the car I stood for a moment looking down at the steering wheel.

'Look here, Kingston,' I said, 'd'you think it's really necessary to go to this place?'

'I do, old boy, I do.' He was insistent. 'It's odd, you know, a stranger hanging about an empty house.'

I got in and began to drive. A quarter of a mile up the road the car swerved violently and I pulled up.

'I say,' I said a little thickly, 'would you drive this thing?'

He looked at me and I saw surprised interest on his round, unexpectedly youthful face.

'What's the matter, old man?' he said. 'Feeling tired?'

'Yes,' I said. 'That stuff must have been frightfully strong Drive on as quick as you can.'

He climbed out, and I moved heavily over into the place he had vacated. A minute later we were roaring down the road again. I was slumped forward, my head on my chest, my eyes half closed.

'Can't understand it,' I said, my words blurred. 'Got to get ol' Lugg. I'm tired – terribly tired.'

I was aware of him pulling up, and through my half-closed eyes I saw a dilapidated little villa, its white stucco streaked with many rains. At the side of the house there was a garage with a badly made little drive of a yard or so leading up to it.

I was aware of Kingston unlocking the doors of this garage

and then I was down at the bottom of the car, my eyes closed and my breath coming at long regular intervals.

Kingston stepped behind the steering wheel again and we crawled into the narrow garage. I heard him stop and then I heard him laugh. It was like no sound I had ever heard from him before.

'Well, there you are, my clever Mr Campion,' he said. 'Sleep sound.'

I think he must have pulled on some gloves, for I was aware of him wiping the steering wheel, and then he dragged me up and pressed my hands upon its smooth surface. He was talking all the time.

'Carbon monoxide is an easy death,' he said. 'That's why suicides choose it so often. It's so simple, isn't it? I just leave you in the car with the engine running, and close the garage doors as I go out and the neurotic Mr Campion has done the inexplicable once again. Suicide of distinguished London criminologist.'

He was some time completing his arrangements and then, when everything was set, he bent forward.

'I was too clever for you,' he said, and there was a rather shocking note in his voice. 'Too damned clever.'

'By half,' I added suddenly and leapt at him.

I hadn't spilt our poor old bearded friend's beer at the 'Dog and Fowl' for nothing. Showing a man something interesting out of a window while you put a spot of chloral hydrate in his tankard is poor chaff to catch old birds.

I caught him by the back of the neck and for a moment we grappled. What I hadn't realized, however, was the fellow's strength. Outwardly he appeared a rather flaccid type, but when we came to grips there was muscle there and weight to back it up. Besides, he was demented he fought like a fiend. I had no longer any doubts about the identity of the hand which had sent that skilful thrust into Hayhoe's neck.

I struggled out of the car, but he was between me and the garage door. I saw his great shoulders hunched against the light. He leapt on me and we fell to the ground. I caught a glimpse of his eyes, and if ever I saw the 'blood light' in a man's face it was then. I nearly escaped him once, and had almost reached the doors when something like a vice seized me by the throat. I was lifted bodily and my head crashed down upon the concrete floor.

It was like going down very suddenly in a lift. It went on and on and at the end there was darkness.

I came up again painfully, in little jerks. I was aware that my arms were moving up and down with a slow rhythmic motion I could not control, and then I was gasping, fighting for breath.

'Look out – look out. You're doing nicely. Don't get excited. Steady yourself.'

The voice came to me like a dream, and I saw through the fog a ridiculous small boy with ink smeared all over his face looking down at my bed in the sicker. Then the boy disappeared, but I still saw the same face, although the ink had been removed. It was Whippet. He was kneeling behind me giving me artificial respiration.

The whole business came back with a rush.

'Lugg!' I said. 'My God, we've got to get Lugg!'

'I know.' Whippet's voice sounded almost intelligent. 'Fellow's positively dangerous, isn't he? I let Kingston get away before I got you out. I mean, I didn't want to have two of you on my hands.'

I sat up. My head was throbbing and there was only one clear thought in my mind.

'Come on,' I said. 'We've got to get him before it's too late.'

He nodded, and I was suddenly grateful for the understanding in his face.

'A fellow came by on a bicycle a moment or so ago,' he said. 'I put it to him and sent him off down, to the village. He's going to send the whole crowd up to the nursing home. I thought that was the best way. I've got my car in the meadow round the back. Let's go to Tethering straight away, shall we?'

I don't remember the journey to Tethering. My head felt as though it was going to burst, my mouth was like an old rat-trap, and I couldn't get rid of a terrible nightmare in which Lugg was hoist on a scarecrow stake which was as high as the Nelson Column.

What I do remember is our arrival. We pulled up outside the front door of Kingston's barrack of a house, and when it wouldn't give we put our shoulders to it. I remember the tremendous sense of elation when it shattered open before our combined strength.

It was a movement on the first floor that sent us racing up the stairs, and, since five doors on the landing were open, we concentrated on the one that was not. It was unlocked, but someone held it on the other side. We could hear him snarling and panting as we fought with it.

And then, quite suddenly, it swung back. I was so beside myself that I should have charged in and taken what was coming to me, but it was Whippet who kept his head. He pulled me back and we waited.

Through the open door I could see a bed, and on it there was a large, familiar form. The face was uncovered, and as far as I could see the colour was natural. But as I stared at it I saw the thing that sent the blood racing into my face and turned my body cold with the realization of the thing I had not dreamed.

The faded grey-black fluff which surrounds Lugg's bald patch was as red as henna would make it. I saw the truth, the body of one fat man is much like the body of another once the features are obliterated, and what time can do can be done by other agencies. Kingston was going to have a body for his 'jolly' exhumation after all.

I dropped on my hands and knees. Ducking under the blow he aimed at me from his place of vantage behind the door, I caught him by the ankles. I was on his chest with my hands round his throat when I heard the second car pull up and Leo's voice on the stairs.

CHAPTER 17

Late Final

It took three policemen to get Kingston into the car, and when he came up before the magistrates there was an unprecedented scene in the court. At the Assizes his counsel pleaded insanity, a defence which failed, and I think justifiably; but that was later.

My own concern at the time was Lugg. Whippet and I worked upon him until Pussey got us a doctor from a neighbouring village, who saved him after an uncomfortably stiff fight. It was chloral hydrate again, of course. Kingston was not mad enough not to know what he was doing. He did not want any wound showing in his exhibition corpse. What his 'finishing' process was to be, I can only guess, and I do not like to think of it even now.

Lugg told us his story as soon as we got him round. It was elementary. Kingston had simply phoned up Highwaters, made sure from Pepper that I was down in the village, and had then asked for Lugg. To him he gave a message purporting to come from me. According to this, I had work for him to do in town, but I wanted to see him first up at Tethering churchyard, where, Kingston hinted, I had discovered something. Lugg was to pack his bag and nip down the field path to the road to meet Kingston in the car. The pound note was to be left for Pepper in case I could not return. That was all. Lugg fell for the story, Kingston did meet him and the reason they had not been seen was that the doctor's car was far too well known for anybody to notice it.

On arrival at Tethering, Lugg was left in the dining-room, where he was given beer and told to wait. He drank the beer and the chloral which was in it and mercifully remembered no more.

Kingston must have got him upstairs alone and have just completed the hairdressing process when I phoned.

It was a pretty little trap, and Lugg's comments on it when he considered it are not reportable.

'You done it,' he said reproachfully. 'How was I to know

you was leadin' the bloke up the garden with your 'come-and-
'old-me-'and every five minutes? You stuffed him full of the
exhumation, thinking 'e'd go for you, I suppose? Never thought
o' me. Isn't that you all over?'

I apologized. 'Let's be thankful you're alive to tell the tale,' I
ventured.

He scowled at me. 'I am. Got to shave me 'ead now. What
are my London friends goin' to think about that? 'Oliday in the
country – Oh, yes, very likely!'

When we reached this point I thought it best to let him sleep,
for there was still much to be done.

During the next twenty-four hours we worked incessantly,
and at the end of it the case against Kingston was complete.

It was on the evening of the day on which the exhumation
had taken place, that Leo and I went down with Janet to Halt
Knights. Leo was still simmering from the effects of that grimly
farcical ceremony which had welded the final link in our chain
of evidence.

'Bricks!' he said explosively. 'Yellow bricks wrapped up in a
blanket and nailed down in a coffin . . . 'Pon my soul, Campion,
the fellow was an impious blackguard as well as a murderer.
Even now, I don't see how he did it alone.'

'He wasn't alone,' I pointed out mildly. 'He had Peters to help
him, to say nothing of that fellow who worked for him – the
builder's son. In country places the builder is usually the undertaker, too, isn't he?'

'Royle!' Leo was excited. 'Young Royle . . . that explains the
key of the mortuary. Was the boy in it, do you think?'

'Hardly,' I murmured. 'I imagine Kingston simply managed

him. He says his master offered to measure up the body while he did a repair job in the house. The nurse must have been an accomplice, of course, but we shall never get her. She and Kingston got the death certificate between them.'

'You're terribly confusing,' Janet cut in from the back of the car. 'How many brothers were there?'

'None,' I said, 'as the clever young man from London suspected after he'd had it thrust well under his nose, poor chap. There was only the one inimitable Pig.'

Janet will forgive me, I feel sure, if I say here that she is not a clever girl. On this occasion she was obtuse.

'Why go to all the trouble of pretending he died in January?'

'Because,' I said sadly, 'of the insurance, my poppet. Twenty thousand pounds . . . He and Kingston were going to do a deal. Tie up with your medical man and let the Mutual Ordered Life settle your money troubles. Kingston met Pig in town and they hatched the whole swindle up between them. Pig invented a wicked brother and laid the foundations by hoodwinking his own solicitors, who were a stuffy old firm at once reputable enough to impress the insurance company and sufficiently moribund to let Pig get away with his hole-and-corner death.'

'Neat,' said Janet judicially, and added with that practicalness so essentially feminine, 'Why didn't it work?'

'Because of the fundamental dishonesty of the man Pig. He wouldn't pay up. Once he had collected, he knew he had Kingston by the short hairs and, besides, by then the idea of developing this place had bitten him. I fancy he kept his doctor pal on a string, promising him and promising and then laughing at him. What he did not consider was the sort of fellow he had to deal with. Kingston is a conceited chap. He has a sort of blind courage coupled with no sense of proportion. Only a man with that type of mentality, could have pulled off his share in the original swindle. The fact that he had been cheated by Pig wounded his pride unbearably, and then, of course, he found the man untrustworthy.'

'Untrustworthy?' Leo grunted.

'Well, he began to get drunk, didn't he?' I said. 'Think of Kingston's position. He saw himself cheated out of the share of the profits and at the same time at the complete mercy of a man who was in danger of getting too big for his boots, drinking too much and blowing the gaff. Admittedly, Pig could not give Kingston away without exposing his own guilt, but a man who gets very drunk may be careless. Then there was Hayhoe. The wicked uncle finds the wicked nephew in clover and wishes to browse also. He even instals a telescope on a neighbouring hill-side in the hope of keeping an eye on developments at Highwaters. There is another danger for Kingston. I think the whole ingenious business came to him in a flash, and he acted on impulse moved by fury, gingered up by fear.'

Leo made an expressive sound. 'Terrible feller,' he said. 'Heighho blackmailed him, I suppose, after guessin' the truth?'

'Uncle Hayhoe was bent on selling his discretion, certainly,' I said, 'but I don't think even he guessed Kingston had killed Pig. All he knew was that there was something infernally fishy about the first funeral. He made an appointment with Kingston to talk it over and they chose the empty villa to discuss terms.

Kingston killed him there and later on carried him to the corn-field where we found him. He left the knife in the wound until he got him *in situ*, as it were; that's how he avoided a great deal of the blood.'

Janet shuddered. 'He deceived us all very well,' she said. 'I never dreamed – '

Leo coughed noisily. 'Utterly deceived,' he echoed. 'Seemed a decent enough feller.'

'He was amazing,' I agreed. 'My arrival at dinner that evening must have shaken him up a bit in all conscience, since he'd seen me at the funeral, but he came out with the brother story immediately, and made it sound convincing. The only mistake he made was in moving the body to the river when I said I was going to examine it. He acted on impulse there, you see; he saw his way and went straight for it every time.'

Janet drew back. 'You ought not to have walked into that last trap he set for you,' she said.

'My dear girl,' I said, anxious to defend myself, 'we had to have proof of murder or attempted murder, for as far as proof was concerned he'd got clean away with his first two efforts. All the same, I don't think I'd have been so foolhardy if it hadn't been for Lugg.'

'You'd have looked pretty green if it hadn't been for Gilbert,' she said.

I looked at her sharply, and saw that she was blushing.

'Whippet and I had a word or two on the phone after Kingston had agreed to pick me up at Highwaters,' I admitted. 'He spotted the empty villa and put me on to it. We guessed if there was to be an attempt on me Kingston would take me there. I shouldn't have been so brave without him. Master-mind is fond of life.'

Janet dimpled. She is very pretty when her cheeks go pink.

'Then you know about Gilbert?' she said.

I stared at her. 'How much do you know?'

'A little,' she murmured.

'My hat!' I said.

Leo was on the point of demanding an explanation when we pulled up at the Knights. We found Poppy, Pussey, and Whippet waiting for us in the lounge, and when we were all sitting round with the ice cubes clinking in our tall glasses, Poppy suddenly turned on me.

'I'm sure you've made a mistake, Albert,' she said. 'I don't want to be unkind, dear, and I do think you're very clever. But how could Doctor Kingston have killed Harris, or Peters as you call him, when he was in this room playing poker with Leo when the vase fell upon him? You said yourself it couldn't have slipped off by accident.'

The time had come for me to do my parlour trick, and I did my best to perform it in the ancient tradition.

'Poppy,' I said, 'do you remember Kingston coming to see your little maid on the morning of the murder? You took him up yourself, I suppose, and you both had a look at the kid? There was some ice in the water jug by her bed, wasn't there?'

She considered. 'No,' she said. 'He came down, and I gave him a drink with ice in it. That was after I'd turned him into the bathroom to wash his hands. I came down here, and he followed me, and after he'd had his drink he look some tablets up to Flossie that he'd forgotten.'

'Ah!' I said impressively. 'Was he long following you down?'

She looked up with interest. 'Why, yes, he was,' she said. 'Quite a while, now I think of it.'

Having located my rabbit, as it were, I proceeded to produce it with a flourish.

'Kingston told us he met Harris, alias Pig, on the stairs, and that Pig had a hangover,' I began. 'The first wasn't true, the second was. Pig was in his bedroom when Kingston slipped in to see him, having first got rid of you. Pig was dressed, but he wanted a corpse-reviver and he trusted Kingston, never dreaming that he'd goaded the man too far. After all, people don't go about expecting to be murdered. In his doctor's bag Kingston had some chloral, which is a reputable narcotic when used in moderation. He saw his opportunity. He administered a tidy dose, and sent Pig to sit out on the lawn. He followed him downstairs, and through the lounge windows saw him settle down. I think his original intention was to let him die, and to trust the coroner to suspect a chronic case of dope. But this was risky, and the position of the chair, which was directly beneath the window, put the other idea into his head. If you notice, the windows on each floor in this house are directly above those on the last, and no one who knows the place can have missed the stone urns. They were originally intended to obscure the attic windows from the outside. It was while Kingston was drinking his highball that he had his brainwave. There were two or three solid rectangles of ice in his glass, and he pocketed two of them. Then he told you some story about forgotten tablets and went up to the top floor again, which was deserted at that time of the morning. There he discovered that, as he had suspected, Pig was sitting directly beneath the box-room urn. He knew he was unconscious already, and would remain so. The rest was easy. He took the urn out of its socket and balanced it on its peg half over the ledge. Then he blocked it into position with the two pieces of ice, and went quietly downstairs. The ledge is just below the level of the window-sill, so the chance of anyone who passed the box-room door noticing that the urn was an inch or so out of place was remote. All he had to do, then, was to wait.'

Poppy sat staring at me, her face pale.

'Until the ice melted and the urn fell?' she said. 'How – how ghastly!'

Pussey wagged his head. 'Powerful smart,' he said. 'Powerful smart. If I might ask you, sir, how did you come to think of that?'

'The moss on the ledge was damp when I arrived,' I said. 'The inference did not dawn on me at first, but when I had a highball here the other day I saw the ice and suddenly realized what it meant.'

'Wonderful!' said Whippet, without malice. 'I was after the same fellow, of course, but the alibi put me out.'

Leo stared at him as if he had only just become aware of his existence.

'Mr – er Whippet,' he said, 'very pleased to have you here, of course, my boy. But where do you fit into this extraordinary story? What are you doin' here?'

There was a pause, and they all looked at me as though I was responsible for him. I looked at Whippet.

'His little hands are sore and his snout bleedeth,' I said. 'This is Gilbert Whippet, Junior, son of Q. Gilbert Whippet, of the Mutual Ordered Life Endowment Company, sometimes called the M.O.L.E. It didn't occur to me until that day at "The

228 MY FRIEND MR CAMPION AND OTHER MYSTERIES

Feathers", and then I could have kicked myself for missing it. You always were a lazy beast, Whippet.'

He smiled faintly. 'I – er – prefer writing to action, you know,' he said, hesitantly. 'I am sorry, Campion, to have dragged you into this, but at the beginning we had nothing to go on at all except a sort of uneasy suspicion. I couldn't very well approach you direct because – well – er – there was nothing direct about it, so I – er – wrote.'

His voice trailed away.

'Both Lugg and I appreciated your style,' I said.

He nodded gravely. 'It seemed the best way to ensure your interest,' he said calmly. 'Whenever I thought you might be flagging, I wrote again.'

'Your people got hold of Effie, and you set her on to me, I suppose?' I said coldly.

'Er-yes,' agreed Whippet, without shame.

Poppy glanced round the room. 'Where is she now?' she demanded.

Whippet beamed. It was the broadest smile I ever saw on his face.

'With – er – Bathwick,' he murmured. 'They've gone into the town, to the pictures. Very suitable, I thought. Happy endings and – er – all that.'

I gaped at him. He had my respect.

When Lugg and I went back to London the next day, Poppy, who had come to Highwaters for lunch, stood with Leo and waved good-bye to us from the lawn. The sky was dappled blue and white, the birds sang, and the air smelt of hay.

Janet, with Whippet in tow, came running up to us just before we started. Her eyes were dancing, and she looked adorable.

'Congratulate us, Albert,' she said. 'We're engaged. Isn't it wonderful?'

I gave them my blessing with a good grace. Whippet blinked at me.

'I'm indebted to you, Campion,' he said.

We drove for some time in silence. I was thoughtful and Lugg, who was as bald as an egg, seemed depressed. As we reached the main road he nudged me.

'What a performance!' he said.

'Whose?' I inquired, not above appreciating a little honour where honour was due.

He leered. 'That bloke Whippet. Come down to a place with Miss Effie Rowlandson, and go orf with Miss Janet Pursuivant . . . That took a bit o' doing.'

'Lugg,' I said sadly, 'would you like to walk home?'

THE END

THE DEFINITE ARTICLE

'My dear man,' said Old Lady Laradine, her remarkable voice penetrating the roar of the Bond Street traffic with easy mastery, 'don't think you're going to get away from me once I've settled down to a gossip. Come back here at once. Dorothea has got her girl safely engaged to Lord Pettering, I see. You know him, don't you? Tell me, do you approve?'

Mr Albert Campion bent his lean back once more and peered again into the tonneau of the elderly Daimler, where the re-doubtable old lady sat enthroned.

His pale, somewhat vacant face, at which so many criminals had laughed too soon, wore a patient but harassed expression as his fifth attempt to escape was again frustrated.

'Forgive me, but you're holding up the traffic rather seriously, you know,' he ventured mildly.' There's a bus having apoplexy just behind you, and I see a traffic policeman gazing over here with unhealthy interest. Does it matter?'

The old lady swung round to peer out of the window above her head with an agility which was typical of her.

'Yes, I dislike the police,' she said briskly. 'They have a mania for motor-cars. Get in.'

Mr Campion drew back involuntarily.

'Oh no, really,' he murmured. 'I – I'm late for an appointment now. Delightful seeing you. Good-bye.'

The car door swinging suddenly open on top of him silenced

his excuses. 'Where is this appointment?' The old voice was commanding.

'Scotland Yard,' said Campion with what he took to be a flash of inspiration. 'Terribly important.'

'Get in then, idiot,' shouted the old lady. 'Bullard!' she screamed to the chauffeur. 'Scotland Yard! – and drive as fast as you like. It's official business.'

A moment later Mr Campion, who had no desire to go to the headquarters of the Criminal Investigation Department anyway, found himself sitting meekly beside his kidnapper as the big car slid quietly out into Piccadilly.

Lady Laradine regarded him with the affectionate pride of an angler for a landed fish.

'There,' she said. 'Now tell me! Your friend Lord Pettering is hysterically in love with Dorothea's girl Roberta, isn't he? How did he get that abominable uncle of his to agree to the match?'

Mr Campion blinked.

'Tommy Pettering?' he repeated with irritating stupidity. 'Has he an uncle?'

Lady Laradine made a menacing noise in her throat.

'Don't you dare to take that line with me, young man,' she said, prodding his knee with a finger which felt as though it had a thimble upon it. 'You know as well as I do that Pettering's mother is determined he shall have a career in the Foreign Office and that old Braithwaite, her brother, who is in the Cabinet, is only willing to arrange everything if he's allowed to keep the whole family under his thumb. Young Master Thomas has to get his uncle's permission before he sells a plater, much less gets himself engaged. How did the boy talk his uncle round? You must know.'

Mr Campion was aware of her small faded brown eyes watching him with a shrewdness which was unnerving, and he stuck resolutely to his usual policy, saying nothing that could possibly be taken down and used against him.

'I imagine the request was purely formal,' he murmured cautiously. 'I don't know Miss Roberta Pendleton-Blake. There's nothing against her, is there?'

'Against Roberta? Of course not!' the old woman snapped at him. 'Dorothea is one of my best friends. But the money in that family did come from frozen meat in the last generation and everybody thought that the old uncle, Braithwaite, would put his stupid feet down on that account. So he would have done, of course, if there'd been any breath of scandal. The F.O. is so pristine, isn't it? But I suppose the meat is something they can bring themselves to forget and forgive. Still, I believe it was touch and go. Tell me, do you like Roberta? She's my godchild, but you can say what you like.'

Mr Campion patiently repeated his previous announcement that he had not met the Pendleton-Blakes. Lady Laradine was shocked.

'Oh, my dear, you must,' she said. 'I'll see you're invited to the dance Dorothea is giving for the girl next week. Mind you come. They're charming, all absolutely charming, even the husband – but he's dead, of course. Dorothea is a sweet creature. So original. She uses all the ideas I give her for her parties. I've told her she must have the psychometrist at the next dance. That's something new to amuse people. It's so interesting, I think, to have something to do, besides watching the younger people dance. It gives one something to talk about afterwards.

You really must meet Dorothea. Oh, how disappointing, here we are.'

Her flow of chatter died abruptly as the Daimler turned on to the Embankment, and her passenger sprang out with uncharacteristic haste. He did not get clean away, however.

'I'll wait for you,' said Lady Laradine, her hand on his coat. 'I want to hear all the news.'

Mr Campion, who had considered crossing the road, picking up a cab and driving peacefully back to Bond Street, was aghast.

'That would be too kind,' he said with earnest conviction. 'I'm afraid I may be hours, literally. Thank you so very much. Good-bye.'

'Good-bye then,' said her ladyship regretfully. 'I shall look out for you at Dorothea's next week.'

Mr Campion smiled a trifle wanly and walked towards the entrance. Since there was nothing for it but a visit to his old friend Superintendent Oates, or undignified concealment behind a gate pillar until the Daimler should elect to depart, he sighed and, waving to the inquisitive figure in the back of the car, he gave his name to the man on the door and sent up his card.

The Superintendent embarrassed him considerably by receiving him at once, having taken his unheralded arrival as a sign of great urgency.

'What's up?' he demanded. 'I've never known you blow in here without making an appointment. Something serious?'

Inwardly Mr Campion cursed all strong-minded old ladies, and after a while he mentioned the fact aloud.

Oates began to laugh. He was a thin grey man with light intelligent eyes and a certain natural mournfulness of expression.

'That's fine,' he said with relish. 'This is just the place for a nice rest in the middle of the morning. Put your feet up. Don't mind me.'

Mr Campion took a silver case from his pocket and drew out a cigarette, which he laid upon the desk with quiet dignity. 'Get this analysed for me, old boy, will you?' he said earnestly.

The policeman's smile faded and he prodded the cylinder gently with a broad forefinger. 'Which is it?' he demanded. 'Drugs or explosives?'

'Heaven knows,' said his visitor seriously.

'Really? Where did you get it?' Oates was as alert as a terrier.

Mr Campion surveyed him affectionately. 'I bought it in an open shop right in your own district. Think that over.'

Oates sniffed at the cigarette suspiciously. 'Righto,' he said, 'I'll send it down. What are your grounds for doubting it?'

'Three extra in a packet and they taste like hell,' explained his visitor affably. 'They're a new brand, advertised all over the place.'

The Superintendent regarded him coldly for a moment or two and finally lit the exhibit, which he puffed contentedly.

'All right,' he said ominously, 'all right, my lad. If you're looking for something to employ your time I'll see what I can do for you. Sit down. I've got something in your line. This'll just about suit you. Somebody wants a miracle. I thought of you when I got the inquiry.'

His guest looked suitably chastened and would have drifted towards the door, but Oates's ferocious good humour increased.

'Sit down,' he repeated, taking up a sheaf of official papers. 'Here's the dope. This is what comes of persuading foreigners to say "Your police are wonderful". They're beginning to take it literally, the lunatics. This is an inquiry from the U.S. The Federal Police are looking for a Society blackmailer who, so they say, always spends October in England. They can't give us any more than that on him. They simply say they'd be obliged if we apprehended him. Obliged isn't the word. They mean staggered.'

Seated on the hard visitor's chair, Mr Campion did his best to look intelligent, and his pale eyes were amused and friendly behind his horn-rimmed spectacles.

'He's male, is he?' he said. 'That's a step. I mean it reduces it from all the population of America to half the population of America, doesn't it?'

Oates turned over the blue sheets in his hand.

'Yes, they seem fairly certain of that,' he said without smiling. 'But you see what I mean when I say the description is slight. This is the story, as far as I can make it out. Late last year there was a fatal accident to the young wife of one of those fabulously wealthy financial men they breed over there. She fell off the roof of a skyscraper, and no one seemed to know why. There was no suggestion of foul play, but the question of suicide was raised. The husband, poor chap, was far too broken up at first to go into the thing thoroughly, but afterwards he seems to have pulled himself together and made several interesting discoveries.

'The first thing he noticed was that the girl died without a halfpenny in her private account, and that there were records of large, ever-increasing sums withdrawn from it to explain this.

'This money had been paid out from the bank in cash and naturally he began to think of blackmail.'

He paused and Campion nodded.

'The girl,' Oates continued, 'was very young, not at all the type to have a dangerous secret, and the whole notion seemed incredible to the husband until he cross-questioned the coloured maid who had come up from his wife's home with her on her marriage. From her he got an interesting story.

'It appeared that the young wife had kept some letters, a sentimental memento of a boy-and-girl love affair which had fizzled out before the older man put in an appearance. The maid thought that someone had got hold of these and convinced the wife that her husband would read a great deal more into them than ever they had originally contained. To prevent this eventuality the poor wretched child ruined herself financially, worked herself into a state of nervous collapse, and finally threw herself off the roof. You know how these things sometimes happen, Campion.'

The elegant personage in the horn-rimmed spectacles did not speak at once. It was an ugly little story, and one which he had heard too often in his career to doubt. Like the Superintendent, he knew only too well that the clever blackmailer who picks the right type of victim seldom has to find anything that is really reprehensible on which to base his threats.

'Too bad,' he said seriously. 'Didn't they get any line on the chap?'

Stanislaus Oates made a few vulgar and not altogether relevant remarks which seemed to relieve his feelings.

'I told you,' he said finally. 'Why don't you listen? They haven't got a sausage, not a whiff, not a faint delicate aroma floating out from the window of a passing car. They don't know anything. And they have the calm impudence to write and say "We hear your Force is wonderful. How about sending this lad along in a plain van? "'

'Yes, I know.' Mr Campion spoke soothingly. 'But they must have something to go on. Otherwise why apply to you? Why not go to the Chinese or to the Nevada Sheriff?'

Oates grunted.

'They think they've got two clues,' he admitted. 'They concede that they're slight. I like that word of theirs, "concede". They're both based on something the dead girl said to the maid. The first one is a remark she made late in the summer of last year, when she first showed signs of worry. "It'll be all right in October," she said. "He goes to England in October." She wouldn't explain herself and seemed to regret the admission of trouble as soon as she had made it. That's the first.'

'The second is just demented. Apparently, on the morning of the "accident", she was sitting up in bed and she said to the maid, who seems to have been a reliable witness, "It's no good, Dorothy, it's no good. It's written in ink. He saw it in ink." And then she went out on the roof.'

He paused and shrugged his shoulders.

'There you are,' he said. 'There's the lot, and I hope it means more to you than it does to me. Written in ink, indeed! What was written in ink? And why was it more important than if it had been written in pencil? Or cross-stitch, for that matter?'

Mr Campion sat looking thoughtfully at the toes of his shoes for some moments.

'This girl who died,' he inquired at last, 'what sort of life did she lead? Was she likely to come into contact with shady characters?'

'No, that's the odd part about it.' Oates studied the blue sheaf again. 'She was one of New York's pampered babies. Looked after as if she was royalty or something. She never went out unescorted and never visited anywhere but in the most exclusive circles. Whoever got hold of her must have had peculiar facilities for getting into the best houses. I think the whole story is scatty. I shall write and tell 'em so, in a nice way, of course, when you've broken a tooth or two on the problem.'

'Me?' Mr Campion seemed startled, and the Superintendent was amused.

'I'll tell 'em I've put a Society expert on the job,' he said, grinning. 'That'll please 'em and keep 'em quiet for a bit. There you are. You came in here looking for something to do and now you've got it. There's a little miracle for you. Pull that off. Written in ink my foot!'

'In ink?' repeated Mr Campion with sudden interest as a chance remark he had heard earlier that morning returned to him with sudden significance. 'I wonder . . .'

Oates regarded him sympathetically.

'You're getting swell-headed,' he said kindly. 'It often happens to amateurs. You're beginning to think you're gifted with supernatural powers. This'll do you good. It's impossible. If you had all the luck in the world it'd still be impossible.'

Mr Campion collected his hat and gloves and wandered to the door.

'I'll let you know if I spot him,' he said.

'Do,' said Oates cheerfully. 'And send me a wreath at the same time. I'll need it.'

His visitor looked pained. 'Do I get a reward if I bring him in?' he inquired.

'You get an illuminated address of five thousand words, written in my own hand and coloured,' said the Superintendent heartily.

Mr Campion seemed both pleased and surprised.

'I shall like that,' he said.

*

He went quietly out of the building, and that evening did what was in the circumstances a very extraordinary thing. After certain elementary researches he wrote a careful and slightly effusive note to old Lady Laradine and begged her not to forget her promise to get him an invitation to the dance in honour of Miss Roberta Pendleton-Blake.

He paid for this fit of apparent lunacy a few days later when he sat beside that paralysing old lady in the corner of a ballroom which was not so much decorated as obliterated with heavily scented flowers and watched a vast throng of young people moving in mass formation on a glistening floor.

Lady Laradine was at the top of her form. She had spent the earlier part of the evening in a black velvet tent in an ante-room of the big Charges Street house consulting the latest Society entertainer, and was bursting with her experiences.

'My dear,' she was saying happily, 'my dear, the creature is too astonishing. Dorothea was *inspired* to engage him. I told her she would be. Look at Roberta and young Pettering dancing together over there . . . aren't they charming? I'm so glad the uncle was reasonable. Dorothea tells me she cried with relief when she heard that the wretched man had consented. Dear me, let me see, where was I?'

Mr Campion had not the faintest idea and was on the verge of forgetting himself sufficiently to say so when she recollected unassisted.

'Of course,' she said, 'the fortune-teller. Quite an astounding person. A psychometrist. Fortunately I'm never indiscreet, but really some of the things he told me about people I know . . .'

Her resonant voice rose and fell, and it occurred to her patient audience that she must have told the seer quite as much as ever he told her. Her flow of chatter was quite remarkable.

'He took my ring and put it in an envelope,' she hurried on. 'I put the envelope under the crystal and then he looked in and told me the most astonishing things about my mother. Wasn't that amazing?'

'A ring?' inquired Mr Campion, pricking up his ears.

The old lady looked at him as if she thought he were deficient.

'I don't believe you've been listening,' she said unjustly. 'I've been explaining to you for the last half hour that Cagliostro is amazing. You give him something that belonged to someone dead, or elsewhere anyway, and he tells you all about them.'

'Cagliostro?' repeated Mr Campion, temporarily out of his depth.

Lady Laradine threw up her small yellow hands in exasperation.

'Bless the man, he's delirious!' she said. 'Cagliostro the Second is the fortune-teller, animal. The psychometrist. The man I've been telling you about. He's in a black velvet tent somewhere in the house. Go and see him yourself. I can't be bothered with you if you don't use your mind at all. All you young men ought to take up Yoga. It clears the brain. Come and see me and I'll put you on to a very good man.'

Mr Campion rose. His ears were singing, but his eyes were alert and interested. 'I'll go and find him at once,' he said. 'I like fortune-tellers.'

The suddenness of his dash for freedom routed the old lady, and he was half-way down the room and out of earshot before she collected sufficient breath to call him back.

Mr Campion went off on his quest with that hidden, almost absent-minded, purposefulness which was his most misleading characteristic. He paused in the doorway to exchange a word with Tommy Pettering and be presented to the entirely delightful Roberta, chatted carelessly with two or three acquaintances, put himself in the good graces of his hostess with a few intelligent compliments, and wandered out into the main body of the house practically by accident.

It took him some time to find the psychometrist and his velvet tent, indeed he became definitely lost in the house at one period before that and came to a full stop in a dark corridor on the floor below the ballroom.

He was standing on the threshold of a small room furnished as a woman's study. The place was dimly lighted and the slender walnut furniture made graceful shadows on the silk-panelled walls. But it was not at these that the tall man with the diffident manner remained to stare with speculative interest.

Kneeling before a bureau on the other side of the room was a girl in a green chiffon dress. The first thing Campion noticed about her was her extreme youth, and the second the astonishing fact that she was forcing the catch of a drawer with a brass paper-knife.

He then saw that her hair was curled on the top of a small and shapely head and that her green dress floated about a slender, childish figure.

As he watched her she slid the drawer open an inch or so and inserted a little inquiring hand.

Mr Campion, deeming that the moment had come, coughed apologetically.

The girl in the green dress stiffened and there was a moment of painful silence. Campion had some experience of the hardened criminal and he thought he had never witnessed such an exhibition of calm nerve. Before she even looked round she opened the drawer a little further and, with a nonchalance that had guilt stamped all over it, drew out a small flat packet which she wrapped in her georgette handkerchief. Then she turned and rose quietly to her feet.

Mr Campion found himself looking into a small, intelligent face which would blossom into radiant beauty in a year or so. At the moment he judged her to be seventeen at most. She was very red and her grey-green eyes were angry and alarmed, but her dignity was tremendous.

Her remark was as bald as it was unexpected, and it had a strong element of truth in it which silenced him altogether.

'It's nothing to do with you,' she said and darted past him before he could stop her, leaving him staring in blank astonishment at her tiny whirlwind figure disappearing into the darkness of the passage.

Mr Campion pulled himself together and went quietly up

to the ballroom. He was mildly startled. Young ladies who open bureau drawers with paper-knives and run off with mysterious packages wrapped in green georgette handkerchiefs constitute a responsibility which cannot be altogether ignored.

He had plenty of fish to fry of his own, however, for he had not braved an evening in the same house with Lady Laradine for nothing. He looked in at the ballroom again and reflected that every woman he had ever met at a dinner table seemed to be present with her daughter, but of the little girl in the green dress there was no trace at all.

Lady Laradine saw him from the other side of the room and bore down upon him like a very small ship in very full sail and he ducked into the first doorway to avoid her, thereby discovering the thing he had sought so unobtrusively for the past hour.

A black velvet tent hung with gilt fringe and topped by a directoire eagle rose up, dark and impressive, in the centre of the high-ceilinged Georgian room. He wandered over to it and raised the flap.

The scene within was much as he had expected, and the sight of it gave him a thrill of satisfaction. One point in particular interested him immensely. A strong overhead light shone down upon a small ebony table which supported a red satin hand-cushion and a black crystal ball.

The man who smiled at him over an unimpeachable shirt-front was unusual. This Cagliostro was not the sleek huckster with the twinkle and the swagger which the credulous public has come to expect in its seers, but a surprisingly large man with thin fluffy hair and prominent cold light eyes. His smile was secretive and not at all pleasant. He did not speak, but indicated the consultant's chair very slowly with a sweeping movement of a great fin-like hand.

Mr Campion would have accepted the invitation but he was frustrated. Lady Laradine pounced upon him from behind.

'Oh, *there* you are,' she said irritably.' Well, I hope you've been hearing something entertaining for it's more than I have. Has anybody *any* conversation at all these days? What did Cagliostro tell you?'

Mr Campion was explaining meekly that he had had as yet no time to consult the psychometrist when he caught sight over his captor's shoulders of a slender little figure in a green dress. There was quite a little crowd in the ante-room and she did not notice him, but made straight for the tent and passed inside.

'Really!' Lady Laradine, who had known by instinct the precise moment when his attention had wandered and had spun round herself, was now looking at him with impolite amusement.

'My dear boy, a *child*?' she burst out in her tremendous voice. 'Well, it's an extraordinary thing to me, but I've noticed it over and over again. You clever men are absolutely devastated by immaturity, aren't you? Still, seventeen… Dear boy, is it wise?'

'Do you know who she is?' Campion got the inquiry in edgeways.

'Who she is?' echoed the old lady, her eyes crinkling. 'My good man, you don't mean to say you haven't even met? But how touchingly romantic! I thought you young people managed things very differently these days. Still, this is charming. Tell me more. You just looked at each other, I suppose? Dear me, this takes me back to the nineties.'

Campion regarded her helplessly. She was like some elderly yellow kitten, he thought suddenly, all fluff and wide smile.

'Who is she?' he repeated doggedly.

'Why, the child, of course,' said Lady Laradine infuriatingly. 'Little What's-her-name. Jennifer, isn't it? To be presented next year when there won't be such a crush. You know perfectly well who I mean. Don't stand there looking like a fish. Roberta's sister, Dorothea's youngest daughter. So pretty. Like some sort of flower, don't you think?'

'A daughter?' said Campion flatly. 'She lives here, then?'

'Of course she does. Where should she live but with her mother?' Her ladyship's eyebrows seemed in danger of disappearing altogether. 'A child of seventeen living alone? Whatever next! She's a charming little thing, although I've never had any patience with schoolchildren myself. Still, she's far too young for you. Put it out of your mind. Let me see, what was I going to tell you?'

This was a secret Mr Campion never learnt. Lady Laradine, who had hitherto accredited him with excellent manners, was deeply disappointed in him. He stared blankly at her for a moment and then, turning away abruptly, strode across the room, passing behind the tent, to the door half-hidden behind it which led out into the house.

Lady Laradine saw the top of the door open and close and assumed that her victim had passed through it, which was just the kind of silly mistake which long experience had taught Mr Campion that most people were wont to make.

The long evening went on according to the programme the hostess had arranged, but there were certain additions to it which were not on her schedule at all. At half-past one in the morning a weary and somewhat stiff Mr Campion made his way gingerly out of the concealing folds at the back of the psychometrist's tent and, slipping into the house, walked quietly down to the little study where he had first met the girl in green.

He went inside and sat down in a wing-chair in the darkest corner. Presently he heard her coming as he knew she would. Her dress brushed the step and he heard her quick intake of breath as she closed the door behind her and, crossing into his line of vision, flung herself down on her knees before the bureau drawer.

'I say,' said Mr Campion, 'I suppose you know what you're doing with that chap downstairs? I don't trust him myself.'

This time his interruption was greeted with interest if not respect. Jennifer Pendleton-Blake screamed and swung round, her eyes terrified. Even so, however, her words were unexpected.

'What do you know?' she demanded.

'Quite a lot.' Mr Campion rose stiffly to his feet. 'I've been standing on one foot, half smothered by dusty black velvet, for an hour and a half.'

The girl gaped at him and he had the grace to look ashamed.

'I've been listening,' he said. 'What did you give that fellow to – er – "psychomet?" I couldn't see. Letters?'

She nodded miserably.

Mr Campion coughed.

'I don't want to seem unduly inquisitive,' he said, 'but I'm out to help in any way I can. Who were they from?'

Jennifer Pendleton-Blake turned back to the drawer and

turned over its contents. The nape of her neck was pink and her shoulders were quivering.

'I don't know,' she said helplessly. 'That's just it, *I don't know*!'

Mr Campion knelt down on the floor beside her and looked into the drawer, which contained as fine a collection of sentimental relics as ever he had set eyes upon. There were several little bundles of letters tied up with different coloured ribbons, a choice selection of dead flowers, a university scarf or two, and quite a quantity of chocolate box lids.

He glanced at the seventeen-year-old at his side and surprised her looking half her age. Inspiration came to him.

'Jennifer,' he said sternly, 'these are not yours.'

'No,' she whispered, her hips trembling.

'Whose are they? Roberta's?'

'Yes.'

Mr Campion lent her the handkerchief out of his breast pocket.

'Let's discuss this,' he said cheerfully. 'I think I'm getting the hang of it. I'll tell you the story as I see it and you correct me when I go off the rails.'

Miss Pendleton-Blake rewarded him with a pathetic acquiescing sniff.

'I don't know who you are,' she said, 'but you seem all right. Anyway, things can't be worse.'

Mr Campion ignored the somewhat dubious compliment.

'When a young woman feels she's grown up, but has only just arrived at that eminence, she often finds herself at a temporary disadvantage,' he began with a certain amount of oracular tact. 'I mean, for instance, when she is faced with the exacting problem of finding something really interesting to take to a psychometrist I can sympathize with her difficulty.'

The young lady looked at him gratefully.

'That was just it,' she said. 'I hadn't anything belonging to anyone whom I really wanted to know something about and I did feel a bit out of it, young and flat, you know. I'm not even presented yet. So I suddenly thought of Roberta's drawer up here, where I knew she kept all Tommy's letters. I thought I'd just get them, hear the low-down on Tommy and put them back. I didn't dream that the fortune-teller would be such a beast.'

'He wouldn't give them back to you?'

'Why, no. It was most peculiar.' Jennifer's face was the complete picture of youthful reproach. 'I put the packet in an envelope and sealed it, as he told me to. He stuck the envelope under the crystal. He told me a lot of silly stuff that obviously wasn't true and then he gave me what I naturally thought was the envelope back. I didn't examine it there, but when I got up here again I found it was only this.'

She opened her green handkerchief and produced a wad of neatly folded newsprint.

Mr Campion regarded the package gravely and with distaste.

'You went back to him, naturally?' he said. 'I heard the whole of that interview. You had to wait your turn to see him, of course. It must have been a trying experience.'

'It was filthy,' said Jennifer violently. 'Did you hear him laugh at me and say I'd made a mistake? Then he congratulated me on my sister's engagement and said he'd be seeing me again. He meant me to realize that he knew all about everything, you see. It wasn't until just now, though, that I realized the frightful thing. Those letters weren't Tommy's. They must have been Bobby Dacre's, or one of her other silly undergrads. They're always writing stupid letters to her because she's so frightfully pretty. Cagliostro must have looked at the letters I gave him and saw that they were written to her and not signed by Tommy, who, as everybody knows, is her fiancé. Now he'll keep them and make a row. What shall I do?'

Mr Campion grinned.

'Hold on a minute,' he said. 'He can't do much, you know, not in this case, although I *can* conceive a situation in which his little conjuring trick might prove decidedly awkward. Who cares who has been writing to Roberta? Not Tommy.'

'Oh, no, not Tommy.' Jennifer was contemptuous. 'But it might be frightfully awkward if he went to Tommy's perfectly revolting uncle. He's a horror. He's just straining at the leash to make an objection to the engagement. Everybody knows that. If this filthy fortune-teller so much as approached him he'd make it an excuse. Besides, you know how frightfully prurient everybody over forty is.'

'Are they?' said Mr Campion, feeling the dangerous age was uncomfortably close.

'Oh, yes!' said Miss Pendleton-Blake. 'What shall I do?' she added after a pause. 'Try and buy them back before he goes?'

Mr Campion regarded her with affection.

'You're what my more vulgar friends would call a proper little mug, aren't you?' he said. 'Our pal Cagliostro isn't so dumb. He certainly knows how to pick his clients. Now look here, we will do that. We'll do just what you say. We'll try to buy them back. But we'll need witnesses and, as we don't want publicity, we'll want the right witnesses. Oates will have to leave his bed, and it serves him right. Look here, can we be certain of keeping Cagliostro here another hour?'

Jennifer glanced up at the sunburst clock over the mantelshelf.

'Oh, no,' she said. 'He's due to leave in ten minutes or so now. Perhaps he'll just take the money quietly and give them back.'

'In view of a rather horrid little tale I heard the other day I think he'll take the money and *not* give them back,' he said. 'And if we don't have the right kind of witnesses there may be a row, which is not what we want at all.'

The girl in the green frock shivered.

'Who's going to keep him here, then?' she said. 'You don't know these entertainers. They'll never stay a second after their time is up. Is it so terribly important?'

'Terribly,' said Mr Campion.

'Then we're sunk.' There was a wail in the young voice. 'Nothing on heaven or earth can detain people like that.'

A beautiful idea came to Mr Campion.

'I know someone who could detain anything,' he murmured, and went off in search of Lady Laradine.

At four o'clock in the morning Superintendent Oates sat in a small room on the first floor of Mrs Pendleton-Blake's house and regarded Mr Campion with a certain thoughtfulness. He was contented to know that in a cab speeding through the quiet streets Cagliostro the Second sat sullen and resigned between two unsympathetic and sleepy police officers.

Opposite the Superintendent stood Mr Campion, looking very wide-awake and wearing an almost intelligent expression.

Jennifer Pendleton-Blake was clinging to his arm, her eyes dancing.

'It *might* be him,' said the Superintendent grudgingly and ungrammatically. 'His papers do show that he only came over from the States at the beginning of the month. Anyway, it was the fairest cop I ever saw. He played straight into our hands. Never having met this little lady before, he felt he was quite safe from any trap, I suppose. He was more astounded than afraid when we walked in on him. Well, we'll keep the publicity right down; it's easy in this sort of case. You played your part very cleverly, Miss.'

Jennifer smiled.

'He was exhausted when I got to him,' she said frankly. 'Edith Laradine had been with him for a whole hour, you know. She did the really clever thing by keeping him here. She's wonderful.'

The Superintendent cocked an eye towards the door.

Through the heavy panels and down two flights of stairs the steady murmur of Lady Laradine's remarkable voice reached them faintly as she recounted her experience to her friend and hostess. Oates listened for a moment and shook his head like an airedale.

'Yes,' he said heavily. 'Yes, indeed. She is. Wonderful is the word.'

Jennifer laughed.

'You were pretty clever, weren't you, bless you,' she said, glancing up at Mr Campion.

'Him?' said the Superintendent. '*Him?*'

Mr Campion remained affable and blandly uninformative until, good nights having been said, they taxied back to Campion's flat together for a nightcap. Then the Superintendent's dignity gave out sufficiently to permit him to ask a direct question.

'Simple, my dear chap,' he said. 'Your police experts *are* wonderful.'

Oates made an unofficial remark.

You come off it,' he said after a bit. 'You know and I know that the chances are a hundred to one on this Cagliostro fellow being the same man I was telling you about last week. We shan't be able to prove it, I don't suppose, but it's clear enough. How did you do it? Luck again?'

'Luck?' protested Mr Campion in pained astonishment. 'My good policeman, when you actually meet brilliant detective work don't let its unfamiliarity blind you to its merit Luck indeed! It was pure deduction and intelligent investigation, backed up by old-fashioned listening at doors.'

'Yes, I know all that.' Oates was irritated in spite of his satisfaction. 'Once you decided to watch your man, the thing was child's play. You spotted his game at once. It was a clever one, mind you. He must have made a point of keeping all letters handed in to him and taking a look at them, giving back the uninteresting ones as soon as his client spotted his "mistake", as he called it. He had a dozen of those little fake packets ready, all shapes and sizes. You spotted that trick all right because you actually saw, or rather heard, him doing it, but what on earth made you suddenly decide to watch a man who was simply entertaining at some wretched party at which you happened to be?'

'I didn't happen to be at the party,' objected Mr Campion with feeling. 'I went there deliberately and at tremendous personal sacrifice in order to find him. I was looking for him.'

'Why?'

'Because you told me to, my dear chap.' Mr Campion leaned back in the taxicab and spoke with weary patience. 'Cagliostro is the only Society fortune-teller to visit these shores regularly every October. As soon as you told me that story the other day it was obvious that he was the man you wanted, providing your tale had any foundation in fact. I wanted to find out if it had, so I went and had a look at Cagliostro at work. Is that clear?'

'Yes,' said Oates hastily. 'Yes, old man. Don't get excited. Yes, I see that. But why a fortune-teller? I didn't mention a fortune-teller. The idea never entered my head.'

Mr Campion seemed to be at a loss, but suddenly he smiled.

'Oh, *that*,' he said. 'Of course. I forgot. You didn't see the significance of the maid's story, did you? She insisted that her mistress had definitely said "It's no use. It's written in ink. He saw it in ink." Now is it clear?'

The Superintendent swore.

'You make me tired,' he said. 'I've never heard such nonsense in my life. That statement was plain idiotic.'

Campion nodded. 'I know,' he said. 'It was. But the maid wasn't idiotic. The maid was a sensible girl, a good witness; you said so yourself. That's why it occurred to me that she must have made a simple, ordinary little mistake, the kind of mistake a sensible person might make. Don't you see, Oates, what her mistress really said was "He saw it in *the* ink. It is written in *the* ink."'

Oates was silent. 'Even so I don't see – ' he began.

Mr Campion chuckled in the darkness.

'You don't patronize fortune-tellers. If you did you'd know

that, while some of them look at cards or peer into crystals, others read secrets mirrored in a pool of black ink. When you told me that story I thought of fortune-tellers, and when I looked into Cagliostro's tent this evening the first thing I saw was a *black* crystal. Then I knew I was on the right track. The unpleasant little trick he tried to play on that adorable guffin, Jennifer, put him slap into my hands. There you are, sir, it's in the bag. When do I get my illuminated address?'

'Eh?' said Oates, and after a second or so of consideration began to laugh. 'I'll hand it to you,' he said. 'You get all the luck, but you have a sort of flair, I'll admit. You'll have to excuse the five thousand words.'

Mr Campion handed him his cigarette case.

'Not at all,' he said firmly. 'I want my reward. Either the address or you take Lady Laradine round the Black Museum for me.'

Oates accepted the cigarette.

'I'll do the homework,' he said resignedly. 'After all, life's short.'